COLD WAR SPOOKS

D1520838

FROM THE
DESK OF

Louis Ball

COLD WAR SPOOKS

NAVAL INTELLIGENCE FORCES INTERCEPT RUSSIAN COMMUNICATIONS—ON LAND, AS WELL AS UNDER, ABOVE AND ON THE SEAS.

A Novel

Tony Seidel

iUniverse, Inc.
New York Lincoln Shanghai

COLD WAR SPOOKS

NAVAL INTELLIGENCE FORCES INTERCEPT RUSSIAN COMMUNICATIONS—ON LAND, AS WELL AS UNDER, ABOVE AND ON THE SEAS.

iUniverse books may be ordered through booksellers or by contacting:

iUniverse
2021 Pine Lake Road, Suite 100
Lincoln, NE 68512
www.iuniverse.com
1-800-Authors (1-800-288-4677)

This is a work of fiction. All of the characters, names, incidents, organizations and dialogue in this novel are either the products of the author's imagination or are used fictitiously.

The maps in this book were designed by my son, Kevin Seidel, to whom I am very grateful.

ISBN-13: 978-0-595-40902-0 (pbk)
ISBN-13: 978-0-595-85265-9 (ebk)
ISBN-10: 0-595-40902-4 (pbk)
ISBN-10: 0-595-85265-3 (ebk)

Printed in the United States of America

Introduction

Peoples of different political persuasions have been spying one upon another since the beginning of modern recorded history. The exploits of the CIA, the KGB, and other organizations are widely known and often the fodder for popular movies and novels. But the accomplishments of other lesser-known organizations such as the Army Security Agency (ASA), the Air Force Security Service (AFSS) and the Naval Security Group (NSG) dedicated primarily to electronic intelligence gathering have gone largely unheralded.

The intelligence-gathering efforts of organizations such as the NSG during the period covered by this work of fiction were silently carried out 24/7 by sailors and marines—"spooks"—at locations all around the world—on land, under, above and on the sea. The work was often mind-numbing but adrenalin-pumping at times and with serious risk to the lives of the participants. The efforts during the Cold War were not without sacrifices.

The rank and file of the NSG of the sixties consisted mainly of bright young enlisted men, often fresh from the recently graduated high school class of a small rural town who were given 10-12 weeks of training and thrust into the world of electronic surveillance. But the most noteworthy characteristics of these individuals are the *esprit de corps*, the pride they took in their work, and the absolute dedication to serve and protect American ideals.

At the peak of the cold war during the 1960s, genuine hot spots such as Vietnam and the Middle East were fermenting simultaneously with our fears of nuclear threat from the Soviet Union. Coupled with the politics of the hot and cold wars was the race by the super-powers to be the first into space. The oft-mundane tasks of the NSG's Communications Technicians frequently resulted in assignments carrying greater risk than these kids had any clue they'd signed up for. And cloaked in the secrecy of the times, they served and sacrificed in silence for a nation that wouldn't even admit to their existence.

The Cold War is generally acknowledged to have begun immediately after the end of World War II in 1945. It was not officially declared over until 1991. During this long period of tense relations between the United States and several major world powers, the intensity of electronic intelligence gathering efforts reached a peak in the 1960s.

Hundreds of members of all branches of the Armed Services put their lives at risk to gather information that would be used to maintain American intelligence superiority. Many put in harm's way lost their lives. Beginning as early as 1950, intelligence-gathering aircraft were shot down by Russian MiGs—one of the first over Latvia, killing all aboard—including U.S. Naval Security Group personnel.

On June 8, 1967, for 75 torturous minutes during the Six Day War between Israel and the Arab States, the American ship *USS Liberty* (similar to the *USS Groveland* depicted in this book) was attacked in international waters by Israeli aircraft and motor torpedo boats. The ship was flying the American flag. Thirty-four young men sacrificed their lives—including 25 Navy Communications Technicians and Marine Corps counterparts), and 172 were wounded defending the ship. Israel claims they mistook the ship for an Egyptian horse carrier that actually was out of service at the time, also claiming that the Liberty was operating in a war zone and not displaying a flag. Israel has never explained or apologized for the incident. The flags that flew on the Liberty at the time are on display at the National Cryptologic Museum, Fort Meade, Maryland and the Cold War Museum near Washington, D.C.

In another incident similarly widely publicized in the world press, the *USS Pueblo* (AGER-2)—a ship similar to the *Groveland* in this story, was attacked in January of 1968 in international waters off the coast of North Korea by the North Koreans, resulting in one death, capture of the ship, and the incarceration of 30-plus crew members, including CTs until December of that year. Today the ship is a propaganda museum still docked in North Korea. The North Koreans claimed the *Pueblo* violated their 12-mile territorial limit.

In April 1969, a Navy EC-121M reconnaissance aircraft on a routine SIGINT (Signal Intelligence) mission off of the coast of North Korea was attacked and shot down by two North Korean MiGs as it turned to return to Osan Air Force base in South Korea. The entire crew of 31, including nine CTs, was lost at sea 90 miles southeast of the North Korean port of Ch'ongjin. A NSA review of intercepted North Korean radio traffic showed that the downing had resulted from a "command and control error" between the North Korean ground controller and the fighter pilots. The "Willy Victor" aircraft—similar to the one depicted in this book, was on a mission graded as "minimal risk" which had been safely flown 190 times during the first three months of 1969 alone.

The Soviets were shocked by the North Korean action and even sent Russian warships to the crash site to help American ships search for survivors. President Nixon's revelation in a press conference that the U.S. had monitored both North Korean and Russian air defense traffic resulted in both countries quickly changing all off their cryptographic systems, operating frequencies and operating procedures which set U.S. SIGINT efforts back for several months.

Hundreds of men gave their lives in the pursuit of preserving our way of life, not only as the result of hostile actions aimed at thwarting these intelligence activities, but aircraft accidents during take off and landing, and men lost at sea and on land. Noteworthy is the loss of 12 CTs who died in a fire while working in the operating spaces of the NSGA Kami Seya tunnel described In this book. The tunnel had only one entrance and exit.

There is no doubt that technology and human bravery played a major role in America's winning of the cold war. While history will largely remember the exploits of James Bond-type agents and real spies on all sides, it was the continuous behind the scenes work of hundreds of "little people" such as the communications technicians of the U.S. Navy that kept America on top. As Isaacs and Downing attest in their book <u>Cold War: An Illustrated History</u> (published by Little, Brown and Co.), "The United States had aerial photographs of Soviet tanks massing against Czechoslovakia in 1968 and Afghanistan in 1979. And detection by Sigint (Signal Intelligence) intercept and computer is supposed to have been so sophisticated as to enable Washington to overhear conversations of Politburo members. *The real penetration of the Soviet Union was made possible by Sigint and satellites, not by agents.*" (Emphasis mine, not the authors.)

Technological advances and recent reorganization and consolidation of intelligence agencies have resulted in the virtual dissolution of the Naval Security Group, at least in similarity to how it existed in the 1960s. Most NSGA bases have been closed, and the remaining organization has been merged with other agencies. But the brave men and women of the NSG and other similar agencies of other branches of service will long be remembered—even though as the message on the wall at NSA headquarters states—"They Served in Silence."

After 70 years in existence, the Naval Security Group was "disestablished"—ceased to exist—on 30 September 2005. At that time, the navy integrated all "Information Operations" under one authority. The new authority became the Naval Network Warfare Command.

CHAPTER 1

▼

"The screeching sound was louder now, and it didn't leave much to the imagination..."

Getting from the coffeepot to his workstation was no easy feat for Walter ('Sonny') Powell, Jr. At six-foot-two, it hadn't been easy for him to master the art of getting through a four-foot high door in a bulkhead by simultaneously lifting his feet, ducking his head and juggling the cup of fairly rancid Navy coffee in hand.

He'd made some progress on the coordination scale since high school—after all, he had been center for Fosston, Minnesota's consolidated high school's basketball team. As a younger man, he couldn't pat his head and rub his stomach at the same time. Indeed, Sonny had come a long way—in more ways than one.

Just being on the *SS Crestfin* was the realization of a dream he'd had since he was a young man on the farm. Sonny was second-generation U.S. Navy, and although he didn't quite follow in his father's footsteps as a full-time submariner, at least his moccasins were on the same path.

Settling into his gray-steel, green-padded government-issue armchair, Sonny placed his cup in the well on the desk of his mini-workstation; the well was designed to keep it from slipping and sliding, a virtual necessity at sea. He knew from his dad's stories that subs were relatively smooth riding—submarines didn't take the beating in a storm that surface ships did, but the normal crosscurrents and thermal changes could shake things up.

The coffee is strong, he thought, and even if it tastes like rusty mud, it's part of the experience. Some of the guys said the shimmer on the surface was an oil slick. He'd brought his own porcelain mug—he'd had it made in Japan. The artist had done a good job of replicating the insignia for his specialty—communications technician, or CT—a crossed feather and lightening bolt—on the unglazed clay before it was put in the kiln. He didn't exactly enjoy drinking hot mud inside a stinking 80-degree oven, but there wasn't a cold beer handy. Actually Sonny thought hot was good, especially in relation to the sub-zero temps that he never got accustomed to in his 22 years in Fosston. And the smells—well, he'd get used to them someday, as much as you ever get used to the pungent mix of B.O. and diesel fuel.

This was his first experience aboard a submarine…or anything on water larger than a canoe in fact. Sonny's father was a retired chief petty officer with 25 years in the submarine service who retired into a comfortable job with the U.S. Bureau of Prisons, and he had endless stories about the camaraderie, adventure and pride he had experienced as a young man on the *USS Narwhal* (SS-167). Harold Senior talked at length about life aboard the *Narwhal* in general, but didn't speak as eloquently or freely about his experiences while aboard at Pearl Harbor when the Japanese attacked in December of 1941. When he had learned that Sonny was being transferred to Japan, his father was ready to grab his .45 Colt and go with him and renew the war. Sonny would learn that his father's bitterness toward Japan was a common taste in the mouths of many veterans of the Pacific war.

And while some of his father's war tales were terrifying, at the same time they had instilled Sonny with a strange desire to have similar adventures and experiences. Life in Fosston was, after all, at the other end of the spectrum from adventuresome.

Funny, he thought as he sat staring somewhat numbly at the oil slick on his coffee—*I could be shaving with part of the very boat that Dad served on*, remembering that his father had told him that the *Narwhal* had been scrapped shortly after WWII and sold to a company to be made into razor blades. Maybe someday, he thought, my own son—if I ever have one—would be shaving with the boat I'm temporarily "riding"—as temporary sub duty was referred to for CT guests like him.

The regular crew didn't associate much with the CTs, or vice versa because of the sensitive nature of their work. CTs also didn't stand fire watches, or chip paint, or any of the other routine but necessary and hated tasks that filled hours of time for the regular crew. It's possible, he thought, that the crew might figure there was little purpose in developing any kind of friendship with their guests who wouldn't be there long enough to make it worthwhile. The popular saying "We eat their food, we drink their water, we breathe their air, but we were never there" pretty much summed up the status of the sub-riding CTs.

"Keep in mind that you won't be real popular with members of the regular Navy," his instructor at code school had told them. "But it's important work. We listen to the conversations of military units all over the world—friendly nations included, and it helps our intelligence effort to be ready. If we'd believed the intelligence we had in hand in 1941, there would have been no Pearl Harbor. We provide an early-warning system that helps us keep both our friends and enemies honest, so to speak." The explanation made sense, and now Sonny was experiencing the consequences of his job first-hand.

His watch had just begun. They were always the same. The working quarters for the CTs were always hot, day and night; there wasn't much room for the air to circulate in a space Sonny estimated to be about the size of two telephone booths. Even the light wisp of air coming through the ventilation system was warm, and there wasn't much point to get up and move around. The irony of sipping hot coffee in these conditions didn't escape him; he leaned his chair back and rested his head on the bulkhead and wished for a cool glass of Kirin. He thought it strange that the steel of the ship remained cool while the air wasn't.

Space was valuable everywhere, but at least he had his own bunk to collapse into, and didn't have to share one with some other smelly crewmember he didn't know. Sharing a bunk, or 'hot bunking' as it was known—with all of its individual aromatic essences, often was necessary because often there weren't enough bunks for each member of the crew to have his own. As one man would come off watch, he'd take over the bunk of someone about to go on watch.

The routine six-hour watch usually passed fairly quickly, although some days it felt like a lot longer when it was over. Tonight there was a slight motion to the boat, but as he had no visible references to judge its speed or even determine for sure if it was day or night, the only indication that he had that time was passing at all was the watch on his wrist. Being submerged for days on end didn't help.

He put his coffee aside and began to get ready for his watch responsibilities. The cup he'd brought was one of the few personal niceties he could squeeze into his sea bag. He couldn't really complain—he had almost everything he needed, and you didn't need much when you were only here for 60 days. Theoretically.

However, he was starting his third month on this cruise, and Sonny was relieved that he finally was on his way home—or at least on the way back to Yokosuka where he'd joined the sub. The cruise had been a good experience, but he had to admit that he hadn't anticipated the eerie feeling he got from not seeing the sky for days on end. At first it had completely upset his system—he didn't know when to be hungry or when to feel sleepy. He still had seven months left to do on his tour of shore duty in Japan, and hoped that after that he would be able to get home to Minnesota before he had to report to his next duty station, wherever it may be.

"How's it hangin,' Powell?" It was the voice of Dusty Rabinovitz, the friendliest of the five other CTs on board, all of whom he'd met for the first time when he joined the *Crestfin* in Yokosuka. The name fit him—his voice was deep and somewhat hoarse all the time. His voice reminded Sonny of someone who'd been working in a grain elevator all day and truly did have a 'dusty' voice. Dusty was walking through the passageway on his way to get coffee. Dusty called Navy coffee the 'black death,' which did little to endear him to the regular crew, other than mark him as not being a serious coffee drinker—ergo not a true sailor in their minds.

Sonny dropped his feet from the top of the workstation and swung around in his chair, but Dusty had disappeared before Sonny could answer. *How does he do it?* Sonny wondered, as Dusty squeezed through the door. He's short and he has to be over 250 pounds, yet he goes through there like a greased pig. At least Dusty was cordial. Most of the regular 80-member crew treated the six enlisted CTs like lepers, if they spoke to them at all.

Growing up on the streets of New York City with only one parent, a working mom, Dusty evidently had seen a lot of life before he joined the Navy at 17. He seemed to have a lot of street smarts for someone so young, but compared to his own rather bucolic existence in Fosston, Sonny figured he had more need for them in New York than he did in Fosston. Survival had a different meaning in the Bronx. Dusty was one of the most resourceful, outgoing people Sonny had ever met. He had an answer for everything, and if asked "How did you know that?" he'd use both hands to symbolically smooth back his straight black hair and reply "You don't get to be fat in New York if you're stupid." Sonny wasn't quite sure what that meant, but he suspected life hadn't been easy for Dusty. He didn't talk much about a home life anyway.

Sonny reached up to the top of the instrument rack for the main power breaker that would bring his workstation to life—a black crinkle-painted mass of electronic equipment stacked on top of one another side by side in a two-bay rack, most of which had to be at least 10 years old. There was some newer gear distinguished by gray paint, such as the R390 model receiver he was using—a distinct improvement over the old model SP600 he'd used when he first got to

Japan. At least it was a little more stable and didn't drift off frequency like the old receiver had. The paint was worn off around some of the dials, so he could tell it had seen hard use. That and the well-worn chair cushion indicated that lots of others had been here before him. There were demodulators, tape recorders, paper tape readers and other stuff for other CT specialties that he wouldn't be using. A small TTY sat on a shelf to his left, against the exterior bulkhead.

By now, in the sub's dim light, he knew how to find every knob, switch and dial—even in complete darkness if necessary—and where every plug should be and what it was for. You learned to know your equipment well when it was all you had to stare at for six hours straight. He could even tell if someone else had touched something in his absence through a subconscious memorization of the position in which he'd left every knob and switch. Most of the gear was still tube-based, so it would be a good five minutes for everything to get warmed up and cookin'. It contributed to the stifling air in the workroom.

The increasingly loud hum of the R-390 receiver through his headset told him it was time to get to work. He began filling out his log—date, zulu time and frequency. Setting the receiver's squelch, gain and the bias, and all of the other knob twisting by now was second nature to Sonny. It was almost an autonomic response to hone in on a target transmission and fine-tune it so he could lean back in the spartan government-issue armchair on rusty wheels and let things run as they would.

He couldn't see Dusty, but he knew he was right around the corner within shouting range. "Hey, Dusty—what's today's date?"

"July 17, why?"

"That's what I thought. It's my birthday!"

"Happy birthday, swab; where's the cake?" Dusty asked.

Yeah, cake, what I'd give for one of mom's angel food cakes right now, Sonny thought. "The skipper's having us up at 1600 for cake and tea. You go on ahead if I'm not ready," Sonny replied, as he filled in the date on his log sheet. The Navy operated on zulu—Greenwich Mean Time—using the 24-hour clock. It eliminated confusion as to whether four o'clock was a.m. or p.m. Sixteen-hundred was four hours past 1200, or noon, and everyone knew it meant four p.m. And here and now, nobody cared.

Everything was working and ready—tape decks were running, the antenna patch plug was in the right hole, and with one spin of the R390's vernier tuning dial, Sonny was on his assigned frequency.

But all was quiet, and it shouldn't have been.

"Shit," he said aloud, "Did I miss their schedule? He should be there by now."

He checked his watch—Timex, but reliable. *No,* he told himself, *I'm right on time.* He tried alternate frequencies and all was dead. Normally the Russian Morse code operators were punctual; they had set times to communicate ship-to-ship or ship-to-shore, and Sonny could only imagine the penalties in the Russian military for things like missing an important schedule. One less ration of boiled potatoes and an ounce of vodka, at least.

And even though they didn't use call sign identifiers, Sonny usually could tell who they were just on the basis of the time, the frequency, and the rhythm and speed of the operator's code, referred to as the 'fist.' Each operator's sending technique was slightly different one from another and after a period of time listening to or 'copying' one individual, Sonny would become quite familiar with him and be able to identify him regardless of atmospheric conditions.

The Russian military stations that Sonny was monitoring usually started with voice or Morse code before switching to other forms of transmission such as Teletype (TTY) or facsimile, and that was the time to identify them. But today Sonny's target either was late or had switched frequencies, which was possible but not common.

So the search was on. And a futile one it turned out to be. The characteristic roar of the TTY warming up was gone and no unintelligible Russian voices were to be heard to tell him what was going on. In fact, the entire frequency band was uncharacteristically dead.

"Dusty, you got anything?" he yelled, unconsciously glancing up at the overhead as he did so, as though Dusty's image would appear and answer him, or maybe the sound would carry better. Sonny's workstation was one thin bulkhead around a corner from the next; it was amazing how they fit six guys in such a small space.

"Yeah, all is well on the Russian front, or at least my piece of it" was Dusty's reply.

"Good for you. Mine's dead." *It must be a loose connection in the antenna patch-panel, or else the entire Russian Navy had gone off to their dachas on the Black Sea. Not likely, even if it was August, the traditional month for vacation, or holiday as most Europeans called it,* he concluded.

Sonny got up and walked the few feet to the central antenna patch panel that the six men shared. It was difficult to get confused, because the choice of antennas was very limited. For the most part, their selection consisted of a few vertical antenna masts mounted above the conning tower, and a few retractable long-wires strung fore and aft from mid-ship when they were surfaced.

He double-checked to make sure his receiver was connected to the right antenna, and it was, so Sonny suspected that he had patched into a dead antenna. He checked his plug, and it was secure. He'd heard stories about antennas getting tangled in fishing nets or snapping off from a variety of reasons, so anything was possible.

He called the duty maintenance tech on the intercom and asked him to check it out. Within minutes, his suspicion was confirmed: a lost antenna.

Switching to an alternate, the band sprung to life. And sure enough, there was 'Ivan' or 'Igor,' or whatever his name was, just a little late. He was right on frequency and getting ready to switch from voice to five-letter coded groups of gibberish—data that hopefully would mean something to someone back at the 'parent company' National Security Agency in the States. It certainly didn't mean anything to Sonny.

"You up yet?"

Sonny nodded to himself. "Yep. Don't bother using A3—it's dead."

After a few seconds, Dusty yelled "What's 'sladiche' mean—or however you say it in Russian?"

"Slidiche means 'change frequency'."

"Great. Just when I had him. Now I don't have a clue where he'll go," Dusty said in a disgusted voice.

Sonny didn't hear him. Mentally, he already was back in Japan. He was eagerly anticipating his body following suit—back to the Bar 'Happy,' where he knew everyone and could count on the security and friendship that liberty with buddies was all about. Not to mention the great draft Kirin beer that had no equal anywhere in the States—especially in Fosston, Minnesota.

Sonny was quite proficient at copying code. He'd actually lapse into somewhat of a half-daze and the dits-and-dahs seemed to automatically transform into alpha-numerics. It was in the middle of this semi-conscious state when suddenly a faint metallic screech echoed through the sub, and snapped Sonny back to the present from his imaginary glass of over-the-top foamy beer. Something was very wrong—the metal-to-metal scraping sound over his head was new to him, and it wasn't a pleasant sound. And it was loud…VERY loud.

Realizing that his earphones had gone dead, he first checked to be sure they were still plugged in, and then it dawned on him that the whip antenna he was using probably had hit something on the surface. "Oh shit," he said, beginning to tweak dials—to no avail. The screeching sound was louder now, and it didn't leave much to the imagination—they'd *scraped something, and now it was more than just an antenna!*

With a loud unfinished "What the…," Sonny jumped up, a reflex action, and then just stood there—listening. He had an overwhelming deep feeling of anxiety, and it was the first time he'd felt any fear on this cruise. Now he was cold, but beads of nervous sweat began to pop out on his forehead, the salty liquid running down into the corner of his eyes. Sonny suddenly felt clammy all over. Dusty obviously had heard the screeching noise also, because Sonny heard him yelling. Hell, the entire crew had to have heard it.

Unbelievable—and unfamiliar loud, grinding and crunching sounds resonated throughout the boat—steel bulkheads were designed to keep you safe, but they also were excellent transmitters of sound. Sonny's workstation was just forward of the conning tower, the tallest part of the sub. The sub was still moving, and the scraping sound continued for at least 15 seconds or more. The screech of metal to metal was now so loud that he ripped off the headset and fruitlessly put his hands to his ears.

We're in deep shit, Sonny thought. And he was about to discover that he was right.

Simultaneous with the end of the scraping noise, Sonny suddenly was knocked to the deck; the headset cord around his neck was still plugged into the receiver and snapped as he fell back against the bulkhead.

All went black. For a brief moment, he thought he'd knocked himself out, but quickly realized that he couldn't be thinking about it if he truly had been unconscious. The power was off. The cube, indeed the entire compartment was pitch dark—the kind of blackness that led you to focus all of your senses on listening.

"Dusty, you O.K.? Dusty, what's going on?" No answer. He grabbed the edge of the equipment bay and began to pull himself up off the deck when he heard a very loud crunch of metal—whatever it was, it had rocked the sub. It felt like something was pushing them sideways. *Hell of a way to spend my birthday*, he thought.

*   *   *   *

Starishy matros (petty officer) Alexi Prilov was beginning to nod off. It had been a long night. He'd been partying in Vlad only four hours earlier, celebrating his last night on shore before a week-long coastal defense cruise. A physically fit 21 year old, Alexi could keep up with the best of them and normally only required about five hours of sleep a night. But tonight was developing into a long one.

He'd only been assigned to the *Novosibirsk* for a few months, and while it was sea duty, it was sea duty with a tight tether to shore. The *Novosibirsk,* a light Russian cruiser of the Sverdlov class, would only cruise off the coast for a week at a time, and then would be replaced by another ship. The theory was that this kept the crew fresh and alert, and morale high. It was viewed as great duty—one week at sea, one week docked, and indeed morale was high. As for keeping the crew alert, that was a different matter.

For Alexi, shore time meant party time, and the first 24 hours back at sea were pretty much a waste. Tonight was no different, except that it was unusually cold on the deck. He'd let his beard grow in the false expectation of enhanced facial warmth, but the reality was that this was not to be—his sparce blond beard wasn't much longer than the short hair on his head, and that wasn't by design either. He wondered if his ancestors had all been bald and if it was something hereditary from generations of potato farming.

It seemed surprisingly cold for this time of the year. His heavy USSR-issue pea coat was warm, but he'd forgotten his turtleneck sweater tonight, and the cold was getting through in patches like pincushions. He paced back and forth on the foredeck, but it was small and there wasn't much room to exercise to keep the blood flowing. The fermented potato-based antifreeze he'd spent hours and many rubles pumping into his system was working against him, and he shivered, never able to get away from the wind. It seemed to come from all four directions at once.

He'd only been on watch for a short time, and knew it was going to be a long, cold four more hours. The *Novosibirsk* was moving pretty fast for this time of night, and Alexi's guess was that she had to cover more patrol area than normal as her sister ship was in dry dock for repairs. Alexi was brought out of his post-liberty vodka stupor when he spotted something sticking out of the water—*too straight to be a tree branch*, he thought.

At first he didn't pay much attention to the object in the water, but it seemed to reflect in the moonlight—maybe even leaving a slight trail of bubbles in the water that was not normal for tree branches. Besides, the water depth here was sufficient for the ship, so nothing should be stuck on the bottom.

There had been a major storm off the tip of the Kamchatka peninsula just two nights previous, and a lot of debris was still bobbing on the surface. This particular piece of debris that Alexi was watching, however, appeared to be moving in an uncharacteristic straight line directly across the bow of the ship.

Alexi stared long and hard, but hesitated sounding an alarm. He had done so once before and that had turned out to be false. As a result he'd spent a week scrubbing pots and peeling spuds in the galley. At least it was something he had experience with, and it was an indoor, sit-down job.

To Alexi, getting transferred from shore duty at the base at Petropovlosk on the Kamchatka Peninsula to coastal defense duty with the Red Banner Fleet out of Vladivostok initially seemed analogous to a transfer to hell. Vlad was almost 6,000 miles from his home. He'd often wondered why he had joined the navy in the first place, given that he liked shore duty better than sea duty. *Should have gone with the infantry*, he thought, however briefly.

He'd been surprised that duty in Vladivostok had turned out to be o.k. He'd been having a good time even though he thought that this business of sailing up and down the coast, over and over, was stupid. Certainly no American ship of any kind would dare approach this closely to the coast of Mother Russia given the presence of the entire fleet and all of the shore defense missiles and other surprises waiting for any intruder.

But he didn't dare risk another transfer. This time he wanted to be sure of what he was seeing before waking half the ship. Besides, he was sure the radar or sonar operators must be aware of this moving object which appeared before him by now; it was only about 200 yards off the bow. If it was more than a branch, for sure it was causing bleeps and raising all kind of alarms in the operations center. If they were awake, that is.

A Russian light cruiser of the Sverdlov class

As the Russian cruiser and the floating object came closer together, Alexi lifted his heavy, gray 50-power field glasses that were hanging around his neck and saw what it was—what it had to be—an antenna, probably from a sub. There was no mistaking it now—it was almost following the moonlight trail across the black water. Alexi quickly grabbed the inter-communication telephone and rang the bridge.

"Moving object in water 200 yards off port bow," Alexi shouted excitedly to the unknown sailor on the other end of the phone. "Da," was the only reply as he hung up the phone. He had sounded the alarm. It didn't matter if it was a Russian or American sub he was seeing—it was dangerously close and about to cross their bow.

The 14-ton cruiser came alive. But 'coming alive' at three o'clock in the morning meant little more than Alexi having time to utter the Russian version of "Oh My God!"

In no time, the sleek cruiser *Novosibirsk* was within yards of whatever it was, and stopping or turning at this point was not a consideration. At 25 knots, all he had time to do was to brace for impact. The slim, knife-sharp edge of the ship's bow, so efficient at parting the sea, was about to slice into a very large, dark object just beneath the sea's surface.

Alexi leaned back against the bulkhead on the foredeck and spread his feet, braced for impact. He watched in horror; they were about to hit something, and he knew it wasn't going to be a floating log. His feet were firmly planted on the deck, and he anticipated a ride up and over whatever it was. He wasn't disappointed.

✳   ✳   ✳   ✳

As Sonny slowly regained consciousness, he was unusually cold—temperature-cold and fear-cold. He quickly became aware that water had risen up to his chest, and when he tried to get up on his knees, he couldn't feel his feet and his legs weren't cooperating. In the total darkness he didn't realize that his workstation had shifted and the tabletop had collapsed and pinned the lower half of his body against the bulkhead. Then he heard a second crunching noise, more like a muffled squashing sound, indicating that the hull probably had been breached. Sonny didn't know it, but about 10 feet of the bow of a very large Russian cruiser was protruding through the hull only 20 yards behind him in the control room.

His "Hey, can anyone hear me?" was met with silence. In fact, other than the sounds of rushing, gurgling water and stressed steel, the sub was silent.

What had seemed to occur over several minutes actually had happened in less than one. The *Crestfin*'s engines now were silent, and other than the eerie noise of stressing steel, the only other sound was that of lapping water approaching his chin from below.

Despite the complete darkness, the cold, and the realization that he couldn't move, an unusual calm came over Sonny. He reflected with amazement at how fast the human mind can process information under stress. He began to accept the numbness in his legs and the silent destitution he faced. He was cold, but the cold was physical. A calming warmth was spreading across the surface of his mind, and with it, memories of home.

Fosston had been cold too. In February it was lucky if it got much above minus-10. Higher than 20 above was considered a heat wave, it seemed—even inside his uncle's grain elevator where he'd worked after graduating from high school. When it was that warm, it was difficult to get his friends onto the pond for a quick hockey game.

He'd given Uncle Martin three years in the grain elevator. The first year was spent at the working end of a shovel. Then he drove truck for awhile, and eventually Uncle Martin moved him into the front office to the boring job of preparing weight tickets and other necessary but dull paperwork. It was difficult for Sonny to believe that Martin and his father were brothers; Sonny's dad had burnt-orange hair, was almost as tall as Sonny, and fair. Martin was dark and short. There was, of course, no question where Sonny's genes came from. His hair was a little less brassy than his fathers, but that probably was tempered a bit by his mother's (once) brown hair. The freckles came from dad, without a doubt.

The three years working in Fosston after high school had been an adjustment for Sonny. Most of his friends were going off to college, joining the service or working for their parents. He wondered about those who went off to the military—how many were in Vietnam now? How many wouldn't be at his next high school reunion? It seemed that the TV network news took an impersonal position on the dead—they were nothing more than a body count. Great stress was put on comparing body counts, as though it was the true measure of success. And of course the U.S. count was always lower than that of the enemy…

Those who were home and working, as he was, didn't seem to have time to get together very often. Most of his friends had serious love affairs in progress; serious in the sense that the high school romances which had survived had developed into something with signs of lasting. At least they were more time consuming, and one or the other of the couple seemed to require more of the other's time. Sonny had thought about college, but his parents really couldn't afford it and he was, by his own admission, little more than a mediocre basketball player, so an athletic scholarship was out of the question.

And then, at age 20 it suddenly was time—time to get out, see some of the world, taste some of the flavors that he knew existed outside of mom's cooking, and—quite simply—time to grow up.

Hoping to minimize his chances of going to Viet Nam—a good bet if he joined the Army or Marines, Sonny readily accepted his father's advice and found the fastest way out of boredom and Fosston was to join the Navy. He'd never been out of the state of Minnesota before and he'd had apprehensions. But to his own surprise, he wasn't homesick after the first few weeks in boot camp at the Great Lakes Training Center in Illinois. But he did miss his dog Radar. While most of his buddies had pictures of girlfriends and wives to share, Sonny had a framed photo of Radar that he carried all the way to Japan.

He took a lot of ribbing about that from his buddies, with most of the comments asking him what his 'sheep's name was.' But he didn't have a particular girl's picture to display; there hadn't been much time for a girlfriend in Fosston, between working in the grain elevator and basketball practices and games. He did have the almost exclusive use of his father's pickup truck, but girls in Fosston were somewhat fussy. The fact that his truck didn't have a windshield discouraged most of his dates, especially when it was raining or snowing—both of which were frequent occurrences.

So with a somewhat vacant social calendar, Sonny had spent many enjoyable off-hours hunting with Radar in the grass and grain fields around Fosston, and as Sonny was an only child, Radar truly was a member of the family.

Radar had been named for his ability to sense the presence of rabbits and game birds even in open grass where everything was otherwise invisible to human eyes. He always found them when Sonny's 16-gauge double-barreled Ithica would bring them down, too. Dad had always told him that a good hunter never abandoned the search for a wounded bird, and with Radar's skills, that search never took long. *Radar was probably missing him too*, Sonny thought.

He reflected on how much he really had wanted to be here on this boat. He'd tried for a full-time assignment to submarine duty right out of boot camp, but he was too tall and he was told he had too many fillings. Replacing fillings and anchoring them to the jawbone to pressure-proof them was expensive but necessary for submariners; sudden loss of pressure on a deep dive could send the little silver fillings flying right up through the brain like .22-caliber bullets. Normally if a submarine candidate had but a few fillings, they'd either replace them or yank them. But in Sonny's case, his was a grin of gold.

He'd been told that TAD could be exciting, but he had found sailing up and down the coast of the Soviet Union and straight into Vladivostok harbor slightly less than thrilling. Perhaps it was best that it wasn't exciting, Sonny postulated. Getting in and out like they'd never been there was, after all, the objective. Sneaking an American sub into Vlad harbor in 1968 just wasn't high on anyone's list of fun things to do.

The port of Vladivostok was home to the Pacific Fleet, the largest of the four Russian fleets. Historically, the fleet's focus here had been on countering both the U.S. and Chinese presence in East Asia. As such, Vlad has been the target of intense attention by U.S. and other nations' intelligence forces, and numerous surveillance missions on, above and below its adjacent waters since as long as surveillance was technically feasible, or necessary.

Located on the northwestern coast of the Sea of Japan, Vlad had the benefit of good strategic access to points in the Pacific Ocean and the Sea of Japan. Vlad's location also was a curse, because it was thousands of miles from Moscow, connected only by the single-track, 5000-mile Trans-Siberian railway, and all practical movement of goods was by sea or air.

The region's other target of significance to the American intelligence effort was the major Soviet submarine base at Petropavlovsk on the Kamchatka Peninsula. All of the Pacific Fleet's nuclear boats were based here. Located about 1500 miles northeast of Vlad, it commanded control over the icy waters of the Sea of Okhotsk where both Russian and American submarines routinely cruised north of Japan's northernmost island, Hokkaido.

Like the Soviet coast facing the Sea of Japan, the frigid Sea of Okhotsk is ringed with defensive radar and communications systems, missile batteries and numerous other fortifications for defense of the homeland.

Most countries claim a 12-mile coastal limit to their territorial waters. The Soviet Union claimed 30 or more, and the internationally recognized limit was three. So by everyone's standards, the sub Sonny was riding was violating all of the rules. But the Russians did it too—subs had been spotted well inside the American territorial limits for years. American subs chased Russian and Chinese subs; Chinese and Russian subs shadowed American subs. It had almost reached game-like proportions. A very deadly game, at that.

The *Crestfin,* an older diesel-electric boat originally commissioned in the early 1940s, had suffered a delay enroute to the Vlad vicinity because of engine problems. As a result, Sonny's tour, originally scheduled to last about 70 days, had now stretched to about 90.

The *Crestfin's* Captain had successfully taken them into the Vladivostok harbor, and skillfully put them on the bottom for three days—snugly nestled between a mothballed freighter and the shore. The sub would surface only long enough to allow its antennas to penetrate the surface of the bay, never enough to permit the silhouette of the boat to be visible. It was quiet there compared to the main channel they had entered through, less than 100 feet beneath an endless and nerve-wracking parade of fishing boats, freighters and what seemed like the entire Pacific fleet passing by overhead.

During the previous 48 hours, Sonny hadn't heard a single screw turning over their heads. He'd even had the thrill of looking through the periscope at the lights of Vlad about 0200 the previous morning right before they departed. Poking their periscope and antennas above the surface was tricky; typically kept up only long enough to get certain scheduled transmissions that couldn't be obtained while submerged. Unfortunately they never were up long enough to take in the precious fresh air that they needed at least every four to five days. So their stay was brief. The new nuclear boats didn't have that problem, generating their own oxygen and remaining submerged for weeks. Sonny understood the new boats created their own fresh water from seawater and showers were possible every day instead of once every week.

The *Crestfin* was moving out, taking it slow—at about ten knots, half the sub's normal submerged speed. The captain was keeping the boat just barely submerged, ready to surface or dive deeper if necessary—on their way out, back to Yokosuka. And eventually back to relative normalcy at the Navy communications station at Kami Seya.

The Captain also was taking a different route back; weather had changed, the tides were out, and they had to find a deeper channel.

Unexpectedly, the bottom was sloping upward as they exited the bay. Charts for this area were unreliable, and the sea bottom subject to change. Evidently silt had built up from a big storm further out at sea, and had blocked their original entrance channel; the hope was that the new route was going to be less of a problem.

The boat was actually following the slope of the bottom, and with a 16-foot draft, they were getting dangerously close to the surface and the possibility of putting the superstructure out of the water. *We're definitely rising*, Sonny thought—*maybe for some long overdue fresh air...or maybe we're switching from electric to diesel so we can go faster and make up some time.*

That had been only moments ago. But Sonny was back in the present, in the dark and alone in the cold. In the water. He stopped struggling, coming to the inescapable conclusion that he wasn't going to make it home to see Radar again. And with seawater now entering his nasal passages, he finally dismissed the cold and accepted the warmth that was entering his soul…

CHAPTER 2

▼

"To make a long story short, we want to know what it's doing down there, so we're sending you and a small team to find out."

"Excuse me, Lelani my precious flower, but duty calls!" With those parting words, uttered with an authentic W.C. Fields inflection, Art Spencer, CT first class, lover of ladies and voluminous repository of fermented malts and other alcoholic beverages, was dragged semi-upright from Oahu's smoky 'Wahoo! Bar' by two much, much smaller members of the U.S. Navy Shore Patrol.

"C'mon, guys, take it easy. I'm going. I'm cooperating. What's the rush? I was just having a quiet beer and therapeutic crotch-rub…"

"Sorry to interrupt your massage, Spencer, but the Operations Duty Officer wants to see you immediately. And he doesn't care about the health of your balls."

A burp or two later, a now more relaxed Art Spencer was helped into the back seat of the topless shore patrol jeep–and they began the short journey back to base. Art was sober enough to realize they hadn't handcuffed him so, he reasoned—he couldn't be in *too* much trouble. The fresh air was helping him recover some of his senses, but not helping a lot with the whirlpool that had engulfed his stomach. It was a typical balmy Hawaiian night: lots of stars, high humidity and a temperature of about 80 degrees. Art had problems keeping his chin off of his chest, but he endeavored to do so if for no other reason than to present an image of sobriety. It was tough. He'd been at the Wahoo! Bar for three hours, or at least that's what his body clock told him. Needless to say his wrist-watch was way too out of focus to confirm that. *Damn cheap Jap watch*, he thought…

"When we get to the base, we'll give you five minutes in the head to clean that lipstick off your face—and wherever else, and then we'll take you to the O.D.," the short but husky navy shore patrolman in the passenger seat told him. Tough as it was to do so, Art instinctively knew this was a good time to keep quiet…Any shore patrol sailor whose sleeve displayed only seaman's stripes and four hash-marks representing 16 years of service wasn't to be argued with.

The ride back to the Naval Communications Station at Wahiawa seemed longer than it actually was. After initially turning his stomach into a large blender, the steady hum of the knobby tires on the cement highway—coupled with the alcohol swimming through his large body—had lulled Art to sleep just about the time the jeep came to a brake-screeching stop just inside the base main gate.

"Get cleaned up and get back here fast. We have 10 minutes to get you there."

Art lumbered out of the back seat of the jeep and tried to make his wobbly legs function fairly normally as he stepped into the bathroom at the base service station. The sink was disgustingly black and hadn't drained since the last similarly blotto sailor used it, but the tepid water was effective in removing the lipstick; he wished it could clear away the imaginary cobwebs from behind his eyes—he just knew they were the sole reason for his fuzzy vision.

Art walked what he imagined an impressive straight line back to the jeep—he was very pleased with his performance, and within a few minutes the jeep arrived at the base operations building—the nerve center of normal Navy operations 24-hours a day. Art gave a half-hearted mock goodbye salute to the two men as they drove away. He entered the building—now deserted and dark except for the single enlisted man standing his duty watch at the entrance, and light from the officer's office down the dimly lit hall.

"Straight ahead, Spencer…" the watch announced, knowing that at this hour the guy being delivered by the shore patrol had to be the one the O.D. had sent for.

Art straightened up and smoothed his wrinkled Hawaiian print shirt as best he could—acutely aware that he reeked of stale beer even though the wetness was now gone. He zigzagged down the asbestos-tiled hall for a few doors and came to the O.D.'s office. He knocked once and the unlatched door to the duty officer's office opened on its own.

"Good Morning, Spencer. Sorry to roust you away from your evening out. Stumble on in here and have a seat." The O.D. was seated, his tie loose around his neck, and his sleeves rolled up. One leg was resting on the typewriter attached to the desk, and the officer appeared about as relaxed as any Art had ever seen.

"Good Morning, Sir. Thank you." Art sat in the chair furtherest from the officer's desk. *Maybe I won't smell so bad from here*, he thought. The office was pretty bare with the exception of the desk, a few files and a single hanging ceiling light. There were no personal items—no family photos, awards, trophies, flags, etc. decorating the office. This wasn't any single individual's office—different duty officers rotated in and out of here many times during a day. Kind of like the parking attendant shack at the pay-lot near the local shopping center.

"Spencer, I understand you're fluent in Russian."

"Yes Sir."

"I also understand that you washed out of the language school at Monterrey."

"Uh, Yes Sir." All of a sudden this casual-appearing officer had his attention. He must know more than your average slob on duty, Art concluded.

"Mind telling me what happened?"

"Not at all, Sir. I was in my eighth week, well into it actually, total immersion and all that, you know. Jesus, I was dreaming in Russian. You know they don't allow you to even speak English at that point…"

"I've heard that. Go on."

Art was prepared to continue, although he wasn't sure what he should or should not talk about. He had no way of knowing what this guy already knew, or even what he was authorized to talk about. "Well, I don't want this to sound egotistical, but I was bored. Most people—Americans anyway—have a real problem learning the Russian language. Naturally the Cyrillic alphabet throws people, but the verb conjugations, etc. are all totally different. Unlike Spanish or French which, like English, are Latin-based…Anyway, it seemed to come pretty easy to me. I got a little cocky—too cocky some thought, and I got into a few disciplinary actions with the instructors, etc. We had a mutual agreement that I probably didn't have the dedication, the patience and rigid discipline that are required to be a successful linguist. I guess I could have worked into an analyst job, but that probably would have meant being stuck at Ft. Meade, Maryland, and that's not why I joined the Navy—to see Maryland. So I was told to go away—as an admin type, and here I am."

"That's about what I read in your service record. You've smoothed it out a little from what I understood, but you're entitled to do that. The dismissal order in your record is the first one that I've ever read that concluded by complimenting your skills and abilities after reaming you a new asshole for your attitude." With that the officer smiled, and Art knew this was probably going to be a friendlier discussion than he had anticipated.

"Yes Sir, I may have left out some of the rough spots..."

"Neither here nor there, Spencer. I think we have a job for you and we're going to overlook the attitude problem. I've been in similar situations where the learning seems to progress faster than the teaching, and it's not easy to slow yourself down.

"Anyway, here's what's going on. Do you understand that the balance of this conversation will be classified?"

"Yes Sir, I have top secret clearance."

"O.K. I'm aware of that, Spencer. Otherwise we wouldn't be having this discussion. Here's the gist of it. We've been tracking a Russian submarine that's been snooping around in some of the old atomic testing grounds. We first spotted it just off Johnston Island to the south of here. We've picked up several of its radio transmissions, some of them sent back to Soviet fleet headquarters in Vladivostok, and some to an unidentified, but obviously mobile station also somewhere south in the same vicinity." The officer paused, partly to make sure that he still had Art's attention, but also to provide the opportunity for comments or questions at this point. Observing Art's complete attention, and silence, he continued.

"Our best guess is that the mobile station is some sort of a supply and refueling ship. The Russian sub is a Foxtrot-class diesel-electric boat, and they couldn't have make it to where they are, that far from home, without getting re-supplied with fuel every once in awhile." Again a pause, an awareness check, and no response from Art.

A Russian Foxtrot-class submarine

"To make a long story short, we want to know what it's doing down there, so we're sending you and a small team to find out. We don't have any official presence in the area, so we want you to accompany two other men and go down there and help us figure out what's going on. The sub is using VHF line-of-sight, low power transmissions most of the time, and it's too far from our NSGA Guam and Hawaiian ears to cover. The two men you'd go with both are communications intercept specialists, experts in both Morse code and radio-teletype, and you'd round out the team by supplying the interpretation."

Art was sober now. The cobwebs were gone, and he relaxed a little in his chair. "Not to be impertinent, Sir, but aren't there better, more qualified linguists here at Wahiawa or on Guam?"

The officer stood, pushing his chair into the desk. "Yes, there are. We have two qualified men here in Hawaii. NCS Guam has one in their analysis section that they say is good. But we can't spare any of them. And quite frankly, those that know you tell us that even though you're a little harder to handle than some would prefer, that sometimes you're worth the trouble. Besides, you're just wasting away here in the base admin department, shuffling paper and getting fat. I think you're right for the job. It's only about a two-month assignment at best, and maybe shorter if the sub leaves the area. What say?"

Art stared at the floor, probably longer than he should have, contemplating his options—the number of which seemed scant—before he looked up at the officer, now standing right in front of the desk—within olfactory-range of Art's beer-soaked shirt.

"You with me, Spencer?"

"Sure. What the hell, I probably don't have any choice anyway…"

"To the contrary," the officer corrected him. "This is a *volunteer* mission. Both of the other men are volunteering as well. You don't have to go—you've been here almost 10 months and you'll rotate out soon…probably to our station in Adak. Alaska needs good men."

Ha, Art thought, *that makes it abundantly clear.* "When do we leave?"

"I thought you'd appreciate the opportunity to get out from behind the desk. And I think this will be a good career move for you, Spencer. I'll see to it that Adak finds someone else to issue their cold weather gear to."

"Come back tomorrow—or rather I should say later this morning—say right after noon chow, and we'll fill you in on the details. Now go hit the rack and get some sleep. And burn that shirt."

With that, Art smiled, got up and said "Yes Sir. See you later," and turned and left the ops building. *Burn this shirt? Bullshit. This is one of my favorites.* CT1/ A-branch Art Spencer was on his way back to his barracks and a few hours sleep. And, he thought, he was on his way to some God-awful hot islands in the South Pacific—islands that shouldn't be too hard to find at night if they flew in as they probably were still glowing from the atomic bomb tests that the U.S. Government had held there since the 1940s.

✻   ✻   ✻   ✻

It was early by anyone's clock, especially the one Art had been operating under for the past few days. No amount of coffee or sunshine could convince him he should be anywhere other than back here where he'd just been six hours earlier in the Ops building. The officer providing the mission briefing droned on in a monotone. *Why do they always select the most inept speakers when the objective is to keep you interested?* Art wondered.

"The Trust Territory Pacific was established in 1951, covers an area of more than three-million miles, has only 97-odd inhabited islands and atolls, and has a population of less than 100,000; the total land mass is only about 700 square miles…"

And all of them now glow in the dark, Art thought.

"The 67 U.S. atomic tests primarily were conducted in the Bikini and atolls of the Marshalls in the 1940s and 1950s, and for the most part ended in 1958. But in 1962, Operation '*Fishbowl*' in the Christmas and Johnston Islands was sort of the last hurrah for the American nuclear program. These tests consisted of missile-launched atmospheric detonations conducted by the Department of Defense at altitudes of from 30 to 250 miles high, and payloads as high as 1100 kilotons.

"U.S. testing ended with a joint Russian-American agreement signed in Moscow in August of 1963. That didn't involve the French though, and their tests in Murakoa, French Polynesia, however, began just recently, in 1966."

With that background explanation, Art now wondered if he'd come home with any hair. He didn't have much to lose—a heredity problem…"Here's our chance to get sterile without an operation!" he exclaimed to the other two enlisted CTs who would accompany him, sitting one on each side of Art and looking about equally enthralled with the proposed mission.

"Yeah, and after watching those Japanese science fiction movies about two-inch lizards that get radiated and develop into battleship-devouring monsters, maybe this isn't a Russian submarine we're looking for after all!" exclaimed CT2/R-branch Chris Noonan, the Morse code expert of the trio.

"Gentlemen, let us continue," the Operations Officer said as the unidentified officer who had delivered the social/political background briefing was ushered out of the room.

"As you know, we have an ocean-bottom network of listening devices known as "SOSUS"—short for 'SOund SUrveillance System,' which basically is an array of seabed hydrophones arranged in a grid pattern that are used to detect and track submarine activity. The first indication that we had Soviet activity was when the SOSUS gear around the Johnston Atoll southwest of Hawaii tipped us off. Then we detected the sub again when it swung further south toward the Marshall Islands. The sub seems to be headed on a straight-line course toward Eniwetok Atoll. Since the testing ended there, we don't have a lot of 'eyes' in the area, so we're not positive of her exact current position right now. Or who she is…

"Without going into a lot of unnecessary detail, let me emphasize that the Russians' presence is not so much of a worry or immediate danger as it is a curiosity for us. For a sub to travel that distance from its home, given the elaborate support required by a diesel boat, is simply very unusual. The area she's in holds no current military significance to anyone, and so we're just being cautious.

"The three of you will be flown to Majuro, capital of the Marshalls, where you'll meet up with an Indonesian-registered freighter known as the '*Malacca Star*.' The freighter should be there when you get there, having recently sailed from Ponape to the West. She's an independent, small, older freighter that's been roaming around through the South China Seas since the end of the war. The captain is a former merchant mariner who bought the ship in the late 1950s to take advantage of the potential trade in the area. He delivers a lot of fuel, food and other supplies throughout the region, and trades on the spot, with no fixed schedule or route. It's the perfect cover for a ship to just roam around with no obvious intended course and—coincidentally—tracking this Russian sub, hopefully unnoticed."

"Your challenge is to locate and identify the sub, track it, intercept any and all radio traffic, identify its supply ship, and report back to us. Basically, we want you to try to find out what she's doing down there. We're hoping her communications will provide the answer. Any questions?"

Any questions? Art thought, like saying *Sure, you got a week?* But he knew, as usual, that he'd be told what he needed to know when he needed to know it. But he couldn't resist asking "Why us? Why not put one of our own subs down there on the Russian's trail?"

"Good question, Spencer. We easily could send a task force down there and drive the sub out, either intentionally or not. But rather than do that, we want to observe her without interrupting whatever she's doing. One of our own boats blowing diesel down her snorkel would be quickly detected and detract the Russians from whatever they're up to. After all, we don't have much more business being down there right now than they do. It's only that their presence is more difficult to explain. Plus, their communications would be more guarded if we were in the area, and they'd probably stop doing whatever it is they're doing until an American presence went away. After all, that boat's come a long way from home, so whatever she's after must be important. Any more?"

"Sir, I have one." CT2 T-branch Mark Krebs, proposed teletype whiz, also on his second tour, stood up and addressed the Operations Officer. "Who do we report to?"

"We gave that a lot of thought, Krebs. In the interest of keeping this operation as quiet and inconspicuous as possible, we decided against sending someone just to function as a team leader. The three of you are all specialists, co-dependent for success. The mission is short, and you won't be in uniform or identified as members of the U.S. Navy. I guess because Spencer is the senior of the three of you, he's the unofficial lead. You do, of course, answer to the captain of the '*Star*' as long as you are his guest, in all normal shipboard matters other than related to your classified activity. The captain—by the way his name is Lawrence Cabot, has been fully briefed on of your task—but only to the extent that he has been directed to locate and surreptitiously follow the Russian. We already have upgraded the ship's radar and installed a new sonar system to help him do that—his ship wasn't exactly a model of modern technology—and by the way—sorry, I forgot to mention this—we're sending a first class electronics technician profi-cient in sonar and radar to work the gear. He reports directly to the captain, and won't have a lot of contact with you gentlemen on anything other than what he can tell you that'll help with your mission. Anything else?"

With a prolonged response of silence, which the officer didn't let drag out too long, he ended the briefing. "Report to this office at 0600 hours the day after tomorrow. We'll supply the clothes you'll need for the mission, so just bring your ditty bags. No personal photos of the honey back home, or anything that con-nects you with the U.S. Navy, and we'll get you on a plane. Thank you gentle-men. Enjoy your vacation in paradise, compliments of Uncle Sam."

The three CTs—Spencer, Noonan and Krebs sat in silence for a moment before Krebs asked, "Well, if we're going to be in civvies, can we be taken off and shot as spies? Actually no, I guess not, because we are in American-controlled water down there, and who's going to take us off the ship—Godzilla?"

The men laughed, and got up in unison to head back to their respective bar-racks. *I hope Captain Cabot isn't Godzilla*, Art thought as he waved good-bye to the other two men. "See you in a couple."

*   *   *   *

Four days later following a six-hour flight, boarding the *Malacca Star* in Majuro made Art feel like he had a part in an old black and white Humphrey Bogart mystery movie from the '40s. The only thing absent was the ever-present movie fog enshrouding the dock and the ship. Secretly he wished it had been there—it might have made the rusting hulk before him a bit more attractive as his future home for the next few weeks.

The *Malacca Star* was tied up alongside an island ferry in probably the most remote part of the harbor possible. It was about 1600 hours and the water was calm, with only the shrill cry of ever-ravenous seagulls penetrating the afternoon calm. The ship truly was a sight to behold. Even the lines, which had her fastened to the dock, looked tired, ready to snap any moment. Art wasn't sure if the dock would hold or float off into the harbor with the ship if a wind came up. The hull originally had been painted a single shade of light blue many years and many barnacles ago, but by now the old ship had been spot-painted its entire length in at least five other different shades of blue and grey—with probably whatever paint they could find when the persistent rust got bad enough to do something about. The ship seemed to be listing to port if Art's eyes didn't deceive him. It certainly was nondescript; NSA couldn't have found a more inconspicuous ship if Hollywood had designed it for them. Art's first thought was that the rough, long airplane ride down here was probably the most luxury they would see for the next several weeks.

Once aboard, it became apparent that with a ship's crew of only 25, everyone on the *Star* would get to know each other very quickly, and very well. Captain Cabot was waiting on the main deck as they climbed the gangplank, leaning over the rail dressed in shorts, a sleeveless tank-top T-shirt, and sporting a Greek fishing hat. He was a short, stocky, yellow-haired man with a very ruddy tan complexion, obviously the result of many years' exposure to the sun. And even though he wasn't necessarily an imposing figure of a man, there still was a distinct air of authority about him, and to Art, he appeared very much in command. He was cordial, and welcomed the men and immediately showed them to their quarters to stow their gear.

"Get settled as quickly as you can, gentlemen. We hope to get underway immediately and your assistance in making that happen would be appreciated. We have word that 'Red Star' is about 300 miles due north of here. It's time to begin the game. Report to the bridge as soon as you get sorted out here."

Without waiting for a reply, the captain left the men and returned to the bridge.

"Red Star? Isn't that original. Well," Krebs said to no one in particular, "I guess we don't get to check out the bars in Majuro before we leave."

"Nope. But I'm sure the lonely town virgin will still be here on the dock waiting for you when we get back," Noonan replied.

Art just smiled. From what he'd seen from the taxi they had taken from the amphibious airplane dock to the freighter, there wasn't anything in Majuro he'd risk his chances of fathering a future generation for. Majuro was largely unpaved streets, some stucco-faced buildings with corrugated tin roofs and ramshackle wooden huts mixed together. Zoning obviously wasn't a big priority with the local council of elders. The mostly-dirt streets all radiated out from the port like spokes from the hub of one-half of a wheel, a testament to the historic importance of the sea trade to the survival of the people.

Within a half-hour of boarding, the freighter's single screw was churning up the shallow muddy bottom and clanking its way out of the harbor. *It still lists to port,* Art thought. The ship quickly cleared the outer marker and poured on the proverbial steam.

Art made his way to the main deck rail and watched land fall behind them. The ship's first mate approached Art—temporarily done with his duties of helping get out of the harbor. "We only do about 20 knots, but that's fast enough. The boat we're following can't go that fast under water anyway, so we can keep up. If it surfaces and we need to chase it, we can gain some speed by lightening up and dumping you guys over." With that and a chuckle, and no time for Art's reply, he put the toothpick back between his two remaining brown upper teeth and moved off to perform some essential duty.

That was an intelligent conversation, Art thought; *and I'm glad I had so much to contribute...*

The water seemed to be a much deeper shade of blue than Art remembered it having been around Hawaii. Art was amazed at how many dinky islands there were, and how close together; *This captain may be in command of a rusty old scow,* he thought, *but he must know his stuff to navigate through here without either bottoming out or running aground somewhere.* Many of the islands, if they could be called that, were low and barely visible until you were right on top of them. Most were barren piles of sand and rock sticking out of the water, with all or most of the vegetation gone; Art wasn't sure if this was the result of intentional gleaning by the natives or the result of years of being bombarded by radioactivity. Some had lone palms, and Art found himself looking for the imaginary shipwrecked sailor leaning up against the cartoon tree on the cartoon island busily throwing message bottles into the waves.

The ship continued weaving through the atolls and islands—some no more than sand bars—for about two hours, when the captain appeared in the men's workspace and announced they had located 'Red Star,' the unimaginative code name that the brass in Wahiawa had assigned to the Russian sub.

The *Malacca Star* zigzagged and wandered through the islands in the immediate vicinity of Majuro for the best part of a week, slowly making its way northwest, to intercept the sub—assuming that it maintained its last reported course. The men early on had confirmed their equipment was operational and they actually performed a few sporadic and brief duty watches. But if the sub was transmitting anything, they weren't hearing it. Or much of anything else for that matter—not even a hum from the radiation that Art was sure was all around them and silently consuming their livers. Or, God forbid, something vital.

On the sixth day out of Majuro, the captain entered the unclassified area of the CT's operations area and told the three men that the sub had been spotted on radar. "We're pretty sure it's her, about 100 nautical miles to the north. She's in open water now, poking along on the surface. We're reducing speed to stay back. We'll wander through some of these channels just so our course doesn't appear suspicious. Everything o.k. with your gear and stuff, whatever it is?"

"Everything powers up, if that's what you mean, Captain. Hopefully the vibrations that are very effective at keeping my feet awake won't shake it to death. Thanks for asking. Keep us informed and if we learn anything helpful, we'll let you know," Art said.

With a laugh, the captain replied "O.K. gentlemen. Don't sweat the vibrations. This tub may not be pretty or smooth, but her engines are sound and we haven't had a major leak in over two weeks. Chow in 30 minutes. You don't want to miss tonight's boiled sea snake and urchin salad. It's the cook's specialty." After a pause to see if they understood his humor, the captain determined from their blank stares that his attempt at a joke had escaped them, and with a laugh at their expense he backed out of the door and turned toward the deck.

"As long ago as two weeks ago? No problem. We just have to keep our gear up off of the deck I guess. Let's see what's on the air," Chris Noonan said, settling into his chair. "Mr. Krebs, we're back to work."

"There isn't much I can do until you get something. I presume you're going to record anything you pick up, but if you intercept something live, give me a shout and I'll jump in and see if I can figure out what's happening," Art said.

"O.K., Spencer. We'll holler loud" Chris said and immediately returned to get the gear warmed up and working. Art sensed that Chris was the senior of the two men, even though both were about the same age and rank, and with about the same amount of experience. Noonan just seemed to have a certain air of leadership about him, Art thought.

"Just bang on the bulkhead. I'm right around the corner."

Art closed the door between the workspace and the living quarters and stretched out on his bunk. The compartment was small—maybe 15 by 20 feet. Two bunks were stacked up along the port bulkhead and one Art claimed which was on the starboard side. Three metal lockers in the middle of the room separated the bunks, and a ventilation fan recessed into the overhead provided a little air movement. The head was a simple stainless steel commode and sink in a partially walled corner of the room. Other than two steel chairs and a steel table bolted to the floor, the room was bare. No portholes, no decorative art. It wasn't a room Art would be spending a lot of time in, he decided.

It wasn't long before evening mess was announced over the ship's public address system, and the three men left together for their first experience meeting the whole crew in one place. "Somehow I don't have high expectations for this meal. I hope I'm surprised," Krebs said as the three entered the mess hall.

To Krebs' and everyone elses' surprise, the chow was surprisingly good, a mix of Polynesian and standard fare, appropriate for the mixed crew that was composed of just about all of the major nationalities in the region. The standard-fixture of the meal was silvery-green slices of roast beef from Australia or New Zealand that seemed to be the most common meat on Navy menus all over the Far East.

The CTs joined the one other American crewmember—the electronics technician working with new navigation gear. They introduced themselves formally, and the four men sat on benches at a stainless steel table bolted to the floor, soon to be joined by four other members of the crew—two deck hands, brothers from Saipan, plus an engineering department member from Palau, and a galley crew member from the Philippines.

Crewmembers evidently had been instructed not to question the Americans about why they were aboard, as no questions were raised. Under penalty of what, Art wondered. He also wondered what the crew *had* been told, but reasoned it better not to ask. The conversations mostly centered on where everyone was originally from, and crewmembers extolling the pros and cons of nomadic sea life.

After chow, the three CTs returned to their quarters. Chris and Mark got back to work and after cleaning up, and Art went up to the bridge to get an update on the sub's activity.

"I suspect they've been recharging her batteries and exchanging old air for new," the captain told Art. "She's been on the surface for about two hours now, so they must feel pretty secure. We don't have a visual on the sub yet, and I want to keep far enough back for awhile. But the electronic picture your buddy is showing us says she's in no hurry to get anywhere."

"Do you think they know we're here?" Art asked. "That's a stupid question I guess—they'd have to be pretty inept to not know," he said, answering his own question.

"Oh, they know we're here alright. But hopefully—and so far apparently— they figure we're just a rusty old hulk wandering through these atolls trying to make a buck. And hopefully we'll keep it that way. We're going to stop just off of Jabwot Island in about an hour just to kill some time. There isn't anything there—basically just a pimple of an island, flat, surrounded by coral. It looks like the sub is turning west now; she's just about 50 miles north of Kwajalein. There isn't much west of there, just a lot of open, deep water. I want to see where she's going before we keep going ourselves."

Art returned and told Chris and Mark the status. "Well," Chris said, "the sub is being pretty quiet. They sent a short five-character code group message on their high frequency link—probably a location/fuel/etc. report back to Vlad, but that's all. And that was more than an hour ago. I guess she's buttoning up for the night. I'm going to keep at it for about another hour, then Mark is going to relieve me for an hour, and then we're going to bag it. We'll leave it in scan mode and record everything."

"Sounds good. See you on deck in an hour or so," Art said and left the two men to go topside. It was a warm night made warmer by the high humidity. *At least there's a small breeze on deck that makes it feel cooler than down below*, Art told himself.

After a brief time on deck he returned to his bunk and slept for about two hours. It was uncomfortably hot in their quarters, but the combination of the hum of the small ceiling fan and the cadence of the ship's engine helped lull him into a light sleep. Just as Art was beginning to drift into deeper sleep, Chris Noonan came in and kicked the bottom of his bunk to wake him. In less than an hour, the *Malacca Star* had come within sight of the island of Jabwot. The freighter had dropped anchor about 200 yards off the coast in 50-foot waters so clear you could see bottom. Off the starboard side was the island with a beautiful white sand beach. The island was relatively flat, treeless and uninhabited. Art wondered if it glowed at night from the radiation.

"Captain Cabot told me that the Russian sub appears to be lying just off Ujae Atoll to the west of Kwajalein. So we're proceeding on to Kwajalein, and we'll stop over there and see what moves the sub makes. At least we'll be closer."

"Thanks for the update, Chris. Now get the hell out of here and let me sleep!"

"I'll wake you in Kwajalein," Chris said with a laugh and left the room.

✳   ✳   ✳   ✳

"Get out of the sack, lardo—we're coming into Kwajalein and I want to show you something topside."

"What is it?" Art sat up, rubbed his eyes and simultaneously slid his legs off the edge of the bunk. He had stripped down to his underwear, so it took him a minute to focus and pull on his pants.

"Meet us topside." Chris left the sleeping quarters as Art drug his 270 pounds out of the sack and tried to wake up. He'd had a good sleep for a few hours and it helped, but it wasn't enough. He could hear a light rain, and it had cooled things off slightly, although the temperature never varied much more than plus or minus 10 degrees, day or night. And the humidity was stifling at times. Rain actually was a relief, which didn't exactly make sense to Art.

As Art's head cleared the hatch at the top of the short ladder to the main deck, he could see a long concrete pier sticking out into the bay shaped like an 'L'. The light rain had made puddles on the deck, and the warm drops hitting Art's face helped revive him. "Look over there," Mark said, pointing off the bow of the ship. Approximately a half mile around the inside of the lagoon, a very large gray tanker flying a Japanese flag was docked at another pier.

"What the hell do you think a Jap tanker is doing way out here?" Mark asked.

"I obviously have no idea, but I bet the captain does. Let's go ask." The men approached the bridge and asked official permission to enter, which was granted. Captain Cabot was standing close to a window, dressed in khaki shorts that had string remnants of a hem hanging from the legs, and a sleeveless undershirt. He wore a Giants baseball hat and was smoking a large, black cigar.

"We're a little busy right now, men, getting this tub in here without wiping out the pier. What's up?"

"Tell us about the tanker, captain."

"Can't tell you much. Never saw it before. She's flying the Japanese ensign, and the name on the stern says '*Yakota Maru*'—that's about all I know. She's probably on her way back to Japan—looks like it has a full load—she's riding pretty low in the water. Most likely a natural gas carrier; there are a lot of natural gas reserves and pumping stations throughout these islands. She also appears to be carrying some machinery topside rear—hard to tell what it is with the tarps over it, and a crane far aft, so she must have some cargo to deliver—probably pumping equipment."

"I don't see any activity—wonder where the crew is, and why they stopped here?" It was more of an observation than a question.

"Good question. There isn't much of a settlement here since most of the people migrated out of here during and after the nuclear testing. Usually the only ships you see here are freighters involved in the copra trade. We won't be going ashore—no reason to. We have some food and supplies to unload for a group of German nuns who run a mission somewhere in the boonies around here, but they're coming down to the dock tomorrow morning to pick it up."

The men thanked the captain and left the bridge, returning to the rail on the main deck to watch the docking process. It was a little touchy—being a dark night with no moon, there were no lights on the pier, and the ship was using its floodlights for visibility. The rain had all but stopped. Prominent scrapes on the pier's bumpers gave evidence that docking here was a common problem. Once the ship was docked and secure, the crew began lowering pallets of supplies using the cranes on the aft portion of the *Malacca Star*.

It took about an hour to get everything unloaded and to secure the crane. According to the electronics technician manning the radar/sonar equipment, the Russian sub was sitting still on the surface about 50 miles west of the harbor. The freighter's crew was finishing up and had turned out the searchlights used to illuminate the dock.

Art remained on deck and Noonan and Krebs returned to the operations area to check the scan equipment and tapes that had been running the entire period they were docked. Ten minutes later, Chris—obviously excited, ran down the deck toward Art.

"Mark and I were on our way to get a cup of coffee and decided to check the monitoring gear. Everything was quiet except an interesting blurb we picked up on the scan about 30 minutes ago."

"Let me grab a cup of coffee too, and I'll meet you down there."

With a short detour to the mess to grab a cup of coffee, Art was back in the operations area, having some of the darkest, most bitter coffee he'd ever tasted. "Jesus, this is worse than in Hawaii."

"Yeah, it's probably made from Java beans—no pun intended—they like it that way down here," Chris stated.

"Let me run this tape back a minute. It's interesting…it's a voice message—most likely from the sub. It sounds like Russian to me, but there's no call sign or any identifier used. Obviously the sender had a scheduled appointment on this frequency and the recipient was waiting, listening. There also is no reply—it's a one-way, low-power, VHF transmission, but it came in clear as a bell, which means that the intended recipient has to be close by since VHF at low power only has a short range." With that unsolicited technical explanation for Art's benefit, Chris rewound the tape to a point he had noted on the analog counter, and put it on play.

Art listened—it was a deep, male voice speaking in a monotone, and the message was very brief. Art asked Chris to rewind it and play it back again. "Yeah, that's sure Russian, and it's a very short, simple message. Not sure we've learned much. In essence, it says 'Hello friend. The horse is in the stable and thirsty. 2200 at coordinates 334Y by 54J.' And that was it. Obviously it was meaningful to the person receiving it. Are you sure there wasn't a reply?"

At that exact moment, the ET knocked on the door of the operations center. "Hey, for what it's worth, I thought you might like to know that the *Yakota Maru* has just started to pull away from the dock. I never did see any of the crew, and the ship has been dark the whole time. We did see some people on the bridge, briefly. Looked at 'em through the binoculars and could only see two people—both Caucasians, both in dark shirts and wool hats. Interesting crew, for a Japanese tanker…"

Art looked at his watch. It was 2030—8:30 p.m. "Hmmm…" he murmured. "Chris, let's send a message to both NCS Guam and Hawaii. Ask them to check the registry of the *Yakota Maru*. I've got a hunch."

Fifteen minutes later, they had a reply. No ship by that name currently listed under Japanese registry.

"Let's go see the captain. My hunch is stronger now."

After calling him on the ship telephone, the three men approached the captain who was relaxing in his private quarters, and who acknowledged them after a brief knock on his door. Art spoke as the three men crowded into the captain's small compartment. "Sorry to bother you sir. We contacted our base in Hawaii and they say there is no vessel by the name *Yakota Maru* listed under Japanese registry. And your bridge watch told us he saw two white men on the bridge as the ship pulled away—somewhat suspicious considering it's supposedly a Japanese ship. We also intercepted a voice transmission from an unknown source that I now think was directed to the tanker, and while it's mostly nonsense to us, they do mention a meeting point and a time that's only an hour and a half away from now, from here. The bottom line is that I suspect that this tanker is the supply ship for the sub, and the crew is probably Russian—they sure aren't Japanese, and I think they're on their way to meet the sub. An hour and a half would give them just about the right amount of time to get there by 2200." Art waited for the captain's response.

The captain sat at a small table, an open bottle of Jack Daniels and an English-language newspaper by his elbow. He was motionless except for running his fingers through his hair, wet with sweat. It was a hot night and his cabin didn't appear to be air-conditioned—or at least it wasn't working very well if it was. It was obvious that he was digesting Art's theory. He swirled his coffee cup, the contents of which appeared to be awfully light in color to be coffee, in Art's opinion…

"Everything you said seems to make sense. I was planning on spending the night docked here, especially since radar still shows the sub dead in the water near the Ujae atoll. But based on what you've now told me, I think we'll only wait here about another 20-30 minutes to give the tanker a good head start. Then we'll angle northwest toward Eniwetok and swing southwest on the opposite side of Ujae. If that's where the tanker is headed, and that's where we think the sub is stationed, we'll end up parallel to both the sub and tanker, but out a few miles. The moon's coming up and it's supposed to be full tonight; that might give us a visual. I'm sure they'll know we're there—you know they have to have been tracking us as much as we've been tracking them since we're the only ship in the area...but that's o.k, because we should appear to them to be continuing our round trip back to Ponape. Sound like a plan?"

"Sounds good to me, sir. Let us know when we're in the area. We'll go back and see if there has been any more communications between the two. Thanks, captain. I have no doubt in my mind now, but we won't be sure until we actually see the two of them together."

The captain lifted his cup in a drinking-salute to the men, and nodded an affirmation. The three left the cabin. Art said, "Let's see if there have been any more messages. Sure wish I knew what that cryptic reference to the thirsty horse meant."

∗   ∗   ∗   ∗

They had some time before they'd be in a position to know if their hunch was correct. Even if it was, Art doubted that they'd be much further along with understanding exactly what the sub was doing there in the first place. The French had just resumed nuclear testing in French Polynesia, a good distance east of their current location. Why the Russians were poking around in this area where testing had ended many years ago was a big mystery.

Art's initial qualms about the captain were ebbing. He'd seen no sign that the captain was unfair or disliked by the crew. To the contrary, Art was surprised that the crew got along with him as well as they did, being the only white face on the ship before the CT group arrived. Evidently the *Malacca Star's* navigation equipment upgrade—courtesy of the USN—was to serve as partial payment for allowing the Americans to tag along and shadow the sub. Art also had noticed a case of Jack Daniels whiskey in the captain's cabin displaying Navy Base Exchange stickers, and suspected that 'Mr. Daniels' was part of the compensation package as well.

Krebs and Noonan manned the headsets in an effort to pick up any possible communications between the two Russians. And then, after they'd been away from Kwajalein Island for about 45 minutes, they did intercept another voice message from one vessel to the other, and this time it was answered.

"Art, come on over here and listen to this. It's probably the sub and the tanker talking." Mark only had to open the secure door and yell; Art was just around the corner in the sleeping quarters.

"Coming," Art replied, and put his novel down and turned out the bare light bulb directly above his head at the end of the bunk.

"I taped it—I think they're done now; at least they haven't said anything for the past 10 minutes. See what you make of it," Mark said as he rewound the quarter-inch wide brown magnetic tape on the large reel.

The voice was clear, and it was the same one Art had heard on the previous one-way transmission. Art interpreted:

HELLO! HELLO! ETA ABOUT 90 MINUTES FROM SOUTHEAST BEARING 140 DEGREES. WE HAVE YOU ON RADAR. NO OTHER VESSELS IN AREA EXCEPT INDONESIAN FREIGHTER NORTH-WEST OF YOUR LOCATION. IT WAS DOCKED AT KWAJALEIN AND DEPARTED AFTER WE DID. IT APPEARS HEADED TO ENI-WETOK. CONFIRM STATUS OF YOUR PREPARATIONS. OVER.

After a momentary silence and some static crashes, the submarine replied:

GOOD. ACKNOWLEDGE YOUR ARRIVAL 90 MINUTES. PREPARA-TIONS READY FOR FUELING. MUST COMPLETE AND TRANSFER _____ URGENTLY. HAVE FREIGHTER ON RADAR ALSO. OUT.

"I didn't understand that one word—what it is that they have to transfer 'urgently'; actually it wasn't a word, it was three initials—Cyrillic equivalents of 'M,' 'P,' and a Russian character for which there is no English equivalent. That sure confirms what we thought though—that natural gas tanker is nothing more than a big barrel of diesel fuel for the sub. I guess I'd better go tell the captain. Sounds like they're not worried about us at all," Art said. Chris and Mark nodded in agreement as Art left the ops center to inform the captain.

He found the captain on the bridge with the ET, both studying the radar screen. "Permission to enter the bridge, sir?" Art requested from outside.

"Of course," the captain said.

"She's still just sitting there," the ET said over his shoulder to Art, entering the bridge.

"Yeah, and she's going to be there for awhile according to what we just learned from communications between the two ships. And they know we're out here too, but they don't seem to be too concerned. There's no doubt now—the tanker *is* the fuel and supply ship for the sub—they were talking about refueling, and that's why they're rendezvousing."

"Figures. The moon's coming up, and I'm a little concerned about getting too close and appearing to be too nosey," the captain said as he continued to stare straight ahead at the relatively calm sea ahead. "We'll be off his starboard side, and unfortunately the moon is to port, low on the horizon and shining right on both of us. Maybe we'll slow down a bit; I'd like to be able to keep moving once we're close and the sub can see us. If we stop, even a few miles away, it might make them suspicious. Half-speed," he ordered the first mate.

"Aye Sir, half speed it is."

Art asked, "How close do you think we can be without being too obvious?"

"We'll have to play that by ear when we get there. I know you want a visual of the two of them, but I also don't want a large hole in my hull. I don't want to go swimming tonight. We'll do the best we can. I'll call you when it's time."

Art took that as a dismissal, so he thanked the captain and returned to relay the information to Noonan and Krebs.

Less than 45 minutes later the captain summoned Art, Mark and Chris to the bridge. The moon was full now, and the calm sea was lighted almost like daytime in a large parking lot.

"We'll be directly opposite the sub and the tanker at a distance of about a mile in 20 minutes. They are side-by-side, according to the radar, and dead in the water. I'm assuming their refueling process has begun. The Ujae Atoll is two miles long, not much of anything except a long, narrow sand bar. It's exactly one mile due west of the two boats. If we hug the western shore and keep moving at about five knots, we should have a solid 15 minutes to observe the ships with binoculars while we're moving."

Addressing all three CTs, the captain said "I would advise you all to find some high vantage points on the ship and get up there with your binoculars. I don't expect you dry-land swabs are too adept at climbing rigging. and my liability insurance isn't too current, so don't fall and make a mess on the deck."

"Roger, Captain, and thank you. We'll make the most of it."

Mark and Chris, each equipped with high powered binoculars, scrambled to the roof on top of the bridge, and Art climbed a ladder up to the main cargo boom located mid-ship. The boom of the crane had a small platform grate about halfway up with railings that was used to maintain the hydraulic system, just large enough for one man to stand and affording a good 360-degree vantage.

In no time, the *Malacca Star* had reached the tip of the Ujae atoll the captain had mentioned. The freighter crept along the western edge of the low land mass at a slow, but constant speed. All ship lights had been extinguished except the running lights and the lights on the bridge, and the view was spectacular. Even without glasses, the men could see the sub—number K-229—and the tanker, side by side, very clearly in the moonlight. The sub, a large black cigar-shaped cylinder with a red hammer and sickle on the conning tower, was riding high on the surface. With the aid of glasses, they could see both sub and tanker crew members at work managing the fueling hoses between the two. Floodlights from the tanker were being used to illuminate the fueling operation, and helped both the Russians and the Americans see what was going on.

"Chris, do you and Mark see that large object on the deck of the tanker, partially covered with a large tarp, just two-thirds aft? We'll have to wait a few minutes until we have a better angle, but it doesn't look like pumping equipment to me!" The object was just aft of the bridge and appeared to be about 10 feet high and about 15 to 20 feet long.

"We see it, Art, and we'll have a better view in a few minutes..."

The words were no sooner out of Chris' mouth when the captain, who was standing on the deck in front of the bridge, called up to Art and said "What you're looking at is a submersible. Probably two-man, electric propulsion, compressed air assisted with a retractable arm. I'd guess it's designed to retrieve things from deep water. I can't imagine what use a tanker would have for it though. It would be used at depths deeper than the sub can go, that's for sure."

It took a few minutes for those words to sink in, when Art exclaimed "A submersible! Of course! They're here to retrieve something from the bottom."

"Gentlemen, we only have about ten more minutes left behind this atoll before we break out into open water and in plain view to the sub. Then we have to pick up speed so we don't appear to have been lolly-gagging and snooping. They're sure to know we're here, but I don't think they're suspicious And they certainly wouldn't consider us to be any threat to whatever they may be up to. I want to get further away before they *do* get concerned."

"Wait a minute!" Mark exclaimed, still looking through his glasses. "The tanker is transferring something over to the sub with that aft crane. Looks like a long, narrow tank or something..."

Art had started down, but climbed back up and took a long hard look through his glasses. "Jesus Christ, Mark, that's no tank—that's the business end of a missile!"

"Why would a tanker be putting a missile on the sub? Don't you figure the sub came with a full complement of missiles? And they surely haven't used any or we'd know it!"

"They sure have a few—it's a Foxtrot-class ballistic missile sub and they have three missiles in silos behind the bridge. My guess is that the missile they're loading from the tanker isn't one of *theirs,* but someone else's. Wait a minute…We've been interested in the wrong ship! I'll bet that the tanker has used the submersible to pluck that missile off of the sea bottom somewhere and is transferring it to the sub. The sub has a dive max of about 850 feet or thereabouts, so whatever they salvaged must've been deeper than that. Besides, even if the sub could go deeper, it doesn't have any means of picking things up from the ocean floor. The sub is nothing more than the delivery boy—probably taking the missile home to mama."

"So all the while we've been interested in and tracking the sub, the tanker has been off somewhere picking up that thing?"

"That's my uneducated guess," Art replied.

"Probably a good bet. Come on down, gentlemen. We're about to break our cover," the captain reminded them.

The freighter had pulled beyond the sand atoll, and now was plainly visible to the sub and the tanker, a brightly lit silhouette against the moonlit sea and the dark distant horizon. They'd increased speed to about 15 knots and were making a direct beeline for Ponape, a good 400 nautical miles to the southwest from their present position. The sub and the tanker quickly faded in the distance, and continued their operation, apparently unconcerned with the rusty old freighter that was ambling by.

The men had climbed down from their perches and immediately went back to the operations area. "I want to make sure we're recording their previous frequencies. Don't want to miss anything," Mark said.

"Yeah, and I think we'd better get a message off to Wahiawa. There's not much more we can do down here, but they might be interested in picking up the track of the sub now that we think we know what she's carrying."

"And exactly what do you think that something is, Art?" Mark asked.

"Well, just putting the pieces together that we've got so far, it's probably the leftovers of a Thor missile that was used to carry one of the atomic warheads into the atmosphere. Most of the latter tests in the Christmas and Johnston Islands were high altitude shots carried by Thor missiles Maybe it was a shot that failed and broke up, or maybe it was just a test shot. Or a dummy. It didn't look entirely intact, but just what part was missing is anyone's guess. I didn't see any tail feathers, so they probably recovered the front-half, which is the business end of course."

"I'll get something encrypted off to Hawaii right away," Chris said.

"Great. Don't be too verbose, but make it clear we're pretty certain it's a missile or part of one; it must be important to the Russians or they wouldn't have come this far to get it. So it *will* be important to our guys," Art said.

The excitement of the night was over. They had reviewed the tapes, and if there had been any further transmissions, they hadn't caught them. The steady drone of the engines and the silence of the night were welcome. Much needed sleep came quickly.

*   *   *   *

Sipping the black coffee that was still bitter after being cut with water, the three CTs sat down for breakfast at a table with the ET from Hawaii and the first mate.

"Good morning," the first mate said with a thick British accent, slightly whistling through the gap in his brown teeth. "I see you've tapped into our own diesel tanks. Wonderful stuff, that coffee. More of it gets used to strip paint than gets drunk."

"I believe it," Art said, "and I wouldn't be surprised if it would ignite if you get your cigarette too close to it. So, where are we? What's happening with our friends?"

The ET spoke up and said, "Well, they're both moving again. Looks like refueling took the better part of three hours last night. They didn't get away until about 0100 this morning. The tanker, or whatever you want to call it, has broken off and set a course due west, probably toward the Philippines and then will head north to the Sea of Japan between Honshu and Korea, back to Russia. The sub seems to be on a straight northwest course that'll take it close to Guam in the Marianas Islands. Once it gets into the Marianas Trench, we'll probably lose it. It's the deepest water in the world."

The first mate interjected: "By our best guess, we should be back in Ponape in 72 hours. The sub is still traveling on the surface—she can go twice as fast as when submerged. She'll probably submerge when she gets closer to civilization and the more traveled shipping lanes—just to avoid potential detection."

"Running on the surface all this time, out in the open, with no attempt to be inconspicuous, probably was intentional," Chris observed. "They wanted prying eyes focused on them, to draw attention away from the tanker and what it was doing. And it worked. Sure wish we could have observed that submersible in action."

"My guess is that they plucked their prize off the bottom before we arrived down here, but of course I don't know for sure," Art offered as he dumped more sugar and milk in his acrid coffee. The ratio of coffee to additives now was probably close to 50-50. "Who knows? We'll let the folks back home figure it out. Gentlemen, we have about three days left to grab some rays on the deck before we hit Ponape. What say we get started?"

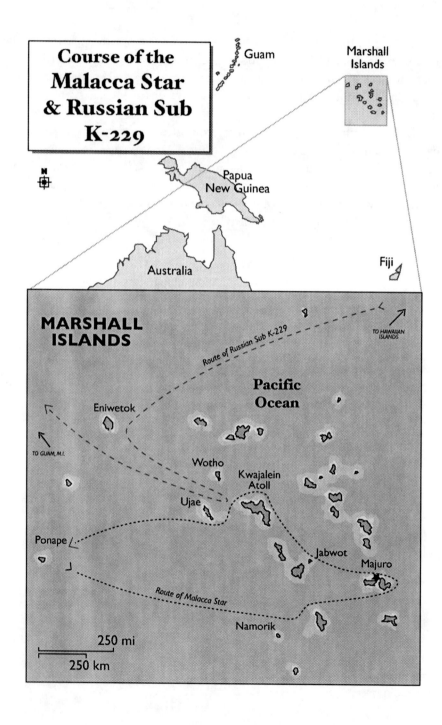

Course of the Malacca Star & Russian Sub K-229

N

Guam

Marshall Islands

Papua New Guinea

Australia

Fiji

MARSHALL ISLANDS

Route of Russian Sub K-229

Pacific Ocean

TO HAWAIIAN ISLANDS

Eniwetok

TO GUAM, M.I.

Wotho

Kwajalein Atoll

Ujae

Ponape

Jabwot

Majuro

Route of Malacca Star

Namorik

250 mi

250 km

CHAPTER 3

▼

Jake had heard of another sailor in Section Three who hadn't come back—back from nowhere, he thought, because they were never officially 'there'.

Communications Technician second-class Jacob "Jake" Morton practically crawled up the steps of the barracks at NCS Kami Seya, Japan, more than ready to crash. Each foot seemed to weigh 50 pounds as he climbed the remaining few steps to the door. He only had one thing on his mind: sleep.

Fortunately, he had a rack on the first deck. It had been a long mid-watch—the shift he hated the most. After a month on this watch rotation—a mix of two-each eight-hour—eve, day and mid watches, with 56 hours off before it started all over again, his body was still not accepting the necessity of sleeping at odd hours.

Sleeping during the day seemed to be the most difficult. He wasn't sure why they'd switched him from the 80-hours off schedule he'd had for the last six months; rumor had it that the military buildup in Vietnam had something to do with it. Increased vigilance and all that. The North Koreans were rattling their sabers too. It seemed that everyone was sticking their chests out, including the Americans, and Jake wasn't sure exactly why.

There were rumors than anyone currently having less than a year to do on their current enlistment was automatically going to be extended for a year. But Jake tuned it out; when he had been at NCS Guam, there had been similar rumors that short-timers—those with less than 12 months left on their enlistment—would involuntarily be extended because of the flare-up (at that time) in Lebanon. Some of his friends actually reenlisted voluntarily to take advantage of the cash bonus for doing so—a reward that they wouldn't qualify for if the Navy had made the decision for them. Then when the threat of auto-extension never materialized, those who had done it for the money were sorry—and stuck in the Navy for another year.

All that particular experience had done for Jake was to reinforce the old axiom that you never volunteer for anything in the military.

This last mid-watch for Jake had been an uneventful, quiet night with not much going on—the kind of watches that were the worst, Jake felt, because time seemed to crawl. Lots of smokes, coffee, walking around to stay awake. The slapping of empty tape reels was about the only action at his workstation; the printers were quiet, and everyone else experienced a similar uneventful night.

For entertainment, the 'salts' had pulled a traditional trick on one of the newer CTs on watch: straightening out the layers of teletype/printer paper. The paper used in the Model-28 printers came in three layers, with two layers of carbon paper between them, for a total of five layers. By peeling the top layer back and tearing it off half way around the roll, the carbon paper appeared on top. 'Newbies' were told that they had to unravel the entire roll and rewind it with the carbon between paper layers. Needless to say, it was an impossible task.

An unraveled roll would run some 100 feet down the aisle of the work area. And, of course, rewinding it by trying to rearrange the layers of paper and carbon would never work. After a lot of laughs at the new guy's expense, someone would show the victim that one wrap around the roll torn-off would solve the problem. Then the crew would go back to work and the new guy would have graduated the initiation, ready to try the trick on someone his junior in the future.

Only one more mid-watch to go and then Jake was off for a while. And since it had just been payday, he felt fairly flush. At NCS Guam, there was less to do during off-hours, and Jake often would get suckered into 48-hour poker games where paychecks were thrown into the pot. *At least here I won't get stuck in a marathon game and lose it all*, he thought.

Once he made it back to his two-bunk cubicle separated from others by moveable six-foot high plywood walls, Jake sat down on his rack and debated whether or not to go to the mess hall. Beat as he was, he wasn't sure he wanted to miss a meal. Food at Kami Seya was outstanding, and unlike most Naval installations, men here actually looked forward to meals. Once a week was steak night—you picked your own and it was grilled to your specifications. The tables were for four, covered with a tablecloth, and usually decorated with flowers. The mess hall even had fish aquariums along the walls for decoration. A Japanese-national (civilian) waitress took your order. And you didn't have to be an admiral either; this was standard in the petty officers' mess.

The base mess had won the fleet-wide Ney Award of excellence several times, an award granted to the best single shore and sea mess hall each year. The brass was proud of their mess, and worked hard to make it the award-winner that it was. And the reason why was no mystery: the Navy had a lot of money and time invested in training him and the hundreds of other CTs on base, and they wanted to keep them relatively happy. By virtue of the Navy's investment, and the critical nature of their jobs, they advanced faster and had better facilities—from the living quarters to the enlisted men's club, the recreation hall, the sports fields, and so forth. Reenlist, son! was the underlying motivation.

CTs were 'special,' but somehow even the prospect of perfect eggs and lean fried ham with blueberry pancakes on the side served at an table by a cute waitress *still* wasn't enough to get Jake on his feet.

Before he crashed though, Jake decided to have one last smoke. It was a habit he'd started in high school, and now he smoked a pack a day. Some of his friends smoked because they thought it was cool, or that it made them look older. Looking older wasn't a problem for Jake. At 16, with his dark wavy hair and chiseled features and deep-set eyes, he easily had passed for 18 or more. At 17 he had no problem buying beer, and became the designated buyer for his crowd.

He usually had a cigarette between his lips when his eyes were still light-limiting slits in the morning. Everyone smoked, and nobody ever told him there was anything wrong with it, or tried to discourage him. Because of fire danger, certain areas were off limits to smoking, such as in the mess and the operations area, but not the barracks.

Jake rationalized that smoking gave him something to do with his hands and it helped make time pass. Although he smoked filters, most of the old timers—the 'salts'—were purists, insisting on popular non-filter brands like Camel and Pall Mall. You had to be tough to inhale the lung-searing strong smoke, trap the bits of tobacco with your tongue, and deal with the hunks of cigarette paper that stuck to your lips. Spitting was part of the process of smoking the strong stuff and the mark of being a salt.

Jake pulled the crumpled pack of Marlboro filters out of his shirt pocket, but didn't light up. For some reason that Jake himself wasn't clear on, he just sat on his bunk and found that he couldn't take his eyes off of the empty bunk in his cubicle—the one he shared with Sonny Powell.

Sonny had been away on Temporary Additional Duty (TAD) aboard a submarine for almost three months now, and about the only visible evidence that Sonny had ever been in Kami Seya at all was the framed photo of the handsome black lab—'Radar'—sitting on the otherwise empty desk.

Sonny's bunk was made up, neat and unwrinkled, and it would stay that way as long as everyone honored the unwritten barracks law that said you never sat on someone else's bed without an invitation to do so.

Jake was beginning to feel like he knew that dog in the picture—Radar—as well as his owner. I've spent more time with Radar that I have with his master—at least here in Japan, he reflected.

Their friendship had begun in boot camp at the Great Lakes Naval Training Center north of Chicago in Illinois. Two kids thrown together in a sea of strange humanity, as Sonny had described it; the two young men, both from small rural communities, had formed a bond. Sonny had gone on to the Naval Communications Station on Adak Island, a very lonely piece of rock near the end of the Aleutian chain of islands off Alaska, and Jake had been assigned to the Security Group station on Guam. They hadn't been reunited in Japan very long before Sonny was off on his first temporary assignment on a sub.

Jake started to undress. He had to get a few hours of sack time now so he could get up and get to the base laundry before it closed at 1600 hours. He was down to one set of clean work dungarees, and couldn't wear his current set a fifth day. With a total of only about four sets of work uniforms, he knew he had to plan carefully: one set you wore, a clean set in the locker, and two at the laundry. Lockers were small—Jake figured that the barracks architects must have been career sea-going 'lifers' that had figured if living out of a shoebox was good enough for them, it was going to be good enough for everyone.

The twenty members of his watch section were all pretty much settled in and asleep by 0830. Of those not hitting the rack, some were off to chow, and some were changing into civvies and primed to hit the bars in Yokohama's "Chinatown" bright and early.

Jack skipped the morning shower and slipped under the sheet and decided that even the omnipresent pungent odor from the nearby Japanese crematorium wasn't going to keep him awake this morning. The stench was particularly bad in August when the air was muggy and still, and at times was so strong that it burned his eyes and nose. And as the crematorium was less than a quarter of a mile from his barracks on the other side of the base fence, there wasn't much he or anyone could do. Closing the windows—a necessity to keep the smell outside, made it even hotter inside. But not as hot as across the fence on the Japanese side, he thought, and he knew he'd rather be here on this side…

He hadn't closed his eyes for more than a minute when he became aware of someone near. Opening his eyes, he saw two marines standing at the entrance of the cubicle.

"Sorry buddy, we tried to be quiet," said the enlisted marine. Jake knew most of the CT-marines, but these weren't 'CT marines,' but rather members of the base Marine Security Force—the base police force. This particular corporal was a stranger to Jake.

The marine officer with him nodded in agreement. "We won't be but a few minutes. We're here to collect Mr. Powell's personal stuff. I'm sorry to tell you that he won't be coming back."

The marines were very respectful and polite, and they understood that no further explanation to Jake was necessary.

"O.K." was all Jake could get out. And the marines didn't find it a bit unusual that Jake didn't ask "Why?" It had happened before.

As soon as he had opened his eyes and saw the marines standing there, Jake guessed why they were there, even before they said a word.

It also was obvious that everyone else in the barracks heard the conversation, and knew what was going on as well, as evidenced by the uncommon silence. Everyone stopped whatever he was doing and stood motionless, all with full understanding of the situation. There were blank expressions and no comments—just silent resignation. Cigarettes dangled from lips. Hands braced on bunk railings didn't move. Those awake but trying to go to sleep didn't even open their eyes—not in disinterest, but in understanding and sadness. Some of those standing slowly sat down. It was a silent acknowledgement of unspoken facts that transcended reality.

Fortunately it didn't happen often, but Jake had heard of another sailor in Section Three who hadn't come back last year—back from nowhere, he thought, because they were never officially 'there'. It was an accepted risk that you knew existed when you signed on for temporary duty assignments and went 'out and about'.

The marines were done packing up Sonny's belongings, and as an afterthought, Jake asked if he could keep the photograph of Radar. The marines discussed it briefly, and when Jake assured them that he'd see to it that Sonny's parents in Fosston, Minnesota would get it back, they agreed and handed it to him.

When the marines were gone, Jake finally took out his flip-top chrome Zippo lighter with the USN anchor insignia that he'd gotten in boot camp, and lit the cigarette he'd been holding between his fingers for the past 10 minutes.

He remembered Sonny as pretty much of a loner. When asked to accompany a group of guys going into Yokohama on liberty, Sonny usually declined. But later they'd often see him in Chinatown, alone in a bar having a quiet beer, never mixing with the local Jo-sans.

Sonny was somewhat of an oddity to the Japanese, mostly because of his height. The bar girls loved to run their fingers through his thick reddish hair. Some actually would ask for Sonny to clip some off for their scrapbooks or something; he really didn't understand. On the rare occurrence when Jake and Sonny would be together in a bar, Sonny got all of the attention. Jake, at five-foot-11, dark hair and more normal at 160 pounds, was far less interesting to them than his friend the giant with the hair on fire.

When he stayed behind on base during his time off, which he often did, Sonny claimed he would hypnotize himself and go home and play with Radar. Sonny swore it worked, and offered to teach Jake how to do it, but Jake was skeptical. Jake had to admit, however, that on a few occasions he had tried to talk to Sonny while Sonny was in his bunk—eyes open and apparently awake, but would get no response from him. He figured that perhaps it helped Sonny cope with his loneliness. But from Sonny's description of his hometown, it sounded like he had gotten used to being alone a long time ago.

He wondered what explanation Sonny's parents would get from the Navy brass. And he wondered if Radar's sixth sense would understand.

Jake forgot he'd lit a cigarette, and it would burn down to the point that it got hot on his fingers, causing him to drop it to the floor. Jake shook his burned fingers for a long time before he took his eyes off the empty bunk. Now Jake's own TAD assignment—coming up in 30 days—overtook his thought processes. Sleep for Jake Morton came slowly that morning.

*   *   *   *

He didn't know if it was the sound of the barracks 'boy' cleaning or his mind working overtime on Sonny Powell, but Jake awoke after only about three hours of sleep. Wide awake, his mind churning with thoughts which changed subject faster than the old MovieTone News clips.

After lighting a cigarette, Jake laid back and stared at the ceiling. It had been three weeks since he'd been told that Sonny Powell wasn't coming back. There had been no further explanation by anyone, and no one asked for one. There wasn't even much discussion among the men in the barracks, because nobody really knew what had happened, and if the officers knew, they weren't saying. Obviously someone knew something, at least those that had determined that Sonny wasn't coming back. But who knew what would never be known. Besides, discussing the risks of TAD just wasn't done. It was one of those things about the job you silently accepted.

There certainly was no mention in the official Navy newspaper <u>Navy Times</u> or the base newspaper, <u>The Daily KamiSeyan</u> about a missing sub or plane or ship, any missing CTs, or any accidents of any kind. Officially it just hadn't happened.

If the Russians, North Koreans or any other nation with whom the United States was conducting a 'cold war' had any involvement in an accident or any other incident involving hostile action, Jake knew they wouldn't break the news. It wasn't in their best interests to acknowledge that an American submarine or ship or plane had penetrated their coastal defenses—if it had. And if it was an accident involving one of their vessels and an American submarine, someone had to be at fault and that would be discussed in lofty government circles with blame decided long before any word leaked out to the public.

Besides, he reasoned, if an incident did involve hostile action, the hostile nation, by not acknowledging involvement, could attempt salvage operations and possibly gain some useful intelligence information—with pretty good assurance that the Americans weren't going to admit their 'aggressive act.'

Jake thought about writing a note to Sonny's folks back in Minnesota, and maybe sending Radar's picture with it, but since he didn't know any details of Sonny's absence—including what details they'd been told by the Navy officials, he decided against it.

After all, Sonny *could* be alive. So Radar continued to be Jake's cube mate, at least for the time being, and that was o.k.—Radar didn't snore like Sonny had.

Jake had just turned 21. He was big for his age—almost six feet tall since he was 18. He'd grown up in a small town located in eastern Pennsylvania's coal regions, where most people were either of Italian or Polish descent. Jake's mother was a second generation Italian from Sicily and his father was of English ancestry. Somehow his father's reserved nature and his mother's often-fiery demeanor complemented each other well, and Jake had come out to be a fairly even blend of the two. He'd done average in school—probably well enough to get into one of the state colleges or universities, but not well enough for the Ivy League. He'd spent too much time on the wrestling team, a real source of local pride as the school had won the state championships for the past two years—before Jake joined the team. Jake's team went to finals, but came in second even though Jake won his match in the heavyweight class.

His parents had encouraged him to go to college, as both were college graduates and more of less felt they owed him the opportunity. His father owned a shoe store and never used his degree in accounting, and his mother was an elementary school teacher who gave private piano lessons for extra income. He had considered college but couldn't decide toward what end, so Jake had joined the Navy right after graduation from high school, accompanied by two buddies. They had hoped to get assigned somewhere together, and his friends had helped get him through the first-time-away-from-home anxieties of boot camp. But after graduation, when his friends went their separate ways to ship duty, Jake was fairly well prepared to face the world.

Boot camp had introduced him to a true sampling of the American melting pot—economic, ethnic, social and racial backgrounds he never knew existed. He had grown up quickly during those fall days in boot camp. From day one at the USN Recruit Training Facility, Great Lakes, Illinois north of Chicago, there were good guys, great guys, and bastards. Just like in real life. It was the freshman year of his Navy education, and he'd graduated with flying colors.

A battery of aptitude tests in boot camp had shown Jake to be a candidate for one of the more technical specialties in the Navy, and that—coupled with the fact he was a 'ham'—an amateur radio operator, resulted in his assignment to several radio and communications-based Navy schools.

After nine or so weeks of schooling at a classified school command in Imperial Beach, California near San Diego, Jake was given his top secret category III cryptographic security clearance and shipped off to the U.S. Naval Security Group's post on Guam outside the capital—Agana. He'd scoffed at the suggestion that the Navy actually went back to someone's home-town and checked on the person's background for the security check. Until he was home on leave the first time, that is, when a former high school teacher approached Jake and was quite animated when he asked "Are you AWOL? There were some Naval intelligence people around here a few weeks ago asking questions about you!" Jake assured him he was home legally.

Jake originally had hoped for an assignment to Adak, Alaska, and was disappointed not to get it. His reasoning had nothing to do with Sonny's assignment there; he simply had wanted to save enough money to marry his high school sweetheart, and had heard that the Alaska duty station was a good place to bank your paycheck. Also, reportedly there was a girl behind every tree in Alaska. And as there were no trees, he'd face no temptation.

*　　　*　　　*　　　*

No duty station could have been more of an Alaskan opposite than was the Marianas island of Guam, where it was 85-degrees day and night during the summer, and occasionally hotter. With rain—incessant rain. And steaming humidity in between.

The small Naval Security Group intercept station was located in a clearing carved out of the jungle, and surrounded by the largest, most voracious population of mosquitoes in the world, as well as other insects and creatures not too common in his home state of Pennsylvania, such as wild boar and six-foot-long lizards. And, of course, cockroaches. Cockroaches—everywhere. Big suckers. Opening your locker at night was an adventure. Normally shy of light, these inch and a half-size mutants had overcome the fear of the bare light bulb put in his locker to help keep mildew to a minimum. He always banged on the aluminum door of his locker before he stood back and opened it. And never in his bare feet.

Jake entertained himself and kept busy in his free time mostly by participating in payday poker marathons, beachcombing and hikes in the jungle. The war with Japan had been over only a little more than 20 years, and the jungle still was littered with leftover reminders of the war of all kinds.

At the Navy's married housing area on the hill overlooking Agana, the capital, a few children were killed every year as a result of digging at play in their back yards and contacting unexploded ordinance. The Navy held an annual cleanup operation and hauled away truckloads of unexploded bombs, mines and shells of all kinds.

Jungle treks during off-hours were equally dangerous, although Jake and his buddies never realized this until years later. Most of their forays into the wild rarely involved little more than taking the well-worn paths to the ocean, which led to some of the most incredible skin diving and shell collecting in the world. Jake tried scuba diving only to discover a mild case of claustrophobia he hadn't known he had. But the swimming was superb, and miles of beaches were empty of all but collectible shells washed up from the recent storms.

Many war souvenirs still lay hidden in the undergrowth, rusting and decaying in the high humidity, and sharing space with large green iguana lizards and squadrons of mosquitoes. You simply didn't go into the jungle with any unnecessary skin uncovered, no matter what the temperature. Sweat beat welts. The large lizards were vegetarians (a comforting thought to Jake), but one whack of their tail could break a man's leg, so green 'logs' were treated with respect.

Collecting war trophies was allowed, as long as common sense was applied. Jake found helmets, a knife, and lots of shell casings. One friend found a 30-caliber machine gun, rusted but intact. Since shipping arms home was forbidden, the friend had disassembled it, cleaned it up, and sent it home in many different packages.

At the end of the 25-plus mile long, narrow island near Anderson Air Force Base was an area where the final garrison of WWII Japanese soldiers had retreated when capture was inevitable, and committed suicide. The bog had preserved many of the bodies almost 20 years later, and out of respect and in concern for safety, the area was off limits to everyone.

The jungles of Guam had been, in the early 1940s, the haunts of Radioman First Class George Tweed. Tweed was the Navy's most celebrated spy as of then, and spent almost 30 months on the island during the Japanese occupation from 1942-1944, radioing information to the Allies about Japanese activities. His hideout, a cave on the northwestern shore of the island, was known by only a few of the Chamorro natives, many of whom died protecting his location. Jake had tried to find it on one of his jungle "boonie walks," but was never successful. Tweed, the last American on the island prior to the invasion of Guam by the Americans was picked up by a U.S. destroyer in 1944.

Jake's more comfortable 'cave' was a square, two-story windowless concrete operations center on base where he worked, about a mile from his barracks. Without a doubt it was the most ugly, nondescript building Jake had ever seen. Rumor had it that the building was purposefully wired with explosives, ready for destruction in the event of capture during a conflict, not a comforting thought to those inside. Jake noted there was only one way in and out, and that was a succession of marine sentry-guarded and combination-lock doors not designed for fast exit.

The op center was located close to the huge antenna field—a 1300-foot diameter wire antenna arranged like a wagon wheel, divided into pie-shaped selectable segments, known as a Wullenweber, named for it's inventor. The huge rhombic antenna array could be used simultaneously as a radio direction finder and receiving antenna. Through communication with other Navy communications facilities such as on Adak and in Japan, they could cooperate with the Guam facility and 'triangulate' on a specific radio signal. Together they 'shoot a bearing' and then could plot the exact position of a transmitter with relatively fine accuracy.

The triangulation process served many purposes, one of which was to identify the location of a transmitter that was identifying itself as a specific station or ship, but suspected of being bogus. It was quite common for the Chinese communists in particular to pretend to be American ships and send phony messages to U.S. ships at sea. It rarely worked as the ChiCom transmitters were very audibly identifiable due to their unstable audio oscillator circuits that produced a distinct warble with each depression of the telegraph key.

Navy busses provided transportation back and forth to the op center for the normal three daily watches. On several occasions, Jake missed the bus and would walk to serve his watch.

This was O.K., but a little nerve-wracking at night, especially after the first incident when a 400-lb. boar and her 200-lb. baby crossed the dark road in front of him. He was following the painted stripe in the middle of the road; it was very dark and the jungle canopy almost touched overhead in the middle over the road. Jake had heard noises ahead of him, off to the side, and walked cautiously. After the boars crossed the road, Jake covered the remaining quarter-mile to work in record time.

On the same road a few weeks later, Jake had an encounter of a completely different nature. That night his island world was brightly lit by a full moon in a cloudless sky, and Jake found the late night hike to work to be quite enjoyable, even if it was still about 80 degrees and humid. At one point the road to the op center swung very close to the ocean, located on a rock cliff some 200 feet up from the ocean's surface below. There always was a breeze coming up the cliffs from the ocean, with the ever-present odors of marine life.

As Jake approached the 'blockhouse' as the op center was commonly known, he glanced toward the ocean.

"Oh my God!" he exclaimed to himself, stopping dead in his tracks as he stared out across the iridescent seascape. There, less than 100 yards from the shore at cliff-bottom, was a Russian submarine. The boat was mostly submerged except for the black conning tower that was sticking out of the water, bristling with antennas, and sporting the unmistakable red hammer and sickle of the Russian navy.

Jake looked long and hard. He didn't see any activity—not a ripple on the sea surface, not a sound, not a moving shadow. He wanted to make sure that what he saw was really what he saw.

One he convinced himself that he wasn't hallucinating, he again sprinted to work, almost knocking over the marine sentry at the door of the operations building.

"Call base security, quick! There's a Russian sub sitting just 100 yards or so off the bottom of the cliff," he told the guard.

"Sure, sure. Just come from the enlisted men's club, did you sailor?"

"No, I'm not drunk and I'm not nuts. Now call security quick or go look for yourself."

Hesitantly, the guard dialed the number for his security command, and relayed the information—in a tone that belied his lack of conviction. Hanging up, the guard said, "You better be right buddy, or we're both in trouble."

Jake went on into the building and to work. After about a half-hour, his supervisor called him over to the watch office. "Well, Morton, you scored one. And just in time. The marines got to the spot you said you saw the sub just in time to see it disappear underwater. They said there was no mistake that it was a sub. They called the Naval Air Station and I guess they're sending a pair of choppers out to see if they can find it and identify it. Are you sure it was Russian, and not one of our own?"

"Oh yeah, I'm sure. Unless our boats are painting hammer and sickle designs on their conning towers too. And I forgot to tell the guard outside, but I did see an I.D. number on the tower: K-229."

The watch supervisor immediately called the O.O.D. and reported the number. "Yes Sir, I'll confirm and get back to you," was about all Jake heard as the supervisor hung up the phone.

"All they want me to do is to verify that you're positive it was K-229?"

I'm absolutely sure. The moon was shining right on it and I double-checked it because I couldn't believe what I was seeing," Jake replied and headed back to work. The incident was met with "What bottle did you see it through?" and "Smoking the nasty weed again, huh Morton?" comments for several days following.

Both sides obviously participated in the cold war listening game.

There were moments of levity at work as well. Early one morning, during the height of one of the many crises in the Middle East, Jake was at work and leaning over a mod-28 Teletype printer reading the UPI news. The printer suddenly stopped printing as the building shook and the overhead lights went out, simultaneously accompanied by a loud noise. The emergency lights came on with their dull yellow glow, but otherwise all power was off.

"We're being bombed!" someone yelled.

Jake smiled and comforted himself with the thought that the one Piper Cherokee that may have existed in the Lebanese air force was not overhead—unless it had enormous fuel tanks.

"It's just an earthquake," someone replied. A large one, indeed, along the Mariana Trench, and it had severed a main power cable on the island that powered the op center.

Power soon was restored, and the watch continued. It was an especially tense time, as the brunt of the communications intelligence effort was focused on Russian space shots. The race to be first in space was as much for political gain as it was to advance technology and man's knowledge of the cosmos.

The Russians had launched cosmonaut Yuri Gagarin into orbit from the Baikonur Cosmodrome near Tyuratem. It was a major coup for the Soviets and one that brought increased pressure on the American space program to catch up. In reality, the Naval Security Group bases located throughout the world had been very involved in monitoring Soviet space shot activity since the late 1950s.

Jake and a lot of other CTs at NSG stations close to the southwestern coast of the Soviet Union were very interested in any transmissions coming out of Kapustin Yar, Alma Ata and Ulan Bator.

The primary difficulty in intercepting this data was due to the fact that the signals often could only be monitored when they were line-of-sight with the ground station. As a result, a network of monitoring stations at various Naval Security Group Activities was established so that when signals faded out of the range of one station, another could assume the responsibility for continued monitoring.

Of specific interest was intercepted telemetry directly from the space vehicle itself—often in plain language. It was this telemetry that would suggest that several Russian cosmonauts had died in attempts to place man in orbit gone wrong. Despite the Russians' claim that Gagarin was 'first in space,' the orbiting wreckage of exploded rockets and space capsules containing corpses of dead Russian men and women was first revealed through intercepted telemetry. Heartbeat, respiration, temperature and other human measurements often were audible to anyone listening to the right frequencies. As Jake would learn, animals—usually dogs—often would be sent up *after* a failed mission had resulted in the death of one or more men and/or women.

During one especially important launch from Tyuratem, Jake's group on Guam was the first to intercept the 'warm-up' transmissions identified with communications surrounding Soviet launches. This particular launch—with a human cosmonaut, followed a fateful launch only a month earlier during which a dog was the guinea pig. The human didn't fare much better and only achieved a sub-orbital position before the test subject's heart exploded.

Because of the importance of the data gathered from this launch, NSA had requested that it be transmitted back to them ASAP, rather than through the normal daily air courier service.

Transmission of data halfway around the world involved setting up a complicated secure Teletype link between Guam and the U.S. The data would be sent encrypted, which meant that the code for encrypting the data on Guam had to be synchronized with the code for decrypting the data in D.C. A team of crypto specialists was busy preparing the data; meanwhile, the teletype link between the two sites had to be established and kept open until the crypto team was ready to transmit.

Jake was watch captain on the mid watch during which the activity was taking place, and—as such—was responsible for maintaining the Teletype link. Normal banter back and forth consisted on "How's the weather in D.C.?" and "How's the weather in Guam?" After about a half-hour of exchanging pleasantries, the crypto team informed Jake they were ready to transmit.

Jake began typing on the Teletype machine's keyboard: "Well old man, the data is ready to send. I'll sign off at this point; I've enjoyed talking to you. Hope your rain stops so you can get your lawn cut at home. CT2 Jake Morton on this end. So long from Guam."

"Roger, CT2 Morton; enjoyed chatting with you too. After a half-hour of this I think I am finally awake and ready to see what you've got to send. Thanks for your help. Good Night. DIRNSA out." And with that, the link was turned over for the transmission of the intercepted Soviet launch data.

"Jesus Christ," Jake exclaimed aloud. "For the last half hour I've been talking about cutting grass and crap like that with the Director of the National Security Agency and didn't know it!"

Jake's 18 months on Guam had been tolerable, even mildly enjoyable. He'd matured, and managed to save some money after all. He saved enough to buy a small diamond at the base exchange, which he mailed to his girlfriend Janice in Pennsylvania. After he figured enough time had passed for her to receive it, he called her on a 'phone patch' made possible through the base amateur radio station, and proposed. She had the ring in the unopened box, which she opened while he was on the phone and slipped the ring on her finger. It was almost as good as being there. Janice officially was his fiancée. Life was good. And it looked like it was about to get better, because his tour of duty on Guam was up and new orders had been cut to send him to NAVCOMSTA Kami Seya, Japan.

*   *   *   *

One of the best benefits of his assignment to Japan was the 30-day leave to go home between duty stations. Catching a Military Air Transport (MATS) 'hop' to San Francisco took a few days of waiting in Agana's quonset hut airport—constantly getting bumped by someone of higher rank, but Jake eventually made it as far as an Air Force base near San Francisco and then to Pennsylvania on a commercial flight.

Jake climbed down the stairs of the Allegheny Airlines DC-3 and spotted Janice behind the fence at the edge of the tarmac; in seconds she was running toward him and in his arms.

"Oh, Jake, I've missed you so much," was about all she got out before Jake put his hand on the back of her neck and guided her lips to his.

"I know, honey. Me too," and he kissed her long and hard. He took her head in both hands and again kissed her on the forehead as he drew her close again. Over her shoulder he noticed both his and her parents waiting behind the fence, and while temporarily slightly embarrassed, it quickly passed. *I love her and I'm about to marry her, for God's sake—I have no reason to feel this way.*

After a brief family reunion, they collected Jake's sea bag and headed for the parking lot. Jake let his father drive the two hours from the airport to home. "I'm rusty, Dad; give me a few days to practice driving at home before I tackle the Turnpike."

Jake and Janice were married less than two weeks later—a hometown church wedding conducted by both Jake's former minister and Janice's pastor. Janice's parents had attended different churches, her mother the Roman Catholic Church and her father the Presbyterian. Janice usually had elected to accompany her father on most Sundays, and consequently had his pastor, not her mother's priest, conduct the service.

After a very short reception at Janice's home, Jake and his bride left for a brief honeymoon at a resort in Pennsylvania's Pocono Mountains. They arrived about two p.m. and didn't emerge from their cottage for more than 24 hours. Having been separated for a year already, with potentially another year to go before they might be together, Jake and Janice had a lot of love to share—and to put in the bank for the future, in a short time.

The atmosphere for their first night together was accented by tremendous anticipation—and nervousness—on both their parts. Janice had strong moral standards and had kept Jake's amorous physical advances at bay for almost three years. Their lovemaking foreplay initially was awkward and—and on Jake's part, perhaps a bit rushed. He was, in short, eager. Janice was a beautiful girl, and Jake had always considered himself fortunate to have her both as a friend and a lover. Fending off competitors had been a constant challenge.

Janice, to Jake's surprise, also was ready, with no hesitation, to make the transition from close friend to intimate lover. She made a point of trying to ease Jake's nervousness in the bedroom and make him comfortable.

"Jake, come here. It's time to come to bed. You've been 9,000 miles away from me and I want to feel you next to me."

Jake moved to the bed and sat next to Janice on the bed. He brushed her shoulder-length blonde hair off of her shoulder and gently kissed the side of her neck. "You've cut your hair," Jake said as he held her head in his hand and lowered her on her back.

"And..you don't like it?"

"Honey, I love it." And he did. It was natural blonde, straight and silky but thick and full, flipped up on the end. "I'd love you bald," and he slowly moved his left hand down and began undoing the buttons of her blouse. He was kissing her full on the lips—they were swollen and hot now, and massaging her ample breasts through the opened blouse.

Janice moaned slightly, and after removing her bra, Jake began caressing her breasts, slowly licking her nipples and gingerly taking them between his teeth. She moaned louder now, and Jake could feel her reaching for his zipper. She was having trouble.

"Here, let me," he said as he unzipped it himself. "I should have worn my 13-button Navy pants...they're quicker." Janice had him full in her hand, and Jake thought he would explode. He had dreamed of this moment over and over for the past year, but for sanity's sake he would quickly put it out of his mind. There was no doing so tonight. His mouth was slowly moving down her breasts and stomach as he reached inside her pants. It was warm and moist.

"You shaved."

"Yes. Just yesterday. I thought you'd like it, Jake..." It was a question, but Jake didn't respond. He was concentrating on other things.

"Oh, Jake, I love you..." she whispered as Jake's fingers found her most sensitive pleasure spot. She moaned a deep, soft sound of ecstasy as he gently massaged her deeper and deeper, and Jake felt her tighten on his fingers.

"You're the first, you know."

"Yes, honey, and so are you..."

Jake slowly slid her pants down her legs and off, and in seconds he was inside her. It was all he could do to hold himself back. For their first time together, Jake wanted to do it right and make it meaningful. For the next hour, Jake and Janice explored the physical side of their love and discovered that it was as deep and satisfying as their emotional feelings for each other.

*   *   *   *

When leave was about to expire, Jake and Janice drove from Pennsylvania to San Diego, California where Jake was to catch his plane to his new duty station in Japan. The plan was to have Janice stay there with a relative and find a job while waiting to join him in Japan, if possible, which Jake would have to try to arrange once he got there.

Jake's flight to Japan seemed like it would take forever, and it did. Turboprop aircraft were state-of-the-art for commercial airlines, so faster travel was an unknown. With refueling stops in Hawaii and on the half-moon-shaped island of Wake, the large four-engine plane finally arrived in Tokyo. The subsequent transfer by bus to Kami Seya in the country near Yokohama hadn't afforded Jake much more than a quick glimpse of the Japanese countryside, but he liked what he'd seen. The terrain reminded him a little of his home in Pennsylvania, and best of all, there weren't any jungles. His initial impression was that he was going to like it here.

And like it he did. The Kami Seya base, even though small compared to other types of Navy facilities, was one of the larger and newer Naval Security Group activities, having been built in the mid-1950s.

After only three months in Japan, Jake missed his new wife terribly, and knew the nine months remaining on this enlistment would be a real test. He'd met Janice in high school—she was a sophomore, he was a senior. Leaving her to go to boot camp was one of the toughest things he'd ever done. Jake was very much in love, and had a jealous streak a mile long. Janice was quite good looking, and Jake was sure every other guy in town would be all over her like a cheap suit as soon as he was out of the way. He wrote to her every few days, and physically ached until he could be with her again. Unfortunately he had been advised that because of the short time left on his enlistment, the Navy would not pay to have her join him. And, as there was no housing on base for married couples, those with spouses at Kami Seya were forced to find private Japanese quarters off base.

Janice wasn't happy when she learned she wouldn't be going to be able to be with Jake, and threatened to come to Japan anyway. Jake had a real shock when, during a mid watch, a message from Janice was relayed to him via the Red Cross saying that she was catching a commercial flight and would be in Tokyo the next morning! Fortunately for Jake, she regained her senses and changed her mind. Had she kept her threat, Jake was three hours away, with nowhere to take her when she did arrive.

So Jake did his best to keep busy, and his mind off of his beautiful new bride when he wasn't working. Kami Seya was about a half-hour drive from Yokohama, surrounded by rice fields and vegetable farms, and along a two-lane road designated as Route 16. 'Gravel-Truck Alley' would have been a more fitting name—based on the constant stream of huge dump trucks hauling gravel to and from where, Jake didn't know. The drivers were paid by the load, so speed limits and anything in their way be damned.

The main gate to Kami Seya was right along the road, and if the liberty bus to Yokohama wasn't there, Jake could always stop in at the Green House bar near the intersection and have a quick beer—and drool over the mama-san's lovely daughter, Midori. The Green House was one of about three local bars situated near the entrance, and frequented almost exclusively by Kami Seya personnel. Midori was unusually beautiful—tall for a Japanese, and possibly more attractive to the Americans because her eyes were more round than traditional for her race. She was lovely, and she knew it.

Jake managed to spend almost all of his free time off base. There was always a party of some kind at a bar in Chinatown. (Every liberty town in the world had its Chinatown—a mixture of bars, clubs, brothels and massage parlors, all of which existed to extract the maximum amount of a sailors pay. If it wasn't 'Chinatown,' it was 'Japantown' or 'Boy's Town' or something similar. The content, purpose and result were always the same.)

Yokohama's Chinatown was world-renowned. With more than 400 bars crammed into a few square city blocks, there was always something for everyone.

Sailors tended to be very territorial and loyal when it came to frequenting specific bars. Each watch section had its favorite, and this served several purposes. If Jake wanted to find someone he knew was in Yokohama, he could usually count on finding him at a specific bar. If not, at least someone there would know where he was.

Also, it was a 'safe' haven. Many bars were officially off-limits to the CTs by orders of the Navy. Rumors abounded of communists attempting to pry information out of drunken CTs in certain bars, stories never confirmed by Jake or anyone he knew.

And then there were the girls, the "Jo-sans." Each bar had its resident girls, and each group of girls had its hierarchy. The number-one girl was the boss (after the Mama-san, of course), and was fairly long-term in one place while the other girls changed bars more frequently.

Many did give or sell their favors, but it wasn't an openly obvious solicitation. Of course there were the well-known prostitutes. Who would ever forget the

'Lady With The Poodle,' or 'Tiger Lady,' or 'Virgin Mary.' They were known as 'roadrunners'.

But most of the bar girls were a bit more subtle. They bore no resemblance to the geishas of old. They weren't trained in any arts—they didn't play instruments or sing or dance; their entertaining skills were limited to conversation and squeezing money from the sailors. They were highly skilled, and successful, at soliciting drinks from their clientele—which was actually mostly tea, for which they got a commission from the Mama-sans—the women who ran most of the bars. Mama-san was law, and was never loathe in demonstrating her position to customer or employee. If the girls' drinks had contained any alcoholic content, they wouldn't have made it past the first hour. Mama-san poured a lot of tea.

Jake being newly married, had a very high dedication to faithfulness. But *Jacob* Morton also was raised in a fairly religious family and that also had a large influence on his morality. Jacob's father worked as a carpenter with a lot of Mennonites in Pennsylvania before opening his retail store, and greatly admired their ethics and morality. "Jacob" had not been a family name, but a common name among the sect his father greatly admired.

A religious fanatic, however, Jake was not. He attended parties, and conversed with the girls. He discovered that it actually was possible to sit in a bar and have a beer, or just have a platonic relationship with a bargirl. He found some of them to be highly intelligent and interesting to talk to. In most cases they respected a sailor's desire for conversation only, and as long as Jake bought them a 'drink' once in awhile to keep the mama-san happy, all was well.

Yoko, as Jake knew her, was one such girl. About 19 years old, slender with long black hair, Yoko had lived above the bar with the Mama-san for at least the past six years. Yoko was a country girl from a large family whose poor peasant farmer parents could not afford to feed all of the children. Consequently, as was quite common, she had been turned over to the bar owner in a form of mutually beneficial servitude. In return for working in the bar and doing housekeeping chores, Yoko lived above the bar and was raised—fed, clothed and educated, by the Mama-san.

Jake enjoyed Yoko's company. She never pressed Jake to buy her a drink although Jake did offer to do so occasionally just to keep the Mama-san happy. Yoko was intelligent, and her English was excellent, the product of many years of entertaining the troops. She provided Jake with a good education about Japan, its culture and customs. And Jake's command of the Japanese language, though limited, would have been non-existent without Yoko's tutoring.

Naturally, the Navy officially frowned upon relationships with Japanese civilians. The security-conscious base officers thought every bargirl was a communist agent. What they didn't realize was that most of these girls only cared about where next month's rent would come from, or getting a new party dress, and didn't give a damn about the Russian Pacific Fleet order-of-battle plan that none of these CTs would have knowledge of anyway.

Jim Strong, whose bunk was separated from Jake's by a four-by-eight foot plywood partition, had taken Jake under his wing when he first arrived in Japan. Going on liberty to Chinatown could be a complicated thing, he explained, if you don't know the ropes. "I want to get you acclimated as soon as I can," he'd told Jake. "I need a new drinking buddy."

"You have to understand, Jake, there are several ways to go on liberty. And as far as parties go, there are several kinds. The 'sayonara' party—that's 'goodbye' in Japanese—are the most elaborate. As soon as someone's due for transfer to another duty station or to be discharged, a sayonara party gets organized. And not to be missed. In fact, Rymond's party is coming up pretty soon. It'll be fancy—lots of hired strippers, a 'happy' coat gift for the departing swab, and large crowds."

"Who pays for all this?"

"Usually we all chip in and buy out the entire bar for about $300 and that way we have a private party with the club all to ourselves. And everyone chips-in for the happy coat. So the more we get to attend, the cheaper it is for all of us."

Jake was taking it all in, and just smiling and nodding. Jim went on for quite some time. "Don't you ever go downtown by yourself?" he asked.

"Sure, but usually it's a party that gets you downtown in the first place. Many parties turn into 'lone wolf' liberties. Every once in awhile you'll decide that the companionship of your buddies isn't enough—possibly some social or deep biological need might arise and drive you to seek companionship elsewhere—often that of the opposite sex. Of course that has never happened to me, being married and all—like you, Jake. But I've heard it happens. Most often a guy just feels sorry for a lonely female spirit that he runs across and wants to contribute to her college fund or something. You can spot the guys coming in the gate—usually hung-over, returning to base alone, just in time to catch the bus to report for duty. And usually they return with a grin on their face and a new rash that has developed where the sun doesn't shine, that'll be there for weeks to remind him what a good time he had. Like every time he makes a trip to the dispensary for his weekly shot. Ha!"

"The 'end-of-the-road' liberty also gets you off base, usually just before pay-day, but normally close to the eve watch when you don't have much time to go all the way downtown. It's always a popular thing to do when you find yourself on base prior to one of the scheduled air raid drills that leaves you sitting in a trench for an hour behind the baseball field. The Greenhouse, Hollywood and Seya bars just outside the gate are always ready for you—and your paycheck, at the end of the road."

"Every once in awhile you'll end up with a bunch of drunks and meet up with lots of other guys from many separate bars at the Club Peanuts, which usually has live bands. Jumping down from the mezzanine onto the stage while the band is playing is always good for laughs...as long as you get away before the Shore Patrol shows up, that is...And of course the bus ride back to Kami Seya can get rowdy as well, usually because the lower-ranked guys who have to be back by midnight (hence the name 'midnight flyer') or guys that have to get back to go on watch and want to cram as much in as they can before they come back."

"What you *don't* want to do is stumble into one of the local bars frequented by the notorious gravel truck drivers—you know, those idiots that own the road between the base and downtown. These guys prize their territory, and they're all well practiced in Karate. I've seen them sitting at a bar just hammering their hands on the edge of the bar to toughen 'em and build fighting calluses. Even the support pillars in these bars are padded with straw and burlap bags so they can practice driving their bare hands, fingers first, into the straw."

"Why?" Jake asked.

"Why the straw? It's practice for jamming their hands into someone's rib cage. And if they really don't like you, once the get their hand inside they grab a rib, twist and break it. 'Nuff said?"

Jake quickly learned that in desperation there was always something to do on base if it was too close to payday or if he just didn't have time to hit the beach. The base enlisted men's (EM) club was cheap food and even cheaper beer. Unfortunately it was American beer, and the formaldehyde-laden Pabst Blue Ribbon and Carling Black Label was barely tolerable after having been introduced to Japanese draft-fresh Kirin, Asahi or Sapporo beer.

On Guam it had been the same story—American beer was 10-cents a can but everyone splurged for the more expensive favorite—San Miguel from the Philippines—for a whopping 20-cents a can.

But life in Kami Seya wasn't all booze, babes and vicarious debauchery Jake learned. The area around Kami Seya also offered quite varied recreation of a more conventional type. Trips to the gorgeous Hakone Mountains were popular, with a stay at the military's Special Services resort that had been 'acquired' from the Japanese at the end of the war.

Climbing the snow-covered slopes of the revered Mt. Fuji was popular, or to the opposite extreme, spending a few days at a beach house. Rentals were inexpensive and it provided an atmosphere that made any unpleasant memories of your work or life just disappear.

Trips to see the Kabuki theater in Tokyo were always fun—even if you couldn't understand an iota of what was going on, and even if you were the only gaijin (foreigner) in the audience. Department stores in Tokyo were fantastic sources of amusement, gifts for the folks at home, and people watching. A tour of the Imperial Palace, with a chance to actually spot Emperor Hirohito when he would make a rare public appearance on his birthday was on everyone's do-it-before-you-ship-out list.

And for the truly lonely, there was the obligatory trip to Tokyo to see the all-girl revue at the Nichigeki theatre, or the classy Mikado that had an elaborate Paris-style stage show featuring pounds of floppy, naked silicone breasts.

CTs played hard, but they worked hard as well. Most of the guys Jake met on Guam and here in Japan were bright, patriotic, and dedicated professionals. Patriotism went with the job—everything done was aimed at continuing to protect what you valued in the American way of life.

CHAPTER 4

▼

"You're part of the Direct Support group now, and about the best I can tell you is that you'll be 'out-and-about'."

Jake found that his early exposure to ham radio had given him a real advantage in his job. Although he primarily operated on—and preferred—'phone,' or voice transmissions, he was proficient at sending Morse code at better than 25 words-per-minute, and receiving above 35 WPM. English was the unofficial language of amateur radio, and he particularly had enjoyed 'DX,' or contacts with operators in foreign countries. Hams generally were a friendly group, very helpful and courteous on the air. Because of the totalitarian regime in the Soviet Union, the few licensed hams in that country were mostly military personnel or well-trusted party members. All spoke English, of course, but QSOs—conversations—mainly were restricted to conversations about the weather, the strength of their relative signals, and vague, general geographic locations. Jake always suspected his conversations with Russian hams were being monitored, because the Russian amateur was always very tight-lipped and seemed eager to end the conversation...but always insisted on a signal strength report. Some people at the American Radio Relay League, or ARRL—the amateur radio association—actually theorized that the Russians were collecting this information on an organized basis; that through some complex computer program, they were factoring in time, distance, origin of transmission, transmission power, etc. to try to forecast optimum future communications. This was never confirmed.

Jake also had developed an uncanny ability to pick a signal out of the noise that other people had a difficult time hearing. Over time, Jake could identify the origin of a Morse transmission by the tone and rhythm of the 'fist' of the sender. No two individuals send a word or a sentence in any language with exactly the same cadence or spacing, and Jake began to know the senders by their fists.

Since call signs were rarely used, differentiating between Soviet and Chinese communist transmitters could be difficult, but Jake seemed fairly adept at doing it. This talent provided invaluable information about the location of transmitters, especially mobile ones, which could have meaning regarding activities such as large military personnel or equipment movement. Formal, technical methods of triangulation and signal analysis were last resorts if Jake couldn't pin an identity on something he heard.

The bands were unusually active one particular night in July, and Jake was kept busy—not just at his own position, but helping some of the newer 'ditty chasers' as Morse code intercept operators were called, with their tasks. He'd earned a reputation for his skills in a short time, and probably would be named section leader shortly.

His section leader, a tall freckled redhead from Nebraska, grabbed Jake on his way back to his position.

"O'Shaughnessy wants to see you topside, so go on up and I'll cover your position while you're gone." Lt. O'Shaughnessy was the division commander, and Jake had only met him once during a surprise walk-through on an eve watch. O'Shaughnessy normally didn't work during mid-watches, so Jake was a bit surprised that he was here.

He worked his way back down the tunnel, through the "H" crossover that had been built to connect the two parallel tunnels in their centers, and up the ladder to the next level. The op center consisted of two tunnels covered over with earth by the Japanese and reportedly used for munitions storage during the war. One rumor was that it also had been a torpedo factory. The Americans had constructed the connecting tunnel in the 1950s when the Navy base was established. Not much had been done to the tunnel since, however, other than improve the sound proofing and lighting. Well-worn green and cream-colored floor tiles were a lovely Navy decorator touch left over from the fifties.

Jake knocked on the division officer's door and was invited in.

"Petty Officer Morton reporting, Sir," Jake announced, standing at attention.

"Good morning, Petty Officer Morton, have a seat."

The division office was small, with lovely period maps for wall covering, furnished with the traditional standard Navy issue gray steel desk and file cabinet, and accented with the homey touch of a few family photos. Jake noted O'Shaug-nessy's wife was quite attractive, and he immediately had a momentary ache in his heart for Janice.

Jake sat in a chair opposite the officer's desk. "Good Morning, Sir," Jake responded. "It's been a busy one so far."

"Yes, it has, and I hear you're doing more than holding up your end. Good work. And that has some bearing on why I wanted to see you," he continued.

O'Shaughnessy was young. His blond hair was cropped short, neatly shaved high on the sides. He smiled often but had an air of authority that appeared beyond his age.

"I want you to begin cross-training with some of the T- and O-branchers for the balance of the week. You're leaving on TAD at the end of the next watch rotation, and I think you'll find what you learn between now and then to be of use," he said.

"I'd welcome that opportunity. I know a little about what the radio printer guys do, but I don't have a clue what the other specialties do. I also don't know where I'm going next week—can you fill me in?" Jake's voice didn't betray the apprehension he now felt. *Why did they pick me for TAD if they needed more than what I now know?* he wondered.

"Sorry Morton, but I can't go into the where or why. Just show up for the bus to Atsugi when you're supposed to, and they'll fill you in over there at mission briefing. You're part of the Direct Support group now, and about the best I can tell you is that you'll be 'out-and-about'," O'Shaughnessy said, standing as he spoke. This was Jake's signal to stand also, and that he was about to be dismissed.

"Meet a first-class T-brancher by the name of Simanski at the entrance of building 42 when you report back for your next eve watch, and he'll take you through it. Any questions?"

"No Sir. Thank you, Sir," Jake responded, and left the Lieutenant's office.

Neither one of them saluted—saluting 'under cover' (with any kind of a roof over your head) wasn't done in the USN, a custom that unfortunately wasn't the case in other branches of the service. While on Guam, Jake had failed to salute a young Marine Corps officer while walking under a covered walkway between the barracks and the mess hall, and was challenged because of it.

"Don't you salute superior officers, sailor?" the marine officer had asked.

"No Sir, not under cover," Jake had replied.

Jake's reply only served to infuriate the officer, who became red-faced and yelled "Well sailor, you'll salute *me!*" And of course Jake did, if not terribly

smartly. Only intervention by a passing Navy officer who reinforced Jake's explanation for failing to salute prevented Jake from being disciplined.

Curious, Jake thought—either O'Shaughnessy doesn't know where I'm going,
or won't say for some reason. In any event, Jake welcomed the chance to learn
more about what the other specialists' jobs involved. He enjoyed his code job,
and even with his amateur radio hobby background, there still were a lot of other
kinds of signals on the airwaves that he had no idea what they were.

Returning to his work position, Jake's section leader briefed him on what had
happened during his absence. It was a busy night and Jake didn't get a chance to
leave his post for several more hours. There was a lot of new traffic, and lengthy
transmissions, and while he tried to copy most of it, he grew tired and relegated
the balance to the tape deck.

Jake was good, could copy code faster than he could send, of course, but never
had mastered typing as well as he should have. The old mechanical Underwoods
were slower than his fingers he rationalized. There was a Naval Radio Station on
base whose main purpose was to monitor the US Navy's own radio traffic—
mostly the ships at sea—for conformance to rules and regulations. They func-
tioned like an 'airwaves police' for the fleet. Jake had heard stories about a Chief
Radioman in that station who could copy 45 words per minute with one hand on
the typewriter and read a book at the same time. He wondered if he'd ever get to
that point where the code would automatically flow from his headset directly to
his fingertips.

*   *   *   *

"Come on, Morton, get with it. The beer's gettin' flat." With those words,
Jake was now awake—it was 1500 and he'd had a solid six hours of rack time
after the mid watch.

"We've got Rymond's sayonara party at the Zebra Club in two hours, did you
forget?" Jim Strong reminded him as he leaned over the plywood partition separating their cubes.

"No, I haven't forgotten. I'll meet you at the bus stop in 30 minutes. I'm out
of smokes, and don't have anything left but a pack of these rotten Japanese
'Hope' weeds.' I'll stop at the PX first," Jake replied as he pulled himself out of
the sack. Somehow waking up at three in the afternoon had a disorienting effect
on his metabolism. He thought he'd never get used to sleeping during the day,
and slowly threw his legs over the edge of the bunk to officially mark the wakeup

process. The subject of the party—Rymond, wasn't a close friend, but a party was a party, and always worth getting up for.

The afternoon sunlight filtering through the filthy barracks windows told him it was a great day, and with that solid sleep behind him, he felt like he was ready for anything. After a quick shower he put on his civvies—a short sleeve plaid button-down-collar shirt and a pair of chinos—complete with buckle in the back, and was on his way out the front gate to meet Jim Strong at the bus stop.

I wish I had a car, he thought, but then realized the folly of his thinking—cars were expensive to maintain in Japan—especially American cars. Plus, the roads were much more narrow than at home, and the locals drove like kamikaze pilots. And the Japanese police were not very forgiving of sailors in wrecks. One sailor had hit and killed a Japanese civilian who was walking down the center of Rt. 16 late one night. He got five years in a Japanese prison, probably an unpleasant equivalent of 10 years in an American prison.

Strong was waiting for him when he got to the bus stop.

"Get your smokes?"

"Yeah, but my ration card is full so I couldn't get a carton. Signed the log and got two packs."

"Wanna grab a quickie at the Green House before we get the bus? We still have a good 20 minutes," Jake asked.

"The only 'quickie' I'd like from the Green House is about 20 minutes alone with Midori," Strong answered.

"I meant a beer, asshole." Jake understood, though; everyone on the base felt the same way. Midori was a very beautiful young Japanese girl, and rumor had it she was dating a marine security guard. Nobody seemed inclined to challenge that.

"Probably for the best," Jim said. "I stopped in here two nights ago and met this delicious young thing. I'd never seen her before—she was alone and just having a drink; she obviously wasn't one of the 'employees.'

"In no time we were in a cab headed for her house. I should have known better. The first clue that I was in trouble was that she spoke perfect English. The second clue was that she had an American-style bed—no futon on the floor for this girl, and an American refrigerator. She screwed like a nymphomaniac rabbit. She actually wore me out to the point I couldn't get it up anymore. Then at five in the morning, she woke me up and told me I had to go—her husband, a military policeman at Atsugi Naval Air Station, would be home soon, she told me. Man, that got my attention. I was up and in a cab back to Kami Seya within 10 minutes."

Jake just smiled. He formed a mental picture of Jim running out the back door in his underwear while the husband approached the front door where his wife greeted him.

The bus into Yokohama was on time for once, and it looked like they'd make the Zebra Club in time for happy hour, the 60 minutes of reduced drink prices beginning at 1600. Mixed drinks were only 20 cents then, and a dime for draft Sapporo or Kirin—a good place to start the evening. Besides, the sayonara party for Dennis Rymond and his wife was in a back room at the Zebra Club and started in an hour, so Jake figured they may as well wait.

Unfortunately Jake didn't have the alcohol tolerance that Jim Strong had, and four 20-cent whiskey sours later, he was feeling little pain.

"Come on, wuss, I'm two up on you," Strong kidded him. But Jake nursed his drink until happy hour ran out, and jokingly told Jim "Oops, too late—can't afford any more. They're 30-cents now."

As it worked out, the sayonara party began shortly thereafter. The honored guests, rotating to the NSG facility at Sabena Seca, Puerto Rico, were welcomed and given the 'we'll miss you' speeches by close friends. A cake was brought out, the couple presented with traditional going away gifts of 'happy coats,' and pictures taken.

And then it was time for the entertainment. A Japanese stripper had been hired from one of the bars to spice up the party with her gyrations to the tune of some American rock & roll. Jake noted that she was unusually well endowed for a Japanese, well before the popularity of silicone. After what everyone thought took way too long, the dancer finally had all of her clothes off with the exception of her G-string. And that signaled the beginning of a moment of fame for Mrs. Rymond that would reverberate throughout the base.

The dancer was greeted by lots of encouragement from the audience to rid herself of that major piece of clothing which blocked an uninhibited view of her crotch—something they all knew they'd see again somewhere that night anyway. By now co-guest of honor Mrs. Rymond was seeing two dancers on the table— very similar to the whisky sour-induced view Jake also had.

When the Japanese girl finally removed the G-string, much to the chagrin of husband CT1 Dennis Rymond, and to the delight of everyone else, the sweet, demure little Jennifer Rymond yelled, "Hell, I had more hair than that when I was 13," and immediately climbed up on a table and began stripping herself. Her disrobing style wasn't as smooth or titillating as the competing stripper, but she was amply well endowed to catch everyone's attention. Husband Dennis had convinced himself that the crowd's attraction to the now completely nude Mrs. Rymond was one of humorous entertainment, not lechery.

Of course that brought the house down, and Jake went to the head—and brought it all *up*. That revived him a bit, and he and Jim left the party—which Mrs. Rymond had all but ended anyway, and decided to check out the action at the "Bar Happy"—their section's hangout in Chinatown. Besides, it was time for a beer.

That decision, about 1800 hours on Friday evening was the last thing Jake remembered until he woke up in his bunk at 0900 Sunday morning with a headache and dry heaves and stomach cramps.

"You really tied one on, pal," admonished his drinking buddy. If they had done a chemical analysis of Jake's stomach, they would have found traces of whiskey sour, Kirin beer, Akadama wine and some Suntory whiskey as well. He was lucky to be conscious, and would never forgive himself for literally losing a day and a half of his life that he couldn't remember.

"Are you going to make it for the physical fitness qualifications this morning?"

The fog in Jake's head began to clear and he realized where he was, but couldn't focus on Jim's face or what the words meant coming out of his mouth.

"You have to at least *try*, Jake, or you'll be washing dishes for a month."

Jake then remembered: President Kennedy had launched a program of minimum physical fitness requirements for all service personnel. Everyone had to qualify periodically by successfully accomplishing a certain number of chin-ups, sit-ups, and run 100 yards in a minimum time.

Forcing a painful and slight smile, Jake told him "I don't think I can get out of bed."

After several minutes of convincing, Jim helped him outside to the lawn area where the qualification tests were taking place. Wobbly Jake started with sit-ups. On number four, he threw up all over the sailor holding his legs, and they drug him back to bed. He'd do 16 hours of exercises in the base gym over the course of the coming month as punishment.

Weak and still dizzy from the hours of recovery, Jake reported for the eve watch the next afternoon, the last round of watches before leaving on his TAD. CT1/T-branch Walt Simanski was waiting at the entrance to the op center, and introduced himself to Jake as they walked through the series of security checks.

Noticing Jake's pale demeanor, Simanski asked, "You sure you're up to this? You look like shit."

"Just a little rough on the edges. I'm looking forward to this; I've been curious about what you guys do at this end of the tunnel."

Simanski, on his second enlistment, was the watch captain for his section of the building. "I don't know how much you can absorb in six watches, but we'll pump it into you and hope some of it sticks. Something may come in handy. I understand you're good on CW, but I don't know if that'll help you with radio printer," Walt told him.

Jake knew a little about radio Teletype, or radio printer as it was more commonly known, having played around with it a little as a ham radio operator before he enlisted. At least he knew the theory part. By the time Simanski was done with him, he'd be able to read baud printouts on paper tape like he was reading the <u>Navy Times.</u>

The next six watches were eye opening to Jake. The equipment was different, the procedures were different, and there was a lot of variety compared to 'chasing ditties.' It turned out that he and Simanski hit it off well; Simanski was a fellow Pennsylvanian from Mt. Carmel, in the eastern-central part of the state, and came from a long line of coal miners.

Jake didn't know where his TAD assignment was going to take him, for how long, or what he'd be doing, but he had to guess that some of Walt's tutoring would have some usefulness. There certainly was a lot more activity here in the op center than he realized. He hoped for relevance in the weeks to come.

CHAPTER 5

▼

When he was airborne, he noticed that there weren't any parachutes on the plane...

The Friday morning bus to nearby Atsugi Naval Air Station was punctual, somewhat unusual for a Navy shuttle. Skies were gray, the air was still, and it was warm—and that made good conditions for thunderstorms, Jake thought, and maybe not a pleasant day for flying. But then that wasn't up to him, so Jake boarded the bus with about 10 other sailors headed for Atsugi, a short ride from Kami Seya.

Jake thought he recognized one of the others who got on the bus—a seaman CT (CTSN). Jake had seen him in Chinatown once but didn't have time to approach him to figure out why he recognized him. He had left early. Seamen were required to be back on base by 2400—midnight—which made Yokohama liberty a bit out of reach unless you got downtown really early. For seamen, it was appropriately referred to as a 'Cinderella liberty.'

Jake approached him from behind. He started saying "Hi, I'm..." when the other sailor turned and Jake immediately recognized him as someone he'd known on Guam.

"Mike! Mike Johnson! Holy shit, I *thought* I recognized you—what's new, other than the long hair?"

"Hi, Jake! Christ, it's good to see you. Yeah, longer hair. Fewer mosquitoes, and it's colder here—gotta keep warm, know what I mean? How long have you been here? I've got a TAD assignment out of Atsugi. Where you headed?"

"Probably the same place you are, out and about. That's all I know. I have a flight out this afternoon. We're probably on the same plane. This is my first TAD, how about you?"

"Well, me too. I hope it's a short one. I've never been much for flying. I've only been in Japan for two months—with the luck of the draw I got Kami Seya. I left Guam before you did—switched from "R" branch to "T" branch. So I spent a few months at Goodfellow Air Force Base in San Angelo, Texas before getting assigned to Japan. My best friend went to Adak, and he's from Miami. *He's gonna have problems!*" Mike said

"Amen. I wanted to go to Adak so I could save money. But I'm glad I came to Japan instead. I hope I feel that way after this flight. How'd you like Texas?" Jake asked.

"I loved it. There were only about 25 of us swabs on the air base, so we didn't get spit on in town like the airmen did. Girls dig white uniforms, it turns out, and the best place to meet them in San Angelo is in church!"

"Church!! Somehow I can't see you in church. But whatever works, I guess..."

"How about you, Jake—how was Guam after I left?"

"I had a good time other than one incident with a very large taxi driver where I almost got religion myself."

"Taxi driver? What was that all about?"

Jake smiled. "I'll try to make a long story as short as I can. I got called into the C.O.'s office one day. They were having problems with Guamanian taxi drivers buying booze for underage sailors in Agana. And they needed a stooge to participate in a sting operation. I was asked to volunteer, being under 21 at the time."

"They wanted me to hail a cab, ask the driver to take me somewhere and buy a bottle of booze for me, and then drop me off at a prearranged destination where the cops would be waiting to arrest his ass."

"All went well. I hailed the cab, got the booze, got dropped outside the Agana Department Store, and took off as the cabbie was surrounded by local Guamanian and Navy police-types."

"And that's the last I thought of it, until about a month later when I was walking down the street in Agana, when this VW bug taxi came to a screeching halt right in the middle of the street; the driver—the biggest Guamanian you've ever seen—and the same one that had purchased my booze for me, jumped out and started after me. Left the damn taxi in the middle of the street with the engine running."

"I never knew I could run so fast. He'd recognized me and took off faster than I knew any 300-pounder could run. Son-of-a-bitch, he could run! We went thru back yards, down alleys, through taro patches, and into the jungle outside of Agana. I thought I was going to die—not from him, necessarily, but from my heart pounding through my chest. He finally gave up, and I snuck back to the bus stop and made it back to base."

"So what happened? Why wasn't he in jail?"

"I asked the same question. As soon as I got back to base, in fact. The official answer was that one of the Guamanian jail guards had drunk the evidence—the confiscated booze, and as a result they had to throw out the case against the taxi driver and release him."

"Give a poor Guamanian jail guard $3.50 a week and all the booze he can drink, and guess what happens!"

"Amen. And it also meant that one Jake Morton didn't set foot in downtown Agana for about four months after that either!"

They continued to get reacquainted during the rest of the short bus trip to Atsugi, and before they knew it, they pulled up in front of the VQ-1 Squadron headquarters building. It was always good to talk to someone with whom you could share memories and experiences; it helped ease the transition to new surroundings. Five CTs got off the bus, and were greeted by an Aviation Boatswains Mate who ushered them inside. The briefing center was pretty basic—a few pull-down maps, several rows of benches, and no windows. Overhead lights hung from single cords, casting a yellow glow over the room. The smell of stale smoke permeated the air. An un-insulated corrugated tin roof about 15 feet over their heads warmed the room to more than it should have been given the outside temperature.

They'd barely had a chance to take a seat when a far door opened and two officers entered; one instructed the men to "Remain seated. Lt. Andrews will conduct the orientation briefing."

The young lieutenant pulled down a map that included a wide area of the Sea of Japan and bordering countries of Japan, North Korea, China, and the Southern coast of the Soviet Union. Dressed in an orange flight suit, the lieutenant addressed the group.

"Gentlemen, welcome to Atsugi, and Fleet Airborne Recon Squadron One. I'm Lt. Robert Andrews, and I'm piloting your Willy Victor today. Some of you have been on these recon flights before, so this orientation will be old stuff for you. For those of you on your first flight with VQ-1, pay attention; the rules apply to everyone."

"Our total crew numbers thirty; three officers including a co-pilot, a navigator and myself. The regular crew will be performing routine electronic countermeasure tests (ECM) and Electronic Intelligence (ELINT) tasks. The complement of five CTs from Kami Seya will be responsible for Signal Intelligence/Communications Intelligence intercept operations, and report to Chief Petty Officer Stanfield."

"For you first-timers, today's bird is Willy Victor 22; officially she's an EC-121M, our version of the commercial four-engine Lockheed super-constellation. This is my sixth flight on number 22; she's a good plane and we've got a decent weather forecast, so I don't anticipate any problems."

U.S. Navy EC-121M No. 22 from VQ-1, Atsugi NAS

"We'll be flying northwest straight across the island of Honshu and over the Sea of Japan to Osan Air Force base. It's right on the 38th Parallel in Korea where we'll spend the night, and take off at 0500 tomorrow. From there we'll head northeast briefly along North Korea and a small slice of the Chinese coast, and then along the coast of the Soviet Union. Somewhere northeast of Vladivostok, we'll be cutting across the sea to Hokkaido and heading back to base."

"The flight to Osan will take about seven hours. If you have any questions, Crew Chief Albers will fill you in. If you'll follow him at this time, he'll get you outfitted. We board in 20 minutes. Thank you, and good hunting."

At this point, Jake and Mike had lots of questions, and knew virtually none would be asked or answered.

"Well, at least we now know where 'out and about' is," Mike said as they both got up to follow the crew chief.

"We sure do. Sounds like it'll be interesting. I guess Chief Stanfield is the guy that's going to fill in the blanks," Jake replied.

The men followed the crew chief out of the building and into another ready-room in an adjacent hut. Before they knew it they were sporting very florescent orange jump suits. Each man also was issued a .32 caliber revolver in a shoulder holster with six rounds of ammunition already loaded in the cylinder.

"What's this for?" Jake asked of the crew chief, referring to the revolver.

"Oh, that's for survival—you know, in case we ditch somewhere, so you can shoot a rabbit or whatever," the crew chief replied. Jake didn't buy the answer the chief had offered—but it was an answer and he knew it was the best he was going to get. Later when he was airborne he brought it to Mike's attention that there weren't any parachutes on the plane.

"Oh well, so much for the survival story," Mike commented.

"Survival my ass. I've hunted rabbits at home with a shotgun and had trouble hitting them, so I don't think hitting one with a pistol is the intended purpose of this pea-shooter," Jake said.

Mike shrugged and replied with a dry "Maybe they'll be big rabbits."

Precisely 20 minutes after the briefing, they were all aboard, and shown to their seats. CPO Stanfield introduced himself to the five CTs, and told them he'd be coming around to each operating position sometime after takeoff to brief them on their individual responsibilities.

Mike and Jake settled into their seats across the aisle from each other. Jake observed that the operating position was equipped much the same as the ones back at Kami Seya, with only one or two pieces of gear that were new to him. Both pieces of gear were newer than the rest of the rack-mounted equipment, and he decided that if he needed to know more, he'd be told.

Mike looked over at Jake, raised his eyebrows and gave a hand gesture that indicated that the equipment was unfamiliar to him also. Both relaxed and listened to the drone of the engines warming up, and the beginning of the taxi down the runway. *I hope he syncs those engines; they're killing my ears*, Jake thought.

The heavily loaded Willy Victor No. 22 finally lifted off after a long run-out. This military version of the commercial Lockheed Super Constellation had more powerful engines than its civilian counterpart, largely to compensate for the nearly six tons of sophisticated electronic gear that had been added. A large 'camel hump' on the top center of the plane held specialized radar equipment, and additional antennas of various sorts were contained in the belly and the nose as well.

Because of the weight and large topside antenna, the plane's maximum speed—about 300 mph, was slower than the commercial version, and consequently the cruising range also was shorter at about 6500 miles. WV-22 could go for 20 hours and that, Jake reasoned, was longer than he wanted to be in the air at one time anyway.

Between the drone of the engines and the early hour he had gotten up for the bus to Atsugi, Jake couldn't fight it and was soon asleep. He didn't know how long he'd slept, but he awoke quickly when he felt the plane begin to descend rather rapidly. He glanced at his watch and saw that he had been asleep only about an hour and a half, so he figured they were about 450 miles out from Atsugi. They'd been cruising at 25,000 feet when the big plane started to descend, circling as it did.

"What's going on?" Jake yelled across the aisle to Mike, who had parted the blackout curtains and was looking out the porthole.

"I'm not sure, but it looks like there are three boats of some kind down there; we must be going down for a look-see."

The plane continued to descend and by the time they were down to less than 1000 feet above the ocean surface, they could no longer see any boats. Lt. Andrews had the put the plane on a straight due-North course and within minutes, the boats appeared on the horizon.

"There they are," Mike exclaimed. "Looks like three fishing boats."

CPO Stanfield came on the intercom and announced that they were going in close to have a look at some fishing trawlers. Jake knew that the Russians often used trawlers as spy ships to keep track of American ship movements, substituting antennas for the nets and rigging that typify fishing boats.

They were coming closer to the boats when the plane climbed again and began a 360-degree turn. The three trawlers were in a group, all headed South—toward Japan—underway at about 15 knots, according to Stanfield's running intercom narrative.

As they circled the trawlers, extending their radius about a mile out as they did, the crew's photographer mate was taking lots of pictures. The photos would be taken back to Atsugi and analyzed so the Navy could keep track of which ships were operating and in what waters.

"We're awfully low for a plane this size, aren't we?" Mike asked.

Jake didn't reply—he was mesmerized by what he was watching outside. The Willy Victor circled the three trawlers at about 500 feet off the surface. As they passed overhead, Jake could see several crewmembers standing on the forward deck of the one trawler, waving enthusiastically to the plane. The Russians were dressed with standard knit blue hats and sweaters and dungarees.

Stanfield came on the intercom—evidently he had been using binoculars and began with a chuckle: "O.K. gentlemen, we'll be leaving now. Russian fishermen my ass. First fishermen I've ever seen who wear black patent leather shoes on deck!" he exclaimed.

After circling four times, WV-22 regained its course and cruising altitude with another five hours to go before they'd land at Osan AFB. Jake and Mike killed some time playing cards and napping, and digging into the box lunch each had been issued at Atsugi.

"Sure not up to Kami Seya mess hall standards," Jake observed.

When they were within an hour of landing, they began to pass over the tip of Southern Korea. CPO Stanfield began making his rounds to brief the CTs on what to expect. When he got to Jake and Mike, he kneeled in the aisle between them and began to explain that they would land at Osan AFB about 1500 local time and they'd be free until takeoff the following morning.

"Remember, we leave early tomorrow. You do NOT want to miss the plane. If neither one of you has ever been to Osan before, be prepared for a shock," the Chief began.

"Osan is a very short distance from the 38th Parallel that divides North and South Korea. It's a forward observation base and in a key location should any trouble break out. You'll be taken to your billet first thing, and then you'll be on your own. The barracks chief will see you get settled O.K. and tell you where to get chow. We take off at 0500, and we have a long day before we head back to Atsugi. So if you decide to hit the beach and try some Korean liberty, don't overdo it. Zero-four-hundred will come very quickly."

The big plane glided onto the runway with a very nice three-point landing and rolled to a stop on the end of the tarmac as far from any buildings as was physically possible. An Air Force bus was waiting for the plane. Jake and Mike boarded the bus to the barracks. Jake noticed most of the regular crew gathered around the nose of the Willy Victor after it landed, and asked the bus driver if he knew what was going on…

"Sure. They're practicing an old Air Force tradition that the Navy has borrowed. Before they left Atsugi, the crew used chalk and sectioned off the nose wheels into pie segments, and wrote each crewmember's initials in the segments.

Whoever's name is resting on the ground when the plane is parked has to buy the first round of drinks at the EM club," he explained.

"Wow. With 20-plus regular crew on that plane, I'm glad I didn't have my initials on the wheel," Mike remarked.

"Not a big deal," the driver added…"drinks are only 10-cents during happy hour."

Shortly after the CTs arrived and checked into the temporary quarters, Jake made a visit to the head. Finding a lack of toilet paper, he went to the barracks office and asked for a roll.

The airman staffing the office handed Jake a clipboard and said "Here. Sign it out. And when you're done, bring it back and we'll check you off."

"Sign out for a roll of toilet paper?" Jake questioned incredulously.

"You going outside the gate on liberty tonight?" the airman asked.

Jake nodded. "I guess so, why?"

"Well, once you're out there, you'll understand."

Strange, he thought…the Air Force accommodations here are better than we have at Kami Seya, so it's hard to understand why they are so tight with cheap old toilet paper.

After returning the obviously valuable half-used roll of paper and having its return officially noted on the lengthy sign-out sheet, Jake continued on to the air force mess hall, where he met and had a good meal with Mike and two other CTs from the plane whom he hadn't met before.

With a 0500 take off, Jake and Mike decided to go on liberty early. As soon as they finished eating, they headed for the front gate and grabbed a cab—a rickety old Nissan belching oil and running on about three of the four cylinders.

They had seen the village from the air, a small community that had sprung up right outside the main gate of the isolated air base. All of the streets were unpaved dirt, and the village didn't seem to consist of much other than bars and small eating-places. There had to be residences, Jake reasoned, though he didn't see any.

His first impression was that the town of Osan was a depressed place, and with a young population. He didn't see many elderly people. He also noticed cats everywhere—and no dogs—until, that is, he passed a butcher shop and then he understood why. Five medium-sized dogs, skinned and gutted but otherwise intact, hung in the window. The shop was closed, and the window display certainly wasn't refrigerated. Flies were everywhere. Cats caught mice, dogs didn't. Therefore, dogs were expendable—as food. These people obviously were poor and were barely subsisting. Other than for some small plot farming, the village appeared to be almost totally dependent upon the air base.

Jake and Mike stepped into a small bar, and although not as lavish as those in Japan, the atmosphere was the same—popular American music playing on a record player, an authoritarian mama-san behind the bar and four or five bar girls. The CTs ordered beer and found they had one choice—"O.B," which stood for "Oriental Breweries," but which the airmen nicknamed "Out Back," referring to where they suspected it had been brewed. O.B. came in green bottles, or so it appeared. Actually it was the beer, not the bottle that was green.

The girls' approach basically was the same—I.e., "Buy me a drink?" But unlike in Japanese bars, it went beyond that. These girls were obviously prostitutes, and the solicitation for sex was much more blatant.

An airman told Jake that when the air base first opened, these girls converged on the small farming village from all over the neighboring countryside. Sex acts of every variety were available for a pack of cigarettes, a *roll of toilet paper*, a candy bar…anything American, he said.

Now Jake understood the toilet paper sign-out experience he'd had earlier. If an American didn't have any cash, he could leave something of value with the girl as credit, and return the next evening with the cash—similar to a pawnshop operation.

It was common for a prostitute to ask for the airman's military I.D. card, he explained, but as these girls couldn't read English, they often got stuck with something official looking but worthless—an expired meal pass, for example. A carton of American cigarettes was sufficient payment to have exclusive services of a prostitute for a week.

Almost all of the bars worth going to were off limits, according to the airmen. But the cabbie knew what to do: he'd drive up to the bar, go inside to see if any Air Police were around. Jake and Mike would then jump out of the cab and make a beeline for the bar's backroom where the police were not allowed to go. When they were ready to leave, the cabbie would scout outside to see if the coast was clear, and Jake and Mike would run to the cab to go to the next bar.

The overall experience—the poverty and the seemingly low value of human dignity—was a little overwhelming for Jake. When Mike elected to stay on, Jake returned to base. He never was so glad that he was an American as he was this night.

CHAPTER 6

▼

"I guess we're more than slightly off course, and that's proba-
bly why we're getting company..."

The overhead lights in the barracks came on at 0330, and that was enough of an alarm clock to wake most of the crew. No rattling of broomsticks in an empty metal garbage can—a sadistic routine the barracks master-at-arms would perform when Jake had been in boot camp. Followed by the M.A. shouting "Drop your cocks and grab your socks," it would bring you out of a dead sleep and on your feet in less than five seconds.

Jake had gotten four hours of sleep and was feeling surprisingly pretty good. He'd gone easy on the O.B. beer, something he didn't have any difficulty in doing, and both his head and his stomach were in good shape. He noticed Mike's bunk was still empty, as were a few others, and though mildly concerned, he figured that Mike would show up in time for the bus.

After a quick shower and packing his small bag, Jake headed for the mess hall, a section of which was always open an hour prior to early flight departures. The choices were limited—coffee, of course, plus cold cereals, scrambled powdered eggs, a sweet roll, some fruit—very sufficient for this time of the day, Jake thought. Just as he grabbed his tray and as he was getting up to leave, Mike came and sat down at his table.

"Morning, Mike—I was just heading out for the bus. You going to make it?"

"Yeah, I'm going to grab a quick cup of coffee and a roll, and I'll be right there. You should've stayed in town—we had a great time after you left. Wait a minute, that didn't sound right…I meant…"

"I understand," Jake said, cutting him off. "No offense taken. I just wasn't into it. Seemed like everywhere you turned, someone had his or her hand out."

"Yeah, they did, and I filled a few of them. I would have made it back earlier to catch some winks, but this sweet young thing just insisted on taking me home to meet her mother," Mike said with a big grin.

"How old was her mother, 18?" Jake asked.

"Something like that. And definitely not the motherly type. The three of us had a good time. Sort of a Korean sandwich. Good thing it's payday in a week."

"See you on the bus," Jake said, shaking his head and heading out the door.

Now he was even happier that he hadn't stayed in the village. *Maybe I'll have time once we get airborne to get a letter off to Janice*, he thought, grabbing his bag and heading for the bus stop. *I don't think I'll mention Osan, or she'll just want to know what I'm doing here*, he told himself. *And since I'm not sure myself, I don't think I could explain it to her*, he concluded.

A few minutes later, Mike joined Jake at the bus stop just as the blue bus pulled up. The rest of the crew—at least those Jake recognized—were already on the bus. It was 0415, very dark, and the bus was very quiet. No one yelled any hearty greetings as they boarded; most of the crew looked to be grabbing a few final winks before takeoff.

The big blue diesel bus roared away from the stop and headed for the tarmac. Their plane was parked as far out from the others as it could have been. No guest privileges on this base, Jake surmised.

In a short 10 minutes or so, they were off the bus and climbing up the ladder into the belly of the Willy Victor. The ground crew was finishing up, and the fuel tanker was just pulling away when they arrived. Lt. Andrews was walking around the plane, making his final visual check as well. Chief Stanfield was waiting for them at the bottom of the ladder, and greeted each CT by name as they climbed aboard.

"You look like shit, Johnson."

"I feel better than I look. A quick nap and I'm ready to go," Mike replied.

Once aboard, the two settled into the same operating positions they'd had before. Chief Stanfield came around and told them to sit tight, take a snooze, and there would be a briefing in about a half-hour after take-off.

Both Mike and Jake took his advice and tried to get comfortable enough to take a quick nap. It didn't work well. Jake had just started to doze off when the sputter and cough of the four turbo-props starting up made it clear he wouldn't sleep. Mike, on the other hand, was already sawing wood and would sleep solidly through the take off.

With little warm up, the big plane lumbered down the runway and immediately poured on the juice and roared up and into the dark, cloudy sky on their way to—*We'll know in a bit*, Jake told himself.

The pilot came on the intercom about 25 minutes into the flight, after he'd gained altitude and cruising speed.

"Good morning, gentlemen. Glad to see you all made it back from outside the gate last night. This morning we're headed east at about 22,000 feet into a headwind that has us only maintaining 280 MPH ground speed. We'll cross the mainland of South Korea until we reach the Sea of Japan, and then we'll bear northeast along the coast of North Korea. We'll maintain a 50-mile distance off the coast until we near the city of Ch'ongin. Then we come a little closer to land and head north again toward Vladivostok, and further up to the entrance of the inland sea between the Soviet Union mainland and Sakhalin Island. When we reach the closest point to Khabarovsk on the mainland, still maintaining our territorial limits, we'll head east again, skirt below the tip of Sakhalin, and a straight southeastern route back to Japan. We should be on the ground at Atsugi in approximately 12 hours. There's a weather system pushing across the Soviet mainland and we'll hit it about the time we approach Vlad. I don't anticipate any problems, but try to minimize moving around. I'll give you an update as we approach Vlad. That is all," and the intercom went silent.

"Well, now we know," Jake remarked to no one in particular. He no sooner had the words out when CPO Stanfield entered the compartment and asked all of the CTs to gather for a briefing.

"I'm going to give out assignments, but before I do, does anyone have any questions about what Lt. Andrews said concerning our course?"

Nobody said anything.

"O.K., then here's the word. As soon as we reach the Sea of Japan, you T-branchers need to begin monitoring and recording anything you hear on the frequencies in your individual logs—which I will be handing out in a minute. Most of the transmitters are high power and should become audible at that point. You'll be busy until after we're on the homeward course.

"As for you R-branchers, you won't have much to do until we approach Ch'ongin and then, as you'll read in your logs, we're interested in the ship-to-ship and ship-to-shore traffic. Same when we approach Vlad; both are major shipping ports and you each have individual targets of interest.

"In the stretch between Vlad and Khabarovsk we'll be sticking as close to shore as we legally can. Both cities lie along the border separating Russia and China, and there's a major railroad connecting them that basically parallels the border. The Russian army transports lots of material and troops along that route, which is about 400 miles long I think.

"We all have specific targets for that leg of the trip, stuff we can't get back in Japan because the railroads use line-of-sight frequencies and low power. They know we can't hear them at a distance, so they generally transmit unencrypted. And you know how much we like plain language. But we won't be in real close, so you'll have to concentrate and pull them out of the mud as best you can. Have a good flight, call me if you need help or have individual questions. That's all—get some rest while you can."

Once again Mike and Jake tried to get comfortable. In an hour or so they'd be on duty. Jake could tell the sun was coming up. Although the portholes had black curtains covering them, he could see the sunlight bleeding around the edges of the one by Mike's position on the port side of the plane. He wasn't sure of the purpose of the curtains—if they were to keep the crew from looking out, or someone from looking in. Neither case made sense to him. Especially at 20,000-plus feet.

They both slept for about a half-hour and awoke almost simultaneously. "Hey, Jake, look. We're over water now. Must be on our way up the coast. I can't see any land on my side, how about you?"

Jake peeked out the starboard port and told Mike that he also couldn't see land. For some strange reason, Jake began thinking about his cube-mate—Sonny Powell—who had never returned, and his dog Radar. Jake had no way of knowing his sudden memories of the two occurred just as the Willy Victor was enroute to the mouth of Vladivostok harbor.

"Let's get Stanfield back here and have him explain this gear we're not used to."

"Good idea—I'll go get him," Mike said, as he got up and made his way to the front of the plane.

Chief Stanfield accompanied Mike back and took about 15 minutes to show the CTs the purpose and operation of the new equipment. As it turns out, it was basically just newer versions of some equipment they were familiar with back at Kami Seya.

"You'll find it easier to use, a lot more sensitive, and that's about it," Stanfield explained. "Why don't you go ahead and get everything warmed up; we'll be close to Ch'ongin soon, and let's see what we can find."

With that said, Stanfield returned to the front of the plane. Jake and Mike got to work and found that they were just approaching the area to be able to copy what they came after.

*   *   *   *

The Willy Victor had been in the air several hours and began to penetrate the fringes of the developing weather system that had been predicted. Dense gray clouds began to obscure any visual ground references, and the pilot attempted various altitudes but couldn't find a clear layer of blue between the varying-degree gray clouds.

The ride was getting a little bumpy due to the inversion layers caused by the cloud cover. Tiny drops of water formed on the outside of the portholes, jerkily skating across the surface of the glass like miniature translucent snails.

Jake and Mike had been constantly busy, with little time for conversation. At one point, Mike remarked that he was surprised at how strong the signals were. Jake agreed, and both went back to work.

Chief Stanfield entered and squatted in the aisle between the two men. He wasn't smiling.

"We have a problem, though I'm not sure how serious it is at this point. Our main navigation system hasn't been working right for the past half-hour and it just went out completely," the chief told them.

Jake knew the system he was referring to; the navigator at Atsugi had explained it to him prior to take-off. The system was similar to a large X-Y plotter, consisting of a three-by-three foot table covered with a map of the area. The course of the plane was plotted by two arms that moved over the map at right angles one to another, with the aircraft's exact position plotted, based—among other things, on a combination of air speed, temperature and altitude. If that system was out, Jake was sure there must be backup systems. *There better be, because you sure can't see through the thick soup we're flying in*, Jake thought.

Shortly after getting back to work, the plane's captain, Lt. Andrews, came on the intercom. Jake removed his headset and listened.

"Gentlemen, we're getting company," the officer said somewhat excitedly. "Chief Stanfield has been monitoring the Russian air-to-ground military frequencies and tells me that the Russians are sending up an escort that should catch up with us in about five minutes. We don't think it's anything to worry about; it's fairly routine on these flights. The Russians claim an unrealistic territorial limit—much larger than international law calls for—and they get nervous when we get too close. We're altering our course and heading further out to sea in the direction of Japan just to be safe. Stand by," he concluded.

Jake wasn't normally the excitable type, but what may be 'routine' for Andrews wasn't 'routine' for first-timer Jake Morton.

"Jesus, what the hell does that mean?" Mike asked, not expecting a reply.

"I don't know, but he's managed to scare the hell out of me so far," Jake said, putting on his headset and getting back to work. *Just my luck*, he thought: *first flight, no parachutes, and a broken navigation system. But I've got my .32 in case we're attacked by rabbits*, he mused.

"My God, Jake—look out the porthole!"

Jake parted the curtain over the porthole and saw their plane had broken into a clearing in the sky—a solid layer of cumulus clouds directly above but none below at this point. "That's *land* down there! I thought we were over the Sea of Japan somewhere near the tip of Sakhalin Island. Obviously not!"

"I guess we're more than slightly off course, and that's probably why we're getting company, as Andrews told us," Jake replied.

And at that moment, both men felt the big four-engine plane make a sharp bank to port and begin what must have been a steep full-power climb. They had been flying level and low at only 5,000 feet. The navigator obviously had been looking for reference points below the thick cloud cover.

Mike and Jake braced themselves, still looking out the portholes. "No wonder the signals were strong back there—we were flying right over the God damned railroad!" Mike yelled, just as Lt. Andrews came back on the intercom.

"Well, it turns out we've strayed a few miles inland from the coastline, and were directly across from the city of Khabarovsk. We have a visual of the coast now, and we're getting the hell out of here. We've contacted the carrier *Kitty Hawk* that's operating just northwest of Hokkaido and requested that she send us some fighter escorts. Stand by."

Within minutes, Lt. Andrews was back on the 'squawk-box' as the crew referred to the intercom system: "Carrier Air Wing 11 has scrambled four A3's from the carrier and they should be here in 20 minutes or so. Stand by," and he was off.

Willy Victor 22 continued in a straight line for the open sea, as fast as Andrews could push it. The sophisticated navigation system was still inoperable, but using other navigation techniques far too mystical for Jake, the plane was headed as far from the Russian coast as it could get. But evidently not far enough, fast enough…

"Here he comes!" Stanfield announced excitedly over the intercom. Jake assumed that Stanfield had taken over the announcement detail because the captain probably was a little busy right now!

"Yeah, and here he IS!! Where the hell did he come from?" Mike yelled as he peeled back the blackout curtain and looked out the porthole.

Jake rushed over and looked out as well. There, leveling off at less than 50 feet off of their wingtip, flying at exactly the same speed as the Willy Victor, was the unmistakable silhouette of a Russian MiG-17. The silver MiG with large red stars on the fuselage and tail seemed to be sitting still. The MiG had a maximum speed of better than 700 MPH and a cruise speed around 450, so Jake wondered how he kept it steady with the lumbering 300 MPH Willy Victor.

A Russian MiG-17

The afternoon sun was on the opposite side of the Willy Victor and shone directly on the MiG. The pilot's face was clearly visible to Jake and Mike—right down to his mustache as he stared at the Willy Victor.

The pilot of the MiG began to flap the jet's wings in the international signal meaning "follow me." Lt. Andrews imitated the maneuver, slowly flapping the big Willy Victor's wings in response, while all the time continuing on his south-easterly path to the seemingly unreachable open sea.

Back on the squawk-box, Stanfield announced that he was still listening to the Russian pilot communicating with his ground control, and had heard the MiG pilot radio back and say (in Russian): "I have U.S. Navy Willy Victor number 22 in my sights, have the means to destroy, and am awaiting orders."

Now why did he have to tell us that? Jake wondered. The 'routine' nature of this flight no longer fit his normal definition of that word. The MiG once again flapped his wings, and Andrews once again imitated the signal.

"MiGs have machine guns and we're unarmed, so I guess he can do whatever he wants. Where the hell are those escorts from the carrier?" Mike's voice betrayed his anxiety.

Jake was a little too numb to reply. After what seemed like an eternity, Stanfield came back on the intercom and told them that the Russian base had radioed back to the fighter and told the pilot to only "follow and observe." The relief in Stanfield's voice was evident, as was the expression on both Jake's and Mike's faces.

Willy Victor 22 was now well out of sight of the mainland—a good 10 nautical miles off the coast, Jake calculated, and the MiG was still parallel with their plane, but it had increased the distance separating the two planes. The MiG suddenly dipped his port wing and peeled off, crossing over the top of the Willy Victor—very closely—close enough that the wake from his exhaust caused the big four-engine plane to rock—and the MiG climbed and disappeared into the cloudbank overhead.

Stanfield once again came on the intercom with a brief announcement—and noticeable relief in his voice—that the MiG was gone and they were resuming their interrupted course back to Atsugi.

"I wonder where he came from?" Mike wondered aloud.

"I don't know, but probably Vladivostok—It's their fleet headquarters and only about 400 miles from where we were before we turned out to sea. I'd say we were damn lucky, especially if we were really so far off course and where Stanfield said we were," Jake answered, adding, "I think that now I have to go to the head."

"I'm right behind you," Mike echoed.

Jake no longer found the endless sameness of the open sea as boring as he initially had thought, as they winged their way homeward, still another three hours away.

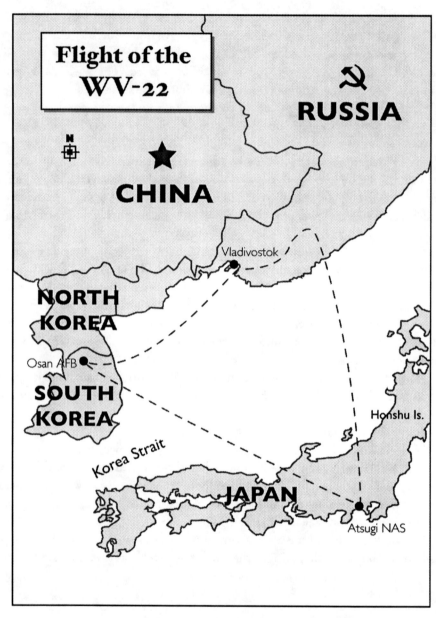

The flight of Willy Victor 22 (depicted by the dotted line)

CHAPTER 7

▼

"Well, I thought I got lucky last night, discovered I hadn't, and then realized how lucky I was."

By early evening, they'd landed back in Japan and parked on the tarmac at Atsugi NAS. The crew was led into a building constructed within a large hanger, and seated while they were debriefed. 'Debriefing' consisted of a short talk by an officer that basically boiled down to telling them that they were not authorized to discuss any part of the mission, including where they had been since departing Atsugi the previous Friday.

After being debriefed, the CTs boarded a Navy bus for the short ride along Route 16 back to Kami Seya. It was late in the day—a warm sunny afternoon, and all Jake had on his mind was a shower and a cold beer, not necessarily in that order. He'd have two days off now, standard procedure for anyone having just returned from TAD, and decided he'd probably head downtown for a few hours right after he got cleaned up.

The bus dropped the men at the main gate. Jake and Mike said their good-byes, expressed intentions to get together sometime soon, and headed for their respective barracks. Because they were on two completely different watch schedules—one was sleeping while the other was working—the reality of seeing each other on base was pretty slim.

Passing the mess hall, Jake spotted CPO Stanfield on his way to the Chief's quarters, and gave a wave.

"Let's do it again sometime," Jake shouted to the Chief.

"Looking forward to it, Morton, but without the chaperone next time, O.K.?" the chief replied.

"Amen" was Jake's acknowledgement as he continued toward his barracks. *Without a chaperone is an understatement*, he thought to himself.

It didn't take long for Jake to realize that he had a new cube-mate when he arrived back at his barracks. *That was quick*, he thought, noticing that what had been Sonny Powell's bunk was not made up and a pair of shoes was on the floor beneath it. Radar's picture was still on the empty desk that the two men had shared.

Jake decided that a shower would take precedence over the beer, and made it his first stop. He remained in the shower for a long time, standing in one position with the water running down his back. He knew it was all in his mind, but Jake felt that the warm water was not only washing away the memories of the cold he'd felt on the plane, but also the tension and anxiety that had built up during the flight. *A good soak in a wooden Japanese hot tub and a massage downtown, with a little Japanese girl walking up and down my spine—would feel good later*, he told himself. It became priority number three, right after a cold one at the EM club.

He'd already decided not to mention anything about the flight in his next letter home; Janice would only worry more than she already was prone to, and have more questions than he could answer. And he probably would describe the TAD as purely routine to his friends on watch, should they ask.

Even though they'd stressed at the post-flight debriefing that the men were not to discuss it at any length with anyone, everyone always did. Most of the men had a fairly good idea what the flyers and 'sub riders' affiliated with the Direct Support operation were doing anyway.

Returning to his cube from the shower, he was greeted by the person he assumed was his new cube-mate sitting on Sonny's bunk.

"Hi. You'd be Jake Morton, right?" He got up and offered his hand to Jake.

"I am. And you?"

"Art. Art Spencer. Arthur, actually. But I go by Art. Nice to make your acquaintance, Jake. I guess we're cube-mates."

"Hi Art. Pleased to meet you. Give me a second to get dressed," is all Jake said as he turned and walked to his locker at the end of the aisle where he kept his civvies.

"I just got off TAD, and was planning on hitting Chinatown for awhile," Jake said when he returned, finishing dressing.

"No problem," Art said, "I've already sort of moved in. Stowed my gear and so on. Sorry to hear about your buddy, Sonny. I don't know any details, but I heard he didn't come back from a TAD. Glad to see you got back O.K."

"So am I. I didn't know Sonny that well; we originally met in boot camp, but got separated until we met up here again. He was only here a short time before he left on TAD. I actually feel that I know Radar—that's Sonny's dog in the photo on the desk—almost as well as Sonny. Radar's been my cube partner for the last three months, a month longer than Sonny."

"Good looking dog. I was looking at the picture a while ago. I never had a dog, but he looks like a good one. Probably a bird dog?"

"Yeah, a black lab I guess, and Sonny named him 'Radar' because he could see things Sonny couldn't," Jake replied, tying his shoes. He noticed that while he'd been gone, the 'barracks boy' had polished the pair of penny-loafers he kept for liberty.

"Yoshi does a nice job on your shoes. Most of us give him a buck a pair. We all chip in once a month and pay him. Yoshi lives right outside the gate somewhere, and comes early in the morning and leaves in the evening. He keeps the barracks clean and anything else you might want him to do, for extra Yen, of course. So where'd you come from?" Jake asked.

"Just transferred down from Sakata up North, if that's what you mean. Originally I'm from Indiana. This is my second enlistment. I'm A-branch."

"A-branch? Interesting. Not many of you guys around. What's Sakata? I've heard of it, but I don't know anyone here who came from there—most of the guys seem to come from Adak and Guam. I'm an R-brancher myself, but just had a few weeks of lessons in T-work before I went TAD, so I have some clue what some of the other branches do, but not 'A-branch.'"

"Maybe I'll figure it out myself some day," Art joked. "A-branch is the admin side of the Security Group. We're similar to Yeomen in the regular Navy, but with security clearances." Art said.

Jake nodded. "O.K., now where's Sakata?"

"Sakata is up north of here. It was a small communications station and it's now officially closed. I helped close it down. I was only there for about six months—kind of a 'vacation' if you will from my last assignment. Actually rode the train down here with the stuff we salvaged—all the classified gear and paperwork, you know. Don't know what I could have done if someone had wanted to rob the train. They gave me a .45 but I didn't even know how to cock it."

"So where were you on your first enlistment?"

"I spent most of my time at Naval Security Group Atlantic, assigned to the Commander-In-Chief's office in Norfolk. Then I got assigned to our station in Hawaii but that didn't last long—I had the dubious pleasure of doing a little temporary duty for about a month down in the Marshall Islands before they sent me to Sakata to help close the station."

"Well, from one big command to a little one and now here. You'll have to tell me what you can about the Marshalls sometime. I was stationed on Guam and got to like that part of the world. I'd guess you won't find Kami Seya much like either of your previous duty stations, but I think you'll like it here. Sure can't beat the food."

"Good. As you can tell by looking at my many pounds of pure unadulterated love, food is fairly important to me. Second only to good cold beer and a hot woman," Art said followed by a hearty laugh.

Jake laughed too. "Let me finish here and we'll go see if we can find one or two of your favorite things. I don't know when you go on watch, but if you haven't been downtown Yokohama yet, and you have time, I'd be happy to show you around a little."

'Hey, that would be great. As for watches, I'm basically a day worker. Actually I got here two days ago, but have been just getting squared away and haven't been anywhere except out at the end of the road for about an hour or so last night."

"So, you've met Midori at the Green House, right?"

"Oh, yeah, I met Midori. When I could fight my way through the other six guys trying to buy drinks for her, that is. She's O.K. And probably untouchable, right?"

"Well, I wouldn't know—I'm married—but that's the rumor. So what'll it be, you got time to come along for a few hours?"

"Give me 15 minutes to change and make myself smell better, and I'm with you. And thanks," Art said as he began to change into his civilian clothes.

*   *   *   *

For the next three weeks, Jake's life at NSGA Kami Seya was quiet. He and Art had become good friends, and spent most of their free time off base together. Art had learned to speak Japanese very well while stationed in Sakata, and that skill made him invaluable when it came to going anywhere off base. His knowledge of the language possibly also saved him from a major bruising one night.

Jake had just come off a mid-watch and was finishing breakfast when Art walked into the mess hall.

"Jesus, Art, what happened to you?" Art was still in civilian clothes, all of which were quite messed up. His eye was black and blue, and his shirt was torn. It was obvious Art had not yet been to bed.

"Hi Jake. Yeah, I'm a mess. And believe me, I could be worse off. You know what it means when someone says 'I got lucky last night?' Well, I thought I got lucky last night, discovered I hadn't, and then realized how lucky I was."

"Sit down. That totally incomprehensible explanation tells me you need some coffee. And tell me about it. Did you just come back from Chinatown?

"Just got back about 20 minutes ago. I really can't stay longer than to have coffee. If anyone sees me looking like this, I might get put on report. I need to go clean up first, and then grab a bite before I go to work. I feel like crap, and I know I look it. But believe me, I think I'm lucky to be here."

"One of the other A-branchers and I went downtown last night about 2100. We hit a couple of bars, and then he got sick and came back to the base. I felt pretty good, so I stayed on. That was my big mistake."

"About two in the morning I stumbled into Club Calmen. Incidentally, do you think the name of that place is supposed to be 'Calmen,' or is this another case of using an 'L' for an 'R' and it's supposed to be 'Carmen?' Anyway, after a couple of beers I met Miyoki-chan. A true vision of loveliness, I thought. I just knew it was love. I had to have her."

"Was she six-foot-five and wanted you too, but for karate practice?" Jake asked.

"Close, but not quite. Sweet cakes told me she had a house nearby, so we jumped into a cab and off we went. I was three sheets to the wind—completely atypical for me, of course, and horny as hell. In no time I was all over her. I mean this little sweetie had a set of mammaries like you've never seen on an oriental, and I couldn't keep my hands off of them.

"I was making out like a champ, about ready to lose my load, and I slipped my hand inside her panties, between her legs. And that's when I found a big surprise. And I mean *big*. I had unconsciously wrapped my hands around a humungous hard-on. I couldn't believe it.

"I think I was more disappointed than shocked. She/he or it was so good looking I couldn't believe it. Just my luck, I thought—if she'd have been a skag, I wouldn't have felt so bad. But then I got pissed. And that's when the fun began. I cold-cocked her/him/it—whatever, right in the mouth, and she let out a blood curdling scream.

"Now the taxi driver is watching all this in his rear-view mirror. And in his mind, here's this ugly American in his taxi—beating up on a poor, defenseless

Japanese girl. So the next thing I knew, he'd slammed on the brakes, rolled down his window, and started screaming in Japanese.

"Best I could tell, he was hollering for help, saying that some foreigner was beating up a woman in his cab. Remember, it was about three in the morning. We were in a residential neighborhood in God-knows where, and out of the woodwork about 10 people appeared who immediately surround the cab. One guy yanked the door open and slugged me—hence the black eye. The rest of the guys looked like a lynch mob. I thought I'd had it."

"So how'd you get out?"

"I realized the cabbie was screaming something about me beating up a Japanese girl. And then it dawned on me I was the only one that knew that she was a he. So I repeated 'Sister-Boy, Sister-Boy' over and over in English and Japanese, and everything else I could think of to make them understand. Finally I grabbed her dress and pulled it up. And there, in all its glory, was this large bulge sticking out of the queer's pants. They got the message."

"By then the crowd burst into laughter. And you know who wasn't laughing? ME! The guy that hit me apologized profusely—I think he offered his sister to me, and said something about the police that I didn't understand. And then the crowd disappeared—leaving me there with my new boyfriend and the driver.

"Needless to say the new boyfriend was scared shitless, and the taxi driver didn't quite know what to do. And then like the Lone Ranger, up drives a Jap cop someone had called. He takes our statements, and the taxi driver takes off with the 'girl,' and the cop gives me a ride back to Chinatown. I got another cab back to base—by myself this time, and here I am."

Jake just smiled, staring at Art, and then broke into uncontrolled laughter.

"Come on, Jake—it isn't funny. I HURT!" But then he started smiling and pretty soon they both were laughing. Not much more was said and the two walked back to the barracks—Art to get ready for the day watch, and Jake to hit the sack—thankful he hadn't been with Art the night before.

Art was always good for entertainment. A week or so later, the Director of the National Security Agency (DIRNSA)—an admiral—made a surprise visit to the base. The Naval Security Group reported to DIRNSA. As was the case for any visiting high-ranking dignitary, a captain's inspection was scheduled for the following morning. This involved a review by the captain and the visitor of all of the base personnel in full dress uniform.

At 1000 hours the following day, everyone was lined up in the street directly in front of the mess hall. The men stood at attention in line, three rows deep. Art, Mike and Jake were side-by-side as the base commander and DIRNSA and an official entourage slowly walked in front of the men, cursorily 'inspecting' the troops. The reviewing party passed by the three men and had gone about five feet when DIRNSA, a rear admiral, stopped, paused, and turned to look back.

"Spencer? Art Spencer? Is that you?" the admiral questioned.

"Yes Sir!"

"Well I'll be," he said, and approached Art and shook his hand. "It's been a long time since Norfolk! Let's see—you went to Wahiawa from Norfolk if I remember right—oh, yes, and then I heard you helped find 'Red Star.' Is the Navy taking good care of you?"

"Yes sir, very good care, sir. And good to see you again, Sir."

"Thanks, Spencer. Come see me the next time you're in the D.C. area," the admiral said, reaching for and vigorously shaking Art's hand again before he turned and continued down the line with the base commander, who was all eyes and ears.

When the inspection was completed and the men were dismissed, Jake turned to Art—who was all smiles at this point, and said "Wow! I'm impressed. How do you know each other?"

"I used to work for him in Norfolk. He was Commander in Chief of the Atlantic Fleet at the time. Looks like he's moved up."

"So what's that stuff about a 'red star'?" Jake asked.

"I think I told you I did a brief TAD in the Marshall Islands. 'Red Star' was our code name for a Russian sub, K-229, that we shadowed for awhile. I provided linguistic support for the intercept ops."

"Wait a minute," Jake interrupted. "K-229? Are you sure of that number? I spotted a Russian sub with that number off the coast of Guam one night!"

"Really? Probably was the same sub. When we stopped following it, it headed in that direction. We figured it was going home, and we had all the info we needed, so we broke off and four days later I returned to Hawaii. I heard later that K-229 disappeared somewhere off Guam, as a matter of fact. I don't know the whole story, but I heard the Soviets sent a lot of ships into the area looking for it. Don't know if they ever did find it. Rumor had it that it had some kind of an accident or blew up for some reason and sank."

"Amazing. We both were looking at the same sub—probably only a week or so apart. And so you speak both Russian and Japanese? I can see that you're going to be a handy person to have around, Art!"

"You think you could fix me up with Midori? Probably not," Art said, answering his own question with a chuckle as they continued back to the barracks to get out of their clean dress uniforms.

*   *   *   *

Jake and Art spent a lot of time together exploring Japan. They hiked to the top of Mt. Fuji—somewhat of a religious tradition for the Japanese, but more of a simple outing for the Americans. They also stayed at the Special Services military resort hotel in Hakone Park, toured Tokyo, and—of course—got to know all of the Mama-sans in the local Yokohama bars. Together they began to get a lot of attention and respect as the bar girls and the bar owners learned that Art could understand and speak their language.

Jake decided that after almost two months and no word of his former cube partner Sonny, that he would drop a note to Sonny's parents in Minnesota, and return Sonny's picture of his dog Radar to them. Art worked in the personnel office on the base and had obtained the address for Mr. & Mrs. Harold Powell Sr. in Fosston, Minnesota for Jake. He assured Jake that the Powells officially had been notified of Sonny's "non-return."

U.S. NAVCOMSTA Kami Seya
F.P.O., San Francisco, CA

Dear Mr. & Mrs. Powell:

My name is Jake Morton. I am stationed at Kami Seya, Japan, and shared a cubicle with Sonny for almost three months. Sonny and I first met in boot camp. I don't have any information for you about Sonny, as all I know is that he went on a temporary assignment and hasn't returned—at least to Kami Seya, to my knowledge.

I wanted to let you know that I enjoyed knowing Sonny. We had a lot of laughs together and he told me a lot about you and his hometown.

Enclosed is a photo of his dog, Radar, which Sonny left here on the desk in our cubicle. I know Radar meant a great deal to Sonny, and I enjoyed hearing his stories about hunting with him. He must be an amazing dog. I hope someday to have the pleasure of meeting you and Radar.

Sincerely,

Jake Morton, CT2

Weeks later Jake had a reply:

Mr. Harold Powell, Sr.
Rural Route 2, Fosston, MN

Dear Mr. Morton:

Thank you very much for your letter. It was very nice of you to write, as it was good to hear from someone who has served with and knew our son, Sonny. The official word from the Navy Department is that he went missing while on a temporary assignment, and is presumed lost at sea. They have not recovered his body. Needless to say we miss him terribly, but we also are very proud of him and hope some day for closure.

We appreciate your returning the photo of Radar. We also look forward to meeting you sometime if you possibly can get to Fosston. We're pretty remote—you have to want to come here to find us!

We look forward to a future visit by you, but unfortunately you will not be able to meet Radar. Radar died, ironically on Sonny's birthday—July 17. We found him lying outside the door to Sonny's bedroom. The vet said it was natural causes. He was only seven.

Having spent almost 25 years in the U.S.N. myself, you have my admiration and gratitude; I know what important work you must be doing which is contributing to our defense effort. Sonny was proud of what he was doing, and enjoyed the Navy very much. Thank you for your note, and we look forward to meeting you some day.

Sincerely,

Harold Powell, Sr.

Sonny was pleased to receive a reply—he really hadn't expected one—but was quite disappointed to learn that Radar had died. He had looked forward to meeting Sonny's folks, someday.

CHAPTER 8

▼

"One of our most important missions here at Kami Seya is the monitoring of Soviet submarine activity throughout the Sea of Japan..."

It was the beginning of September—Fall on the Kanto Plain, and the crisp air hinted that a season change was eminent. The dew on the grass was heavy this morning, but the sky was clear and Jake knew it would warm up by noon.

Before heading to the enlisted mess for a light breakfast, Jake re-read Janice's letter that had arrived the day before. She was still in San Diego, working for a real estate firm, and very upset that she had to wait there for Jake's return.

Janice was living with her Aunt Faye, and the arrangement had started with the understanding that it was temporary until Jake sent for her. But now that it was clear that she wouldn't be going to Japan, Janice hadn't made the move to find her own apartment if she intended to stay on the west coast.

Janice and her aunt got along o.k. but when Janice wasn't working, she complained that her aunt used her as a babysitter for Janice's two-year old nephew, Brian, and Janice felt taken advantage of. Faye was a 40-year-old divorcee, and Janice understood that Faye needed some time on her own. Being a single parent to a two-year-old was not easy while holding down a fulltime job in the insurance office of Rohr Aircraft in Chula Vista.

Jake understood Janice's frustration—especially because of the distance between them and his inability to provide moral support or advice. By the time their letters crossed in the mail, many things would change and make any previous suggestions obsolete. It was especially hard on both of them, newly married and separated almost immediately afterwards.

On one hand Jake felt that Janice would be better off in an apartment of her own, but also realized that she was a 'people-person' and would get lonely very quickly. Aunt Faye did fill the need for a warm body to at least talk to.

He folded the letter and put it in his drawer. As was customary, Jake had written a reply the night before and planned to mail on his way to work. He'd learned his lesson when he was stationed on Guam that it was wise to let a letter to Janice rest for a day before mailing it; thoughts written in haste or during a temporary peak in loneliness often got changed before the envelope was sealed.

After a quick bite at the mess hall, Jake headed to the tunnels and the first in the rotation of two-day watches. Art worked days and had gotten up early enough to get through breakfast and drop some uniforms off at the base laundry before he had to be to work. Jake was surprised to find Art still in the chow hall when he arrived.

"Thought you had to get to the laundry?"

"I did. They were open so I went there first. I had the hours wrong; thought they opened later."

Jake joined him and ordered some fried eggs and bacon. At least he knew they were real eggs—or at least he thought they were; the scrambled eggs tasted like powder and he was sure they weren't fresh.

Art looked around carefully to see if anyone was in hearing range before he asked: "I suppose you heard we're on Alert Level Three, right?"

"No! What happened? When did that happen?" Jake asked.

"Better not go into it now. You'll find out when you get to work. Lots of rumors, but you know—working in Admin, we don't get all the skinny on technical stuff. And I probably wouldn't understand it if we did," Art said with a grin.

Jake finished eating and resumed the walk to the infamous tunnels. He had no sooner passed through security and arrived at his watch station when he was told that O'Shaugnessy, the Division Operations officer had summoned him to his office.

It had been more than four weeks since his TAD assignment out of Atsugi Naval Air Station. The normal routine was for one brief TAD every month, or one long one every so many months. Jake had no idea when his next assignment would be, or where, but he had a hunch he was about to find out.

"Good Morning, Jake. How have you been?"

"I've had a good month or so since coming back from my last assignment. I have a hunch you called me here to tell me it's time to go again."

"Very perceptive of you, Morton. Yes, we do have another assignment for you. But this one is going to be a little different. I can't give you specific details, but I can give you a little insight into what we have in mind," O'Shaugnessy said, getting up out of his chair and sitting on the edge of his desk facing Jake.

It was a cool morning. Jake felt a chill and couldn't decide if it was caused by the weather or by Lt. O'Shaugnessy's attitude. The Lieutenant looked quite tired, or serious, or both, Jake thought.

"You know we went to a level-three alert last night on the mid-watch, don't you?"

"Yes Sir, I heard the rumor, but I don't know any of the details."

"Well, we've been on Level II alert status since last month's incident in the Gulf of Tonkin, when the USS Maddox was attacked by North Vietnamese patrol boats when she was on a recon mission. The first attack on the second of August was minor, but then evidently she was attacked again two days later by gunboats with torpedoes and heavy arms fire. Luckily the carrier Ticonderoga was in the vicinity and provided air support.

"The Pentagon has felt like their hands have been tied for a long time in Vietnam. This was kind of the last straw. As a result of pressure arising from this incident, Congress passed the Gulf of Tonkin resolution giving President Johnson broader powers, so I think we'll see increased activity in that area.

"Right now, though—as you know, one of our most important missions here at Kami Seya is the monitoring of Soviet submarine activity throughout the Sea of Japan and the South China Sea. We have a separate section assigned to doing nothing but keeping track of communications between subs, and between them and their bases. Since the Cuban missile crisis two years ago, Soviet and Chinese sub activity here in the Pacific has tripled. And with the reality of intercontinental ballistic missile capabilities on nuclear subs, the importance of keeping track of their activities is greater than ever."

"I was supposed to get involved with that section before I went on TAD, Sir," Jake said.

"Well, now you're going to have your chance. We get a lot of key intelligence from monitoring their communications. And keeping track of their movements, sub by sub, may give us a heads-up, God forbid, if they ever decide to escalate into a full-blown war."

"As you know, every deployed Soviet submarine is required to send a report back to its fleet headquarters every 24-hours and provide key data such as location, course, speed, fuel availability, and so-on. Intercepting that information also allows us to keep track of where they are, and then by plotting course information, a good idea where they're headed as well."

"I presume the reports are in Morse code, and that's what those brief encrypted transmissions of five-number code groups are that we copy?" Jake asked.

"Right. And the network of NSG facilities all around the Pacific Rim coordinates and compares data so we have a pretty good idea of which sub is where, when, and where it's headed. By the use of Radio Direction Finding and triangulation on signals from three or more NSG facilities, we can pretty well pinpoint the exact location of a transmission, and hence, the sub itself."

Jake had been involved in copying some of this 'traffic' as it was known, and participated in triangulating several transmissions. Before this, however, he hadn't understood the scope of the operation or the importance of the information the process provided.

O'Shaughnessy continued, saying "Well, that was yesterday. Last night we lost contact with virtually all of the 30-or-more Soviet subs actively operating in this theater of operations. The last transmission any COMMSTA heard was from a sub we have code-named 'Blue-Dot' at exactly 2350-Zulu. I hope you understand the significance of what has happened."

"Yes Sir, but do we know why?"

"We have several theories. At one extreme, it could signal the beginning of a major Soviet exercise. But based on other intelligence, we don't see any large troop build-up on any of the borders, and we haven't detected any unusual land or sea activity. Radio traffic on most other Soviet army and navy links appears to be normal.

"At the other extreme, and the one we think is most logical, is that they have made a major change in their communications systems, and—at the very least—they've gone to a new set of operating frequencies. It would be a smart thing for them to do, of course; they've been using the same freqs for a year now, and they must realize we know them by heart."

"So what are we doing about it?"

"Going to Alert Level Three is the first step. It dedicates all available lower priority resources to solving this puzzle, and DIRNSA is adding manpower to speed up the analysis of the traffic backlog they're sitting on."

Jake interrupted: "I can imagine that backlog is huge, just based on what we send them every week, and multiplying that by all of the other stations that do the same."

"Precisely. The second thing we're doing is dedicating more personnel here, with longer hours, to try to find the new frequencies. The transmissions are on a set schedule—or at least I should say they have been, but those schedules are blown now. And since they never identify themselves with call signs, the job's even tougher. About the only thing we can do now is to use signal analysis and voice prints to compare transmitter characteristics with those we've identified and categorized on file."

"What about identifying the sub by the fist of the operator? I've had pretty good success in doing that in the past. Some of those guys have very individual and identifiable sending techniques, and unless they're moving operators from sub to sub, that should help, shouldn't it?"

"Yes, but just like signal analysis of transmitter characteristics, those techniques are only good if we once again catch someone sending something, and if the person finding it recognizes it. And right now we're still searching. Which in a very long-winded, round-about way brings me back to you," the Lieutenant said.

"CINCPACFLT and NSG H.Q. have ordered formation of a task force consisting of three ships—the Groveland—AGTR-33, a technical research ship, plus a carrier—the *USS Oriskany* for tactical support, and a frigate—I'm not sure which one at this point. A complement of 15 R- and T-branchers from this station will be assigned to this activity, to be supported by an additional five I- and M-branchers—20 total CTs. I want you to be part of that team aboard the *USS Groveland*. A number of Electronic Technicians (ETs) also will be assigned to the ship. Neither the frigate nor the *Oriskany* will be sailing closer than within 50 miles of the *Groveland*, but both will be well within range to lend quick support if necessary."

"What's the task force's mission, sir?"

"To be perfectly honest, I'm not sure. We've put men on AGTRs in the past, and never had escort vessels assigned to them. It's true that things are heating up in the region, but it is somewhat unusual to dedicate that many resources for a routine intelligence mission. I can honestly say that I haven't been made privy to the mission; just the personnel requirements needed from Kami Seya."

"Sounds interesting. I've never been aboard ship before. When do I leave, Sir?"

"You'll report to the *Groveland* no later than 1500 hours on Tuesday, a week from today. She's at sea now, but will be pulling into Yokosuka for supplies two days before you're due to report."

"How long is this assignment, Sir?"

"I can't say for sure at this point, but probably two months. Your orders will be ready for you to pick up in the morning. I'm not privy to all the details behind this particular assignment, but I sense it's pretty important to involve both NSG and Fleet Command. It may be related to the heightened alert status, but maybe not. Even if we solve this current crisis quickly, the situation calls for increased surveillance. The Pentagon has increased our commitment in Southeast Asia recently. In addition to the Vietnamese situation getting dicey, the North Koreans are becoming a problem as well. The Sea of Japan is a very volatile place right now, and we need to be there. Any other questions I can answer?"

"I don't think so, Sir. I'll wait for my orders and get back to you if I have any, if that's o.k. Thank you, Lt. O'Shaugnessy. See you in a few months."

"Good luck, and be safe."

Jake left the Division Commander's office and started back to work, his first thought that he should get another letter off to Janice today, because there won't be another chance for quite awhile.

"Morning, Jake," said Walt Simanski as he walked by. Walt had his trademark coffee mug in hand—identifiable by the CT1 insignia and chevrons (stripes) painted on it by some local Japanese firm. Jake was surprised to see Walt in this part of the tunnel.

"Hi Walt. What are you doing here?

Simanski, who had briefed Jake prior to his previous TAD assignment, had been transferred and named section leader for Jake's section. Jake was pleased, because he liked Walt and knew that Walt knew his job very well.

"Adamson, your previous section leader, left on TAD, and I just got back from one, so here I am—musical chairs," Walt replied.

"Glad to have you. What's all this about a new alert?"

"Well, I just started this morning and all I know so far is that the brass is in a panic. We can't locate any of the sub radio traffic—they've just dropped off the face of the earth. I have five guys in the T-branch section frantically searching as well. We're bringing in some new gear that supposedly will let us automatically scan and record multiple frequencies, but I'm not sure when it will arrive. A bunch of civilians from the States are due in the next few days to install it.

"Stick to your regular assignments and let me know if you hear anything unusual. One thing I can tell you is that direct support flights have increased significantly; lots of guys rotating back and forth to Atsugi," Walt said.

"How'd your last one go, Walt?"

"It was short and relatively uneventful, thank God. We did have one very interesting contact one morning about 0330—it was a dark one with no moon and lots of cloud cover when we were headed back to Atsugi. We encountered a Russian 'Badger' in what they call the 'Badger box' about 500 nautical miles east of Japan."

"What's a 'Badger'?" Jake asked.

"I don't know why it's called that, but a 'Badger' is a Tu-16, a two engine Russian turbo-prop bomber. The Russians use them and another plane known as a 'Bear,' a Tu-95, which is a larger four-engine prop-job designed for long-range bombing and recon flights. Usually find them in pairs; they patrol a certain corridor in the Sea of Japan to monitor American battle groups transiting the Pacific—probably mostly interested in troop movement to-and-from Vietnam. Pretty rare to find one as low as he was too; they normally fly at about 38,000 feet—he was at 20,000.

A Russian Tupolev Tu-95 "Bear" long-range bomber

"Anyway, we came up on this guy from behind, and I honestly don't think he knew we were there. We approached his starboard rear—the big brown tail with the red star was about all I could see. Someone in the cockpit of our plane turned on a spotlight to read the identifier number on the tail, and when our light came on, it was right in the tail-gunner's face."

"He sits in a plastic bubble right on the tip of the tail of the plane; probably the most boring job in the world, and I'm sure he was asleep when the light came on. I don't know what went thru his mind, but I know what I'd think if I was awakened at 20,000 feet with someone shining a light in my eyes at three in the morning, just 100 feet away!"

"Jesus, I bet he messed his pants!" Jake commented.

"I bet he did. We didn't stick around very long in case he had a nervous trigger finger. I do know the Badger immediately changed course, so maybe we woke up someone in the cockpit too."

"Anyway, I've gotta get to work. Talk to you later," Walt said and walked toward the supervisor station.

A Russian Tu-16 "Badger"

Three days later, on the mid watch, Jake was composing another letter to Janice. He didn't like to write before he received a letter—he liked to address points she made in her letter rather than just have them crossing in the mail. But he knew he had to somehow explain that he wouldn't be writing for quite awhile, and knew that she would be very unhappy. So this was a long one.

By day four of the Level III Alert, the mystery of the soviet submarine radio silence still had not been solved. Every effort was being made to find the new frequencies—assuming that changes were the cause of the radio silence. Specialists from other NSG activities had been brought in and a NSA representative was ever-present. The analysts were working overtime, and communication between Kami Seya and NSA headquarters at Ft. Meade, Maryland was hot and heavy.

One of the standard procedures involved scanning a portion of a frequency spectrum and recording anything and everything heard. Normally an operator would have to manually stop the scan and begin a recording when something was detected, but with all available manpower dedicated to solving this mystery, that wasn't possible to do—and perform normal duties at the same time.

With the new equipment that had arrived the previous day, each operating station was now able to scan and record continuously, with no interruption. Every conceivable signal and static crash was recorded and analyzed. The necessity of recovering the lost transmissions was becoming critical at all levels. Recorded tapes were literally snatched off of the machines as soon as they were full. Men were assigned to do nothing but run tapes to the analysis section and to return erased tapes to the operators for reuse. One of the runners entered Jake's workspace and reinstalled an erased tape on a machine for re-use.

"That last one sure had a lot of static. You sure your antenna is o.k.? You might want to check your connections," the runner commented.

"Static? That's odd. The section of the band I'm monitoring is typically pretty quiet. I'll physically listen to it for the next half-hour or so and see what's going on," Jake said.

Once he had his earphones on and all of the controls set properly, Jake started the recording and simultaneously listened to what he was recording. *Most of this sounds normal to me*, Jake thought, after listening for several minutes. Then there was an unusually loud and sharp static 'crack'—so loud that Jake turned down the gain. *Strange*, he thought; *must be a storm going on.*

After checking with other operators, Jake determined that there were no storms. Indeed, the weather at Kami Seya was clear and calm with no rain activity anywhere on the Kanto Plain. He continued to listen and then to question his equipment. He changed antennas and even switched to a different R-390A receiver. The audio quality and tone was exactly the same, and the band was just as quiet as before. In fact the most unusual thing about the band was how signal-free it was. The only sound had been the static crash.

But then again after a few minutes he heard another static burst of about the same intensity. And later on, another. Jake called the watch supervisor, Walt. "I think I have something you should listen to," he said, and waited for Walt's arrival.

Walt put on the earphones and listened to the recording Jake had been making over the past 30 minutes. There was no mistake, he told Jake—"There does appear to be a pattern to those static crashes."

"Yeah, and they sound almost too perfect. Each one is nearly identical to the other in length and intensity," Jake noted.

Jake rewound the tape to the beginning and both he and Walt put headsets on and listened again. Walt used his watch to time the interval between the unusual sounds, and determined that there were exactly nine minutes between each crash. Walt's first reaction was to check with other operators and ask if they had experienced anything similar. No one had, but Walt had their current tapes rushed for analysis and advised everyone on this project as to what to listen for, and to clock the intervals between bursts.

It was only an hour or so before the end of the mid-watch, and Jake was exhausted. He now would have 48 hours off and was anxious to get back and get some sleep. Art would be at work by the time Jake returned to the barracks, which ensured a good solid six hours of sleep. After that the barracks-boy would have arrived and begun his daily chores of cleaning the head, sweeping floors and, of course, shining shoes. And although he was fairly quiet and respectful of the guys sleeping, there always was some noise—and after six hours of sleep, it didn't take much to wake Jake.

As he finished filling out his logs and readying his workstation for the next person on the day watch coming up, Walt and Lt. O'Shaugnessy came to his position.

"Jake, congratulations. The mystery is solved!" the Lieutenant said excitedly. "Thanks to you, we now know what the Soviets are doing and we can resume monitoring the sub traffic."

Looking a little puzzled—perhaps more surprised than anything, Jake asked "So what did I do? I gather it has something to do with the static crashes I recorded for you?"

"It had everything to do with them. It turns out they weren't 'static' per se, but a very clever use of suppression techniques and Morse code. From what we know so far, the Russians simply record a normal position/fuel report in standard code groups and then compress it to a 'burst' of less than two seconds, and send it. Apparently the transmissions are broken into segments—otherwise the single 'burst' would be too long and unnatural sounding, and the recipient knows exactly when and where to listen for them.

"All the recipient has to do on the other end is to record the message on high speed tape, then play it back slowed-down. They were even so confident this wouldn't be detected that they haven't even encoded the transmission—so far all of the transmissions we've intercepted have been in plain language!

"Fantastic job, Jake. You're excused from the rest of your watches before you leave for your TAD assignment. Thanks again. You'll be hearing more from me later on. Go get some sleep and I'll see you before you take off for Yokosuka."

"Thank you, Sir. Glad it worked out. And you won't have to tell me twice to get some sleep—I'm half way there already!"

Late Thursday afternoon, Jake received word from Lt. O'Shaugnessy via Art Spencer that his presence was required in the base commander's office at 0900 Friday.

"What's this all about, Art?"

"All I know is I was told to tell you to be there before you get on the bus for Yokosuka. The bus leaves at 1015 so you shouldn't have a problem. And wear your blues—we've switched to winter uniforms now. You'll need them to go to Yokosuka to meet your ship anyway."

After a quick breakfast at the enlisted mess, Jake made the trip to the C.O.'s office in the administration building. The building, a two-story large white wooden structure adjacent to the tunnel entrance, was one of the newer buildings on the base. It had been constructed about two years ago when the former building burned down. Everyone considered it extremely fortunate that the fire hadn't spread to the tunnel itself, which even though constructed of cement covered almost entirely with earth, it did have a wooden entrance shack.

Entering the commanding officer's outer office, Jake announced himself to the yeoman who served as the C.O.'s secretary.

"Petty Office Morton reporting as ordered."

"Have a seat Morton. The C.O. will be with you in a moment."

Jake looked around the office. It was furnished a little better than the Lieutenant's office, he noted, with softer plastic seats and padded armrests on the chrome chairs. There were several framed award plaques on the walls, commemorating everything from their league softball championships to the perennial awards for the best fleet mess. The black-and-white checkered tile floor was heavily waxed and spotless; Jake was glad he wasn't responsible for keeping it that way. Several current issues of the Navy Times newspaper were on the coffee table, one of which Jake had just begun to read when the C.O.'s yeoman told Jake he could go in.

Jake knocked on the door first, and opened it. Stepping inside the C.O.'s large office, he was surprised to see both his watch supervisor, Walt, and the division officer—Lt. O'Shaughnessy inside.

"Petty Officer Morton reporting as ordered, SIR!" Jake announced, snappily coming to attention but not saluting.

The commanding officer, a short and rather rotund Captain was already standing, talking to Simanski and O'Shaugnessy. "Welcome and good morning, Mr. Morton. Stand at ease," the C.O. said. Jake was surprised at the use of the address 'Mr.' which normally was reserved for officers.

Jake relaxed a bit in the 'at-ease' position with feet a little further apart and hands folded behind his back. "Thank you Sir."

"Lt. O'Shaugnessy and Petty Officer Simanski have told me what an outstanding contribution you made to solving the recent situation involving the submarine communications issue. You have my sincere thanks on behalf of the entire Naval Security Group, from me personally, and from all the other CTs who can now get some rest after that intense alert period!" The C.O. said with a laugh—a laugh that was shared by all in the room.

"Thank you very much, Sir. I'm as glad as everyone else that we all can relax a bit now."

The C.O. approached Jake, putting one hand on his shoulder and shaking his hand at the same time. Lt. O'Shaugnessy and Walt Simanski followed suit.

"I'm placing a Commanding Officer's Letter of Commendation in your service record, Mr. Morton, and sending a copy of it with a personal note to your parents. Naturally we'll have to leave out some details," the C.O. said with a grin, "but we want them to know that these honors aren't handed out lightly, and that your actions made a significant contribution to the communications intelligence mission of this command. Congratulations again; I understand you're about to leave on TAD, so I won't keep you. And smooth sailing," the C.O. concluded.

"Thank you very much sir," Jake acknowledged. The silence that followed was brief, but Jake knew it was time to leave. A sailor didn't just walk out of his commanding officer's office without permission, and Jake wasn't sure what to do next when Lt. O'Shaughnessy said "Congratulations from all of us, Jake. I'm going past your barracks; would you like a lift back?"

A relieved and more relaxed Jake replied affirmatively, and walked out of the office.

In the Lieutenant's car, Jake told his division officer that he was glad that was over, and honestly didn't see that what he'd done warranted all that attention.

"After all, I just pointed out some noise to the analysts—they're the ones who figured it all out."

"Nonsense," O'Shaughnessy said, with a correcting tone to his voice. "Sure, maybe we would have figured it out sooner or later—most likely later. But you saved us a lot of time and allowed us to capture of lot of information in the meantime that we would have missed. None of us took that lightly."

"Yes sir," Jake said as they arrived at the barracks. "And thanks for the lift."

"My pleasure, Jake. Have a safe assignment. I understand this is your first time at sea, so remember: never puke into the wind."

"I'll try to remember that," Jake said, getting out of the car and waving as the Lieutenant drove off. *I hope I can remember that when I need to, if I need to, and I am sure I will,* he told himself.

CHAPTER 9

▼

Jake soon learned that Lt. O'Shaughnessy's parting wisdom about not throwing up into the wind was valuable advice.

"Well, buddy, I wish you well. Actually, I'm looking forward to having this entire cube to myself for a while. I may even rent out your bunk. Maybe I can move it out and put in a few kegs and a cooler…"

"Just be safe, Jake, and send me a postcard sometime and let me know what it's like on this rust-bucket you're going on. I'll have an extra steak for you every Friday at the chow hall."

Jake smiled, grabbed his sea bag and slung it over his shoulder. It was light—not much in it for a couple of months on a ship except underwear and work clothes. He wouldn't be using his dress uniform on the ship. He was ready to go meet the bus. "The rack is all yours. Maybe if you're lucky some night you can coax Midori up here from the Green House. I'm sure if you put in a little hot plate, she'd whip up some gomoku-yaksoba, just like you scarf up on the 'Cho. Take care yourself—see you in a few months." And with that, he shook Art's hand and headed out of the barracks to the bus stop.

Moments after boarding the bus and taking one of the front seats, Jake was greeted with "Oh crap, not you again!"

Turning around, he was pleased to see a smiling Mike Johnson seated right behind him.

"Well I'll be damned," Jake said. "You old lush, I haven't seen you since we got back from the last trip. What've you been up to?

Mike leaned forward and placed his arm over the seat and across Jake's shoulder. Without saying anything, he pointed to his new third class petty officer stripes.

"Hey, congratulations. When did that happen?"

"Just got the stripes sewn on about a week ago. Feels good. Best thing is that now I get to eat in the petty officer's mess with you and the rest of the white folk," Mike joked.

"Fantastic. It also means you get to buy the beer as soon as we get back. Where you headed?" Jake asked.

"Got a date with a scow in Yokosuka called the *Groveland.*"

"Well pal, don't let anyone hear you call it that once we get there—they may not take kindly to it. And if you point out any rust, you may end up painting it. That's the Navy way! Incidentally, that's my ship too; let's see if we can stick together."

The rest of the trip to Yokosuka was spent discussing what each had been up to since they'd parted ways after returning from their last TAD. Jake was pleased that Mike had advanced in rank; it would mean more privileges for him, a bit more money, and he wouldn't be the low man on the totem pole. Both men were happy they were starting out a mission with someone they each knew, had confidence in, and could share the loneliness with.

"Probably the best thing about getting my first crow* is that it means no more Cinderella liberties! I get to stay out with you big boys. But for awhile, it'll be good to have some time away from the temptations of Chinatown and the 'Cho,'—and time for my sore dick to recover," Mike said with a laugh.

"What's wrong with 'junior'?"

"Let's just say that I've learned to keep it away from virgins. A young sweetie named Mitsui or something like that was too small for me and ripped my foreskin. I'd never been circumcised as a kid, so they did it in the hospital at Yokosuka last week. It's healing, but I still have stitches and have to keep it down so I don't pop 'em."

Jake just shook his head in disbelief. "Mike, you horny bastard. The hardest thing for me to believe is that you could actually find someone that your puny dick could get caught in!"

"Very funny, Morton. At least I get to *use* mine, Mr. Old Married Man."

Jake didn't have a retort. *There was some truth in what Mike said*, he thought.

---

* (The shoulder patch for all petty officers features a spread-wing eagle insignia—the 'crow'—with the individual's specialty insignia directly beneath it—

in the CT's case, a crossed feather and lightening bolt. Below that there are one, two or three V-shaped stripes that signify rank. Reaching E-4 or third-class, the lowest rank petty officer to deserve a patch with an eagle, is referred to as 'getting your crow'. It came with one stripe. E-5 had two, and E-6 had three.)

The *USS Groveland*, an 'AGTR'—Auxiliary General Technical Research Ship, was one of several similar older ships built during WWII that had been retrofitted and outfitted to function primarily as floating electronic intelligence gathering vessels. Their missions varied, but generally were based on not just communications interception, but also radar defense evaluation, electronic countermeasures, and other intelligence aimed at providing our ships at sea with ammunition to defend against potential enemy incursions.

AGTRs were deployed in the South China seas to support American offensives in Vietnam, in the Sea of Japan to counter Soviet threats, and deployed off the coasts of Latin America and in the Middle East as hot spots would develop.

Compared to the carrier she was berthed next to, the *Groveland* almost looked like a toy. With a length of less than 450-feet, AGTR-33 looked more like a motor whaleboat for the carrier itself. She had a small personnel complement, and was relatively slow with a top speed of only 11 knots.

The slow speed plus a relative lack of armament (i.e., only four 50-caliber machine guns) made her very little threat to any other craft.

An AGTR, similar to the U.S.S. Groveland

"Is that our ship or a tug for the carrier?" Mike asked as they walked down the pier toward the *Groveland.* "Fortunately I don't see any rust, so I guess we won't be doing a lot of scraping."

The two men walked part way up the gangplank to board the ship, faced the flag and observed the Officer Of The Deck (OOD) watching them.

Both men came to attention and saluted the OOD.

"Petty Officers Morton and Johnson reporting as ordered. Permission to come aboard, Sir?" asked Jake, and received a confirming nod and salute from the OOD. They continued up the gangplank. Our orders, Sir," Jake said as he and Mike handed the envelopes containing their written orders, service record summaries and other identifying matters to the OOD.

The OOD took the envelopes, checked the writing on the outside, and handed them back to the two men. "Very well gentlemen. Welcome aboard the *USS Groveland.* Report directly to the Division Officer, Mr. Hopewell, on deck three aft. And if this is your first experience aboard a ship, that means three decks down toward the rear," the OOD said with a grin.

"Thank you Sir," Jake responded as they again saluted and headed for a ladder and hatch leading below.

"That went well; let's hope it stays that way!" Mike said as they started their descent to deck three.

*   *   *   *

One more cruise. My last. Back to my family and the relatively comfortable life afforded to a 'Hero Of The Soviet Union' with the Order Of Lenin and the Gold Star. The old man is coming home from the sea. Life at home in Kiev should be good. My cousin's vodka, my horse, my darling Svetlana…

These were the thoughts rambling through the mind of Soviet submarine K-229's Captain Go Ranga (First Rank) Yuri Lishchenko as his boat slid silently out from its berth at Petropovlosk into the familiar Sea of Okhotsk.

Good to be getting away from Petropovlosk for a while, too, he told himself. Even though he hadn't been in port long, he wasn't anxious to stay much longer either. Winter was coming. His last mission had taken him to tropical waters and had made him question the sanity of his plan to retire in Kiev. The crew had been given leave while the boat was being outfitted with some new equipment, and Lishchenko had enjoyed a few weeks on the Caspian seashore—not exactly like the Marshall Islands, he acknowledged, but as close as he'd get to warmer climes in Soviet territory.

Petropovlosk was home to most of the nuclear Russian subs in the Pacific Fleet. It was located on the eastern shore of the Kamchatka peninsula, 1350 miles northeast of Vladivostok, and already it was getting cold. In a month or so, there'd be heavy ice to contend with—although not a major concern for the nuclear boats that could stay submerged indefinitely. That wasn't the case for Lishchenko's older diesel/electric boat.

Captain Lishchenko, WWII veteran, age 59, was on his last cruise, and he was tired. His orders from the Admiral, Fleet Military Council were still sealed. But he figured it must be a relatively routine mission, and that within two months he would be back with his wife of 39 years in Kiev—a retired Captain First Class. Maybe if he did a good job this last time out, he might be promoted to Admiral. The importance of that meant nothing more to him than a larger pension, Lishchenko reasoned. But the immediate future was largely out of his control, and promotions in the Soviet Navy were very political. Yuri pretty much abhorred politics, and knew he hadn't always been a model communist, a fact that unfortunately was fairly common knowledge among his superiors.

Standing in the open air on the bridge of the conning tower of the submarine as it departed Petropovlosk harbor, holding onto his cap against the cold breezes, Yuri Lishchenko reflected on a remarkable career. It was still Fall and in less than a month, the spray and the sea breeze that he now relished soon would form ice crystals on his three-inch long gray beard and mustache. He had seen worse weather though, and this cruise was going to be easy, he told himself, and took comfort in the fact that he'd be warming his arthritic feet before the wood stove in Kiev before the really cold weather set in.

He was happy to be leaving the military. Politicians, he thought, are waging this cold war, and the military has very little influence in how it is carried out. It's a battle of words more than skill and strategy.

Lishchenko had been awarded the 'Hero Of The Soviet Union' medal—one of the highest accolades afforded a Soviet citizen, and it had been accompanied by the Order of Lenin and the Gold Star. He didn't minimize his own accomplishments during his career, but he did believe that these commendations were now being awarded far too freely. Yuri Lishchenko saw the main benefit of the honors to be the extra rubles it would mean for his pension. Promotion to admiral would almost double it.

Yuri basically was a simple man. His roots sprung from a peasant farm family in Kiev, where he had attended a technical institute before he joined the merchant marine as an engineer in the mid-1920s. He was the first in his family to acquire a technical degree; his 95-year old mother still cared for the family garden back in Kiev.

He'd spent more than 10 years on oilers and cargo vessels throughout the Pacific and Asia, and eventually accepted a position with the Ministry of Defense for about five years. Longing to return to the sea and the outbreak of WWII soon had him enrolled in the Navy of the Soviet Union, eventually with his own command of a submarine.

During World War II, as Captain Third Class and commander of an attack submarine operating out of the Baltic Sea, Lishchenko had sunk two German destroyers, three German submarines, seven or eight assorted other German navy vessels, and eight German cargo ships.

His award as 'Hero Of The Soviet Union' was largely based on his rescue of 35 men in 1943 from a torpedoed and sinking American minesweeper off the coast of England. Immediately after rescuing the survivors, Captain Lishchenko hunted down the German U-boat that had sunk the American ship, found it on the surface and forced it to surrender before it could submerge. Before sending it to the bottom, he captured several members of the crew as well as codes and other documents that proved to be invaluable to Soviet naval intelligence officials. Keeping the captured Nazis from being killed by the rescued Americans on board was the biggest challenge, he had told the Soviet Minister of Defense who presented him with his commendation.

Before long, he had become a Captain Second Rank in charge of a division of six submarines.

Lishchenko was no stranger to the cold war either. In 1957, while on patrol in the Sea of Japan, he had detected another sub along his starboard side about five miles away. He attempted to exchange communications signals with the sub, but to no avail. He followed the mystery submarine, recording the sound of its screws and sonar pings and developed a unique 'footprint' to add to the extensive Soviet library of cavitation identifiers.

After three hours of following the mystery sub, it entered Russian territorial waters. Lishchenko contacted fleet headquarters, which in turn alerted a task force of Russian destroyers that had just departed Vladivostok. The ships quickly located the sub, and trapped it within the territorial limits right outside Vladivostok harbor.

The sub was quickly cornered and mercilessly depth-charged by the Russian destroyers. After 30 hours, the non-nuclear sub finally was forced to surface to restore its air supply. The submarine was identified as American as it breached the surface. It was still intact and capable of fighting, a move the American commander decided against considering the overwhelming odds he faced. After a tense four or five hours, the American sub eventually was allowed to withdraw.

No mention of the incident was ever reported in the press. As it turns out, Lishchenko was instrumental in convincing the Soviet Military Command that releasing the submarine was the only reasonable political and military solution.

But now, a Soviet navy burdened with paperwork and endless bureaucracy had reached its limit, and Captain Lishchenko was ready to retire. Despite the many brave and dedicated men in the Soviet submarine service, he thought that there was way too much politics and corruption. And because the Soviet economy was so tenuous, the inferiority of the equipment they had to work with was a constant danger to the men themselves. *Yes*, he thought, *it's time*.

The Admiral, Pacific Fleet, had one last mission for Captain Lishchenko. As he cleared the Petropovlosk moorings, Yuri opened his orders:

TO COMMANDER SUBMARINE K-229
01 OCTOBER
YOU ARE DIRECTED TO PROCEED TO PACIFIC FLEET HEAD-QUARTERS VLADIVOSTOK AND REPORT TO COMMANDER SUB-MARINE FLOT TWO NO LATER THAN 1700 10 OCTOBER FOR FURTHER ORDERS. THIS, AS ALL FUTURE OPERATIONS, IS CLAS-SIFIED OF THE HIGHEST ORDER UNLESS INDICATED OTHER-WISE BY COMMANDER FLOT TWO.
(Signed) ADMIRAL VASILI SUPOLOV, CHAIRMAN
PACIFIC FLEET MILITARY COUNCIL

Rather vague, Lishchenko thought, but probably routine enough. The 300-foot boat continued toward Vlad on the surface where it could make maximum speed—about 15 knots, and save its batteries. Weather was calm, seas four to six feet, and they would have no problem reaching Vladivostok on schedule.

*   *   *   *

As the *Groveland* left Yokosuka at about 1600 hours local time on the 11th of October, she was trailed by the guided missile frigate *USS King, DLG-10*, one of her designated escorts. The King, fully armored with Terrier Missiles and an ASROC antisubmarine warfare system, could cruise at 33 knots and was very maneuverable.

Once clear of the harbor, the King was ordered to maintain at least a 40 and not more than 50-mile distance between her and the Groveland.

The other support vessel, the carrier *USS Oriskany (CVA-34)* already was at sea and under the same orders as the King to maintain a distance of approximately 50 miles. And like the King, the *Oriskany* also had a top speed of about 33 knots, and was fully capable of reaching a trouble spot with amazing speed for a carrier of her size.

Much to Jake's and Mike's surprise, they initially found that they were subject to the same watch schedule as the regular crew—at least until they were on station, they were assured. Reportedly the captain had a problem with men coming off watch and wanting to sleep; the sight of occupied bunks during the day bothered him. Fortunately both men were assigned to the same watch section, which meant that they were on and off watch at the same time.

As the ship was operating under Condition IV—peacetime cruising—only necessary personnel stood watch while the balance were in reserve, as needed or as cruising conditions changed. The CTs also were subject to the same musters, drills and inspections as the regular crew.

The first day out was one of adjustment for Jake and Mike. Life aboard ship was definitely more structured and demanding than shore duty. They also observed that the purpose of many assignments—watches included—seemed to have no purpose other than to keep the men occupied. To a certain extent, Jake didn't mind this as he found life on a routine patrol had the potential of being pretty boring.

Jake soon learned that the parting wisdom of Lt. O'Shaughnessy—"Don't puke into the wind"—was valuable advice. Within 10 hours of departure, both Mike and Jake found themselves hanging their heads over the rail. But surprisingly, seasickness never was a problem for either of the men after that.

On the morning of the second day at sea, they found they were alone; the *Oriskany* and the *King* both had disappeared from view. At 0900, the Communications Officer, Lieutenant Maxwell, called a meeting in the Operations Department to be attended by all TAD personnel. This was the first time that all CT, ET and other temporarily assigned 'dirt sailors' had been gathered together as a group.

Lt. Maxwell called for order and began his briefing with "Welcome to the *USS Groveland*, Gentlemen. My name is Maxwell, and I am the Communications Officer aboard. As such I have overall responsibility for all visual and electronic communications and of classified material and equipment. The signal officer, radio officer and security officer report to me. Many of you aboard for the first time have very specialized duties. As many of your responsibilities fall outside the mainstream routine communications functions of the ship itself, you will find yourselves under the direct authority of specialists in your respective fields—that is, someone other than myself. Under all situations, however, maintaining the integrity of communications security and procedures, and integrating communications activities—among all departments—is my responsibility."

Jake and Mike understood this to mean that while the ship's communications officer had overall, general authority over all communications on board, but the specialists—CTs and Electronic Technicians (ETs), would report directly to someone else who probably had different—higher—clearance levels than the Comm Officer himself. The fact of the matter was that the Comm Officer—indeed even the ship's captain—did not have adequate clearance to even set foot in the CTs' operating areas aboard the ship. This served to further isolate the CTs from the regular crew.

"I'm now going to run down the details of our course with you. Any questions regarding this should be directed to your department officers as I do not have details on your individual missions for this cruise."

The Lieutenant pulled a map down from the ceiling that showed the entire Asian coast, the Sea of Japan, and more. "We will steam southwest along the southern coast of Japan, around the tip of Honshu, and north through the Korea Strait into the Sea of Japan. We will continue up the east coast of Korea, along the eastern Russian coast, past Vladivostok, and enter the La Perouse Straits between the northern tip of Hokkaido and the southern tip of Sakhalin Island. Once we are in the Sea of Okhotsk, the *Groveland* will pass through the Nemuro Strait between the southern-most point of the Kurile Islands and the northern Japanese island of Hokkaido, to return to Yokosuka."

Jake traced the route on the overhead map with his eyes and mind as the Lieutenant continued. "We do anticipate some heavy seas, particularly as we enter the La Perouse Straits where currents can sometimes be quite rough. Have a good cruise."

"Kind of an officious little mouse, isn't he?" Mike said, describing the communications officer. Jake agreed, and thought he did look a little like a mouse, with close-set dark eyes, a pointed nose, and a scraggly mustache that appeared to be just starting (but which probably was years old). Just so he didn't cause them any problems; sometimes non-cleared regular ship personnel could be nuisances, always somewhat envious of the secrecy of the operations they didn't understand or have access too. Or so he'd been told.

Back in their quarters, Jake prepared for the fire watch he'd been assigned to for the next four hours. It'll be a pleasant break, he reasoned, and give him an opportunity to see more of the ship, and as the watch is on one of the weather decks, an opportunity for some fresh air. He started through the door to the ladder and decided to use the time to work out a reply in his mind to Janice's letter that had arrived before he departed Yokosuka.

Janice said in her letter that she had decided to return home to Pennsylvania. Living with Aunt Faye wasn't working out, and she didn't want to spend the money to get her own apartment. Besides, she'd said, she missed her folks, her friends, and she was lonely. If Jake agreed, she'd written, she would leave in a week by train. Her parents had told her that she could stay with them until Jake returned.

While he understood her reasoning, Jake didn't think that Janice would get along with her folks much better. Her father was a fairly quiet and easy-going man, and her mother was controlling and vocal. Janice got caught in the middle and wasn't happy with the situation in the past.

At any rate, it was too late now. There was no outgoing mail for a while, and she'd be on the train—or already home, before any letter from Jake could reach her. He decided to let it rest and see how it worked out. As a last resort, she could find someplace else to live back there and most probably would get her old job back.

His thoughts returned to the present, the fire watch he was conducting, and what might lie ahead in the Sea of Japan.

CHAPTER 10

▼

"Remember Captain, this is a very sensitive exercise you're about to undertake, the nature of which is known only by a handful of us in the Ministry."

The two Russian trawlers were in position at the entrance to the Korea Strait between Japan and the South Korean peninsula. The Soviets had built and launched a large number of these ships during the late 1950s and early 1960s. Protected by thick armor plate, the ships were designed to both fish and fight as was required. Most were equipped with light armament (typically 50-caliber machine guns) and some of the most sophisticated sonar and radar technology available at the time. The trawlers were fast, agile and perfectly suited to 'fish' for intelligence as well as marine life.

According to her orders, the trawler *Riga* was on her assigned station by 0500 precisely 30 miles south and east of the tip of the Korean peninsula in the western channel of the Korea Strait. Her sister trawler, the *Tallin*, was similarly located 30 miles off the northwestern tip of the southern island of Honshu—also in the Korea Strait.

An intelligence-gathering Russian trawler similar to the Riga and Tallinn

Separating the two ships, directly in the middle of the 125-mile wide strait, was the Japanese island of Tsushima.

The two east and west channels on either side of Tsushima Island were the only entrances or exits through the Korea Strait. The two ships were positioned so that no surface ship could enter the Sea of Japan to the north or the China Sea to the south without being detected by one of the trawlers. The Trawlers were operating under orders to look for a specific U.S. Navy vessel: the *USS Groveland*, AGTR-33. Two other U.S. ships, the *Oriskany* and the *King* both were approaching the deeper western channel of the Korea Strait to enter the Sea of Japan, and the *Riga* knew the slower *Groveland* couldn't be more than eight hours behind.

*   *   *   *

On all three days since she had departed Yokosuka, the southeastern shore of the island of Honshu had been visible to the *Groveland* the entire time, somewhat of a comfort to Jake who finally was beginning to get his 'sea legs.'

"We should be around the southern end of Honshu by mid-afternoon."

"I guess I'll miss the excitement. I start my four-hour watch at noon," Mike replied.

"I thought you just stood a fire watch last night?"

Mike pointed to his bright, new third-class 'crow' on his arm and said "I don't have a *fire* watch. It's time to go to work. We're officially on station now and our responsibility to stand fire watches is over. CTC Stanfield says it's time to start paying attention to the North Koreans at this point."

"*Stanfield* is on the *Groveland?* Is it the same Stanfield that flew out of Atsugi with us?"

Mike nodded. "One and the same. I saw him at chow this morning. I guess out of all of the CTs aboard, he's our senior enlisted man. I don't know who he reports to. Probably no-one."

"Ah-sooo!" Jake said, mimicking the Japanese phrase for 'oh, yes.' "I forgot. I start watch this afternoon myself. See you there," and Jake started to the mess for breakfast.

By 1145 both CTs had settled in and begun their first watch aboard the *Groveland*. The seas were calm but the sky was gray and the Korea Strait was engulfed in a thick fog as they passed through it into the Sea of Japan.

The channel was wide enough that the fog wouldn't be an issue. And it was deep—from 300 to more than 700 feet deep in a trough close to Tsushima Island. Radar had shown only one vessel—a small ship, probably a Japanese fishing boat they were told, about 20 miles off their port side. The radio bands were relatively static-free, and before long both Mike and Jake had comfortably settled into a routine intercepting and recording North Korean military traffic.

Analysts on board sampled intercepted radio traffic, but most was simply collected and transferred back to NSA in Maryland. Most Naval Security Group stations, both land-based and mobile, were not equipped with personnel capable of breaking codes, for example. Linguists were able to read plain-language (unencrypted) text and analysts could spot irregularities, however, often yielding clues that resulted in specific messages receiving higher priority attention.

On their second day after transiting the Korea Strait, one of the analysts came to see Jake.

"Yesterday, one of the messages you intercepted was a brief coded Morse message consisting of alpha-numeric groups of five characters each," the analyst told Jake. "The signal was strong, so it most likely was fairly local. Based on the uniformity of sending, my guess is that it was machine-sent, not a hand-keyed message. There were no call signs used, but that's typical of messages sent according to a pre-determined schedule between two stations; they agree on a time and a frequency, and if there's nobody else there, they use it."

The analyst continued, explaining the significance of the message to Jake. "Normally, because it is encrypted, we'd just send it back to NSA. But I was looking at the coded groups and in the middle of the message, which was only about 40 groups long, was one significant five-letter group with two numerals, the number 33," he said.

"Jesus. That's our ship's number!"

"Yes it is. I don't know if it was coincidence or not, but those were the only numbers in the entire message. It could mean that someone is talking about us, and possibly tracking our movements. Other than that, I haven't a clue, but I'm expediting this message back to NSA to see if they can figure it out for us. I'll keep you posted," the analyst said as he left the workspace.

Jake paid more attention to what he was copying for the next few days but never noticed the ship's identifying number in any further communications.

Two days later, when the *Groveland* was off the coast of South Korea, another message was received which sparked the analyst's attention. This message didn't contain the "33" cluster, but was sent on the same frequency and at the same time as the previous message that had included the cluster.

"We're sending it to NSA for a quick look too," the analyst told Jake. "We've heard back from them about the first message, and evidently it was nothing more than a report of our position. For whom, from whom—and why, NSA couldn't tell us. But we're going to have Kami Seya and Osan Air Force Base monitor that frequency and record anything else that's heard—especially since this appears to be a regular schedule they're keeping. If we're lucky, between the three of us, we can use radio direction finding and see where it's coming from."

Two days after this report, a message was heard on the same frequency at the same time. The *Groveland* was unable to get a fix on the signal's origin due to the short nature of the transmission. But Osan and Kami Seya were successful in triangulating on it, and reported that the transmission was coming from somewhere very close to the entrance of the Korea Straits. The presumption was that the signal originated from a ship that was reporting back to its base.

"What that means," the analyst explained, is that it's most likely the Russians are tracking our movements. Why they're so keenly interested in us is puzzling, though; these AGTR cruises are fairly routine—it's not like it's the first time we've been over here."

*   *   *   *

The weather in Vladivostok harbor was cold—unusually so for October, Captain Yuri Lishchenko observed. The skies were still gray—everything in Russia seemed to be gray; there was a light fog hanging over the water, and the wind had come up. There were white caps on the surface, but the seas were light with swells of only about five to eight feet.

Submarine K-229 pulled into port under diesel power, spewing black smoke from the aft exhaust, and located its assigned berth. Yuri eased his boat alongside the pier and was tied up before nightfall, which came quite early in the evening in this part of the world with sunless skies. It was dusk, with a gray pallor over everything in the harbor, which seemed lifeless. Rusted ship hulls were everywhere, and Yuri wondered about the readiness of the mighty Pacific Fleet.

To Captain Lishchenko's surprise, there was a navy staff car flying an admiral's flag at the dock. Lishchenko descended the ladder from the bridge on the conning tower to the deck of the sub. He could see three officers in heavy, long gray overcoats standing on the dock waiting for him. Normally he performed a cursory inspection of the sub's deck before going ashore, but because of the waiting greeting party, he assigned this duty to his second in command and walked briskly down the gangplank.

The captain approached the men and saluted. By the epaulets on their overcoats, Yuri quickly realized that the men included a two-star admiral and two staff adjutants, one a captain second-grade, and the other a more junior Capitan-Lieutenant. The three officers returned the salute, and the admiral extended his hand, greeting the captain.

"Welcome to Vladivostok, Captain. You had a safe and uneventful voyage," the admiral said, more as a statement than a question.

"Yes Admiral, very normal—just the kind an old sea dog going out to pasture welcomes."

"I understand you're very close to retirement, Captain. You've earned the right to slip quietly into civilian life, but I predict it will be short-lived. You'll long to return your hand to the helm before you know it."

"You're probably right, Admiral. To what do I owe the honor of being greeted by the vice-commandant of Fleet Two?"

Taking the captain by the arm, the admiral said "Come, Yuri, let's sit in the car and talk. This wind is going right through to my old bones. Too many years behind a desk—I never have gotten accustomed to this weather."

"After my mission to the Marshall Islands, I now know for the first time exactly what you mean. I'm rethinking going home to Kiev."

"Ah yes, Kiev. Don't know it well. I'm from Baku, right on the Caspian Sea. I understand you recently spent a brief holiday near there?"

"I did. You'll have to tell me more about Baku sometime. Maybe I could persuade Svetlana to leave Kiev."

The two aides remained on the dock, each lighting a Belomorkanal, the popular black Russian cigarette. The admiral and the captain entered the back seat of the shiny black four-door Zil. Standard issue for Russian military brass, the Zil was a poor Russian imitation of a Cadillac.

The admiral spoke first. "Captain, I know this is your last voyage, and that you're eager to retire and grow fat and lazy. But we have an important job for you—a job that carries some risk. And we know you're not adverse to risk—you're to be congratulated on your successful recovery of the package from the Marshall Islands. I'm told it resulted in some very good intelligence for our missile technicians in Moscow. I also understand that a large whale sacrificed its life for you to our American friends somewhere off the Mariana Islands. Is that true?"

"We did have a bit of a run for it for awhile; we were aware of several shoots by the Americans and did hear an explosion, but I guessed it was one of their torpedoes hitting an undersea rock formation or something."

"Well, it was a successful in all regards and you have your country's gratitude. For this new assignment, we will give you all the support you need. I believe, based on your record, you are ideally suited for it."

"I'm at your command Admiral. I appreciate your confidence in me, and I am still on duty and eager to support anything that the Motherland needs me to do." Lishchenko almost chocked on that last statement.

"Thank you, Captain. I knew you'd accept any challenge we gave you in the spirit of further glorifying the Soviet cause. The reason I wanted to meet you as soon as you arrived is because there is some urgency to this mission, and your stay here in Vladivostok will be very brief. I want you to stay on the base tonight, and get a good night's rest in the officer's quarters. You sail again at 0930 tomorrow."

Captain Lishchenko's expression betrayed some surprise and disappointment. "That's unexpected, Sir. I was anticipating a few days here before executing further orders."

"I know, Captain, and I'm sorry. But we're on a rather inflexible schedule, and unfortunately the mission is being dictated by someone over whom we have no control." The admiral reached into his coat for a long, black cigar, and offered it to Yuri.

"No thank you, Sir." Yuri found significance in the Admiral's statement that the mission was controlled by 'someone over whom we have no control,' instead of the standard 'higher authority' wording.

The admiral lit the big cigar, and the thick, acrid smoke filled the car; Yuri lowered the window to let some of the smoke escape, hoping the admiral would not be offended.

"No offense, Sir," Yuri offered as an apology.

"None taken, Captain," the admiral replied, and continued with his explanation of the mission. "I know it's a foul smell, but it's getting harder to get good cigars from our friend Fidel these days. Your supplies, on the other hand, will be replenished tonight, and your crew will be restricted to the boat. We should have you refueled and ready to go by 0900 tomorrow. At that time we will load your final cargo and you will have your sealed orders delivered immediately before you sail. I apologize for being so secretive, but the reason will become obvious to you when you open your orders on board at 0930 tomorrow. Do you have any questions that I can answer now?"

"I'd like to know where I'm headed. I was hoping to dispatch a message to my wife tonight and at least give her an idea when I would be arriving back in Petropovlosk."

"You may draft a message to your wife and my adjutant will see that it is sent. You will be headed back, indirectly, to Petropovlosk and you should arrive there in a week to a week and a half. I'm sorry but for tonight, that is all I can tell you," the admiral said, flicking his cigar's inch-long ash onto the carpeted floor of the Zil.

"Thank you sir. That's better than nothing. I don't have any other questions. I am sure it will all become clear to me when I open my orders in the morning."

"Very good, Captain. I will be delighted to deliver you to the officers' quarters, and I will see that your personal effects follow immediately," the admiral said, extending his hand once again, which Captain Lishchenko shook.

"Thank you sir," Yuri said, as the admiral signaled to his aides that he was ready to leave.

As the admiral dropped Yuri at his quarters, he rolled down the window and said "Remember Captain, this is a very sensitive assignment you're about to undertake, the nature of which is known only by a handful of us in the Ministry. Let's just say that we probably wouldn't have total agreement by everyone in the party that it's a positive move. But you know the old saying: 'The punishment after the fact for doing something without permission is often less severe than the pain it takes to get that permission in the first place.' So good luck, and send me an invitation in the Spring to come to Kiev and meet your lovely wife. Maybe I can help you convince her to move south."

With that and a wave, the admiral drove off into the ground fog, and Yuri, now more curious than ever, retired to his quarters. *Damn*, he thought to himself. *I never got that message written for my wife. Maybe in the morning.*

There was no time for letter writing in the morning, as Captain Lishchenko headed back to the dock and his final voyage in command of a submarine. The morning fog was even thicker than the previous night, but the wind had died and there were patches of blue beginning to show through the overcast skies. The fog will lift quickly, Yuri told himself, as his driver dropped him off at the entrance to the pier and to sub K-229. Based on the empty trucks parked near the sub, he could tell that the sub had been re-supplied. The tanker truck was just disconnecting the diesel fuel hose when Yuri reached the bottom of the gangplank and was met by the admiral's senior aide.

The two men saluted each other, and the aide handed the captain his orders in an official sealed envelope. "Your cargo is aboard, your second in command has readied the boat, and you are free to disembark as soon as you're aboard and ready, Captain."

"Thank you Capitan-Lieutenant," was all Yuri said as the aide returned to his waiting car on the dock, and Yuri turned and entered the door on the side of the conning tower. Once inside, his Exec assured him that, upon Yuri's order, the boat was ready to depart. Yuri thanked him, told him to stand by for a few more minutes, and immediately went to his cabin to read his orders.

> 11 OCTOBER
> From: Admiral Plotnovich
>   Ministry of Defense
>   Fleet Headquarters, Vladivostok
>
> To: Captain First-Rank Lishchenko
>   Commander, Submarine K-229
>
> Subject: Deployment Order
>
> You will proceed submerged to grid point 343E on map 600 dated 21 July 1963, to arrive no later than 1600Z October 21. You will remain submerged except as necessary for replenishment of air and fuel; you will observe radio silence until the above time and date other than to transmit position reports to this command every 24 hours. Once you arrive at the grid coordinate above, you will remain there until the American navy spy ship USS *Groveland,*

AGTR-33 arrives within 10 miles of your location. A background briefing on this vessel is included with these orders.

You will be kept advised daily of the AGTR-33's position by the trawlers *Riga* and *Tallin* following the American ship at a distance of 20 miles. These trawlers will be following communication protocol Y22 and using code book 56. Once interception of the American ship has been made, you will follow and observe it from astern, maintaining a distance of five miles. When the American ship has reached grid point 355E on the map referenced above, you will—

Captain Lishchenko read on. There were two more pages of orders, excruciatingly finite in detail, and now he understood the admiral's serious tone when he explained the importance and 'sensitive nature' of this mission. And he also now understood exactly why *he* had been chosen to carry it out.

The background sheet on the *Groveland* provided information that the ship was built in 1945 as a liberty (transport) ship and converted to a 'technical research' ship. It noted that there also was an AGTR operating in the South China Sea to gather intelligence in support of the American operations in Viet Nam. It also included statistics on length, tonnage, armament, personnel complement, radar and sonar systems, and specific information on the current commanding officer of AGTR-33.

Yuri Lishchenko felt more comfortable after studying the information in his orders. At least it didn't appear that the *Groveland* was much threat to his retirement plans. *One hell of a way to 'slip into retirement' as the admiral had put it*, Lishchenko thought to himself. The mission was delicate and if anything went wrong, he knew the repercussions would vibrate through the major capitals of the world. *Damn this cold war*, he said to himself.

Captain Lishchenko got on the intercom and summoned his second in command. "Make preparations to get underway, but first I want to see the cargo before we depart."

*   *   *   *

"It looks like we have company," the Radarman second class (RD2) called to the Executive Officer. "I have two small ships 50 miles apart, both about 25 miles astern, speed about 10 knots. They appear to be on a course tracking ours, but I can't be positive of that."

The *Groveland's* Exec ordered that the two ships' positions be marked on the charts and that their progress be monitored and reported to him hourly. There didn't appear to be any other ships in the immediate vicinity—*King* and *Oriskany* were well forward of the *Groveland's* position, and the presence of these two ships would not interfere with the surveillance activities, the Exec reasoned.

After barely a week at sea, the *Groveland* had cleared the Korea Strait and was headed northeast along the South Korean coast, about half way to the 38th Parallel, the dividing line between the communist North and South Korea. At 2200 hours, the radar showed three small vessels approximately 20 miles west of the *Groveland* along the coast in the Ulchin/Samchok area of South Korea.

The vessels were not visible to the naked eye due to the distance and the darkness, although the skies were clear and there was a full moon that amply illuminated the surface of the sea. The vessels evidently were running with no lights, and were stationary when reported by the radarman on duty.

The *Groveland* continued its northern course and didn't alter speed or direction. Within minutes of first noticing the unidentified vessels, the radarman reported that two of them had begun moving in a northerly direction paralleling the *Groveland*, now at a distance of only 10 miles. All three vessels were well within the Republic of South Korea territorial 12-mile limit.

The skipper was cognizant of the territorial limits claimed by both North and South Korea, and reconfirmed the *Groveland's* position well outside of both. Radar reported that both boats were heading on a course directly toward the *Groveland*.

The radio room attempted to make contact with the vessels, but received no reply. In response, not knowing the nationality or intentions of the vessels, the captain ordered the crew to Condition One, or General Quarters, while maintaining course and speed.

Within 15 minutes, the forward lookout reported a visual on the two ships. In anticipation, the captain ordered that the Comm Center send a message to the *Oriskany* and the *King*, both of which were about 50 miles forward of the *Groveland*:

```
18OC 2230Z
FROM CIC GROVELAND AGTR-33
TO CIC USS ORISKANY, USS DLG KING
CLASSIFICATION: UNCLASSIFIED
TWO VESSELS UNKNOWN IDENTITY APPROACHING GROVE-
LAND FROM WEST, APPROXIMATELY 20 MILES AT HIGH SPEED.
SUBJECT VESSELS UNDER 100 TONS EACH. REQUEST FIGHTER
INTERCEPTORS AND COVER SUPPORT AS MAY BE NECESSARY.
END.
```

The message was sent, and immediately replied to by the USS *Oriskany*:

FM CIC ORISKANY TO CIC GROVELAND: THREE A-4 SKYHAWKS ENROUTE, ETA 15 MINUTES. STANDING BY FOR OTHER SUPPORT IF REQUESTED. AIRCRAFT WILL CONTACT YOU DIRECTLY WHEN IN AREA. END.

With that, the *Groveland* continued on its assigned course with the crew at a relaxed general quarters. While this ship condition did not involve Jake and Mike, the complement of CTs was alerted and monitoring attention was diverted to any frequencies and traffic that may have related to the two vessels approaching their ship.

The bridge intercom came alive: "I have two unidentified motor patrol boats approaching from the West at 23 degrees, speed 40 knots!" the radarman reported to the bridge. With the crew at general quarters, all eyes now were on the two smaller boats approaching the ship from the west.

"They're both P-4 class torpedo boats, North Korean ensigns displayed," the Officer of the Deck reported excitedly to the bridge.

The Executive Officer quickly relayed the information to the captain, advising him that each craft was armed with two antiaircraft guns and two 21-inch torpedo tubes.

The captain, who had been seated, arose and picked up the handheld microphone for the ship's intercom system. "This is the captain speaking. We have two North Korean torpedo boats approaching us at high speed. Stand by your stations and be alert. We don't know what they're up to. Gunners hold your positions and don't fire unless ordered to do so. That is all." With only four 50-mm guns, the *Groveland* was in no position to spar with the faster, heavier armed boats and certainly not eager to start an international incident by firing first.

North Korean torpedo boat
(Courtesy of the Seoul Times)

"According to my charts, they're now in international waters, and we are well off the coast of South Korea—well outside both the official and unofficial territorial limits," the Exec reported. He was very aware of the danger inherent in being in these waters—the *U.S.S. Pueblo* had been captured not too far from here by the North Koreans some nine months earlier. It, and more than 30 of its 83-man crew were still being held captive in North Korea despite ongoing international diplomatic efforts to have them released.

"And don't forget, they have every right to be here, just like us," Captain Chandler replied. He knew when he said it that it sounded hollow; perhaps that's because he was only making an obvious statement of fact. Secretly he wished he were commanding a destroyer so he could blow them out of the water and never tell anyone.

The two 60 to 70-foot fast-boats, each with a crew of 15 or so, circled the *Groveland*. There were no shots fired, and the semaphore and signal lamp requests for them to identify themselves and their intentions were ignored. The men assigned to the four 50-mm machine guns followed the boats with their guns, and with knuckles as white as their hats.

The *Groveland* trained its inadequate firepower on the two patrol boats as they circled, for five minutes before three Skyhawks from the *Oriskany* came screaming out of the northeastern skies.

The approaching Navy Skyhawks were flying low, at about 400 feet over the surface of the sea. Two Skyhawks circled the patrol boats while a third jet flew under the other two and passed directly between the two patrol boats, both of which had slowed to half speed as they circled. The pilot had his plane so low that the wash from his engine rocked the two boats. The *USS Groveland* continued its attempts to communicate with the patrol boats by signal lamp, but received no reply.

Given the presence of the jets, the two North Korean patrol boats stopped circling the ship and executed a 180-degree turn back toward the South Korean coast.

"NOVEMBER-BRAVO-TANGO-ZULU, THIS IS SILVERFLY. GOOKS ARE HEADING BACK TOWARD THE MAINLAND. WE'LL HANG AROUND A FEW MINUTES AND KEEP AN EYE ON 'EM. IF YOU DON'T THINK WE'RE NEEDED, HOME WE'LL GO. SILVERFLY OUT," radioed the pilot of one of the jets.

The three jets climbed to about 1000 feet and flew in concentric circles over the patrol boats as they made a parallel beeline for the coast. When the patrol boats were about five miles away from the Groveland, the two jets peeled off and headed back to the carrier.

A few minutes later, the pilot radioed back to the *Groveland*: "N-T-B-Z, THIS IS SILVERFLY. BE ADVISED THE TWO BOATS HAVE JOINED A THIRD ABOUT TEN NAUTICAL MILES OFF COAST AND ALL THREE HAVE PEDAL TO THE METAL HEADING BACK NORTH. RETURNING TO ORISKANY. GOOD SAILING. SILVERFLY OUT."

The officers on the bridge were now relaxed a bit. The captain had taken his chair again and the Executive Officer radioed a 'thanks' back to the fighters and ordered the ship to stand down from general quarters. He then instructed the Communications Officer to contact Republic of Korea (ROK) defense forces and inform them of the incident.

The ROK command later contacted the *Groveland* to thank them and to inform them that they had pursued the North Korean boats back to the 38th Parallel. The ROK contact advised the *Groveland* that they suspected the North Koreans of attempting to infiltrate South Korea and land enemy agents. This evidently was a frequent occurrence at the location the boats had originated from before engaging the *Groveland.*

✳   ✳   ✳   ✳

"What's wrong, Morton—don't like green meat?

"Well, hi, Chief. I heard that you were aboard. And no, after 18 months on Guam, I've had my fill of shiny roast beef."

"I know what you mean. I don't know where they get this stuff. But when it's an iridescent green like that choice morsel you're having, I'd pass it up too." The chief continued: "So, we had a bit of excitement today. What is it with you—does this kind of thing follow you wherever you go?'

"No, I thought it was your fault. So which one of us is going to get off the ship?"

"Not me. I don't swim well. And I don't think that'll solve the problem," the chief said. "Let's hope it's a little quieter the rest of the way home."

"Amen to that."

"Time for me to get topside. The communications officer wants to have a word with me. I think it's beginning to bother him that we won't allow him into our spaces, and he doesn't know what we're doing in there. Check you later, Morton," The chief turned and left the mess hall.

Two more days and we'll be directly east of Vladivostok, Jake thought. And once again his thoughts drifted back to former cube-partner, Sonny Powell. Jake didn't know why the mere thought or mention of Vlad brought memories of Sonny into his head; it also had happened when they were flying near Vlad, he remembered. Jake had just finished his dinner—leaving some of the silver-green slices of roast beef for the fishes, when Mike approached his table.

"Evening Jake. Not a big fan of silver beef I see. What's wrong with you? In the days of 'wooden ships and iron men,' you'd scarf that down like it was chocolate cake."

"Hi Mike. Yeah, I know. Spoiled, aren't we? I guess we have to keep reminding ourselves we aren't in the Kami Seya mess anymore."

"No shit. I'm on my way to catch the evening movie. I hear they're showing "High Noon" or something equally exciting. Wanna join me?"

"I'll pass. I have a day watch tomorrow so I'm going to read my Navy correspondence course on 'culinary arts at sea' and hit the rack. See you tomorrow sometime."

"Watch out. When you graduate, you get a free reenlistment with a four year cruise as cook on a tanker in Haiphong harbor," Mike said with a smile, and left to go catch the 'High Noon' flick.

Haiphong, Jake thought. *Thank God I didn't join the marines,* he thought, as he headed back to the petty officers' quarters.

*   *   *   *

The Sea of Japan was unusually calm for late Fall. Early storms with high winds, which normally cause high seas this time of the year, were absent—so far. The color of the sea—a direct reflection of the sky—was no longer blue, but a gunmetal gray that almost matched the ship.

Never more than 30 nautical miles from landfall, the *Groveland* became a stopover for wildlife, mostly gulls, trying to rest up on their quest for food. Other land birds that had ventured too far out to sea also found the ship's rigging a temporary haven from the wind and their fatigue.

The crew found the tired birds far tamer than they would have imagined, and—of course—always hungry. A palm full of bread crumbs was certain to attract some form of bird-life and the inevitable photo opportunity for the folks back home.

Jake reveled in his time at sea. He discovered certain magic about standing on the open deck, with the salt breeze in his face, and the ever-present odors of sea life. He often spent hours on deck reading or simply day-dreaming/dozing in the afternoon sun, when there was one. Memories of Janice would flood his mind and bring the calm and relaxation called for after a stressful day.

And such a day was October 20. After 24 hours off duty, Jake had returned to the eve watch shortly after his evening meal. Cruising some 30 miles off shore, due east of Vladivostok, Jake's former cube mate, Sonny Powell, came to mind. "*Why now?*" Jake would ask himself. Jake had been working for an hour or so when CTC Stanfield entered the area.

"Hi Jake, do you have any unusual traffic on the VHF frequencies?"

"No, nothing unusual. Maybe a little busier than the last time I was on watch. Why do you ask?"

"The Duty Officer tells me that our shadows are still with us, back about 50 miles. They've been there since we cleared the Korea Straits."

"Any I.D. on them yet?"

"A VQ-1 flight on its way back to Atsugi radioed that they spotted two trawlers in the general vicinity yesterday, so it's probably the same two that were in the Straits."

"I guess it's normal for the Russians to keep track of us, but I didn't know they actually followed our ships to do so. They have radar and radios just like we do, and we're well within range of their coastal defense monitoring systems."

"Yeah, you're right. I guess we just wait and see. Keep your ears open and let me know if you pick up anything suspicious."

"Will do," Jake said, as CTC Stanfield left. Jake got up and went for a fresh cup of coffee. *Amazing how you get used to something* he thought; *it doesn't taste like mud any more—closer to motor oil*, he'd guess.

"Morning *Petty Officer Third Class* Johnson."

"Hey, that sounds good. I think I'm getting used to it. Hope I get back to Japan soon so I can spend the extra $10/month I'm now earning as a third-class."

"Just bank it. You'll need it for bail or something as soon as you're back," Jake said, filling his cup half way and adding some water to dilute the syrupy thick coffee. Even here it seemed to have an oil slick floating on top.

"Stanfield asked me if I had heard any unusual activity on the ship-to-shore VHF frequencies. I haven't, have you?"

"No unusual volume, but I did have an especially strong message come thru earlier today. I'll see if I can find it on the tape and let him know. May be nothing, but you never know," Mike replied, as they both returned to work. The watch would last another four hours or so before they would be off until the eve watch the following day.

Within another hour, CTC Stanfield would return to tell them that the message Mike had intercepted earlier in the day was significant. "We know it was from one of the trawlers that are shadowing us, but without call signs we don't know who they were sending it to. Like the previous messages, it consisted of coded groups and one of them included '33'again. So all we know is that someone is interested in keeping track of where we are."

Jake and Mike returned to work, now more intent than ever in trying to identify the recipient of the mystery messages. Being one-way communication, however, with no response, it was virtually impossible to identify the recipient. Radio direction finding could pinpoint a transmission if the recipient would acknowledge receipt of the message by sending one.

As the days drug on, there were two additional messages similar to the first two intercepted—again with no acknowledgement by the recipient. But the CTs were now certain that the two trawlers following them were the originators of the messages, and they were still shadowing the *Groveland*.

CHAPTER 11

▼

"The Russian trawlers were following us for a reason. Why? They weren't just out fishing and happened to be going the same direction we were…"

The captain's second-in-command, Captain-Lieutenant Alexinov, awakened Captain Lishchenko at 0600 local time.

"You wished to be advised when we had arrived at the assigned grid point. We are here my Capitan."

Captain Lishchenko rubbed his eyes and threw the thin blanket down to about his waist. As he slung his leg over the edge of the bunk, Alexinov saw several large scars on the captain's lower leg—probably from World War II, Alexinov thought.

"Very well, Grigory. Send a message to Fleet Headquarters and advise them that we have arrived at grid location 343 as instructed. And make sure you tell them we have seen no sign of the fucking oiler that was supposed to be here to refuel us. Also send a message to the trawlers *Riga* and the *Tallin,* and advise them we have arrived. Get an update from them on the exact current location of the *Groveland,*" Lishchenko ordered. "Do we have them on radar yet?"

"Nyet, Capitan, we have not identified them on radar. With your permission, I will return to the bridge and carry our your orders, Sir!" Lishchenko nodded and Alexinov left the captain's quarters.

Lishchenko sat on the edge of his bunk, still trying to clear the sleep from his head. *Where the hell is that oiler?* he wondered. *If we miss our schedule because of them, I'll sink the bastards..after they fuel us, of course,* he told himself. And then he chuckled aloud.

After a quick shave and some cold water splashed on his face from the tiny stainless steel bowl in his cabin, the captain arrived on the bridge about 15 minutes later and assumed command from Alexinov. "Bring us to periscope depth, Grigory."

"Da, Capitan," his second in command said as he issued the orders to bring the sub close to the surface. There was a loud noise as the huge compressed air tanks began to purge the seawater from the ballast tanks that had been filled to make the boat submerge. Within minutes, the conning tower broke the surface and the captain ordered "Up periscope."

A quick 360-degree scan of the choppy surface confirmed what the sub's radar and sonar operators had advised—the area was clear of any other vessels at least as far as visibility would allow him to see. Even though the surface was moderately rough and the sky overcast, visibility was good for at least several miles—or as far as it was possible to see before the curvature of the ocean surface obscured vision.

The captain ordered "Down periscope. Surface," an order that the second in command repeated to the seaman operating the controls, now pumping more water out of the tanks.

"The fuel ship was supposed to be here before us; have we had any reply from Flot H.Q.?"

"Nyet, Captain. But it has only been 30 minutes since we transmitted, so I would recommend we wait a little longer, Sir!"

"Agreed," the captain said, adding "But if we don't have a reply within the next 30 minutes, send another message and ask the status. I'll be in my quarters. You are in command of the boat, Grigory," the captain said as he left the bridge to return to his cabin.

"Da Captain. I will advise as soon as we have word."

*   *   *   *

"Chief, this is Jake Morton. I think we have something. You should come down here ASAP," Jake spoke into the ship's telephone.

Within minutes, CTC Stanfield entered Jake's secure work area. "This better be good, Morton—I haven't had my fourth cup of coffee yet," he joked.

"Well, 'good' is a relative term. I think we just intercepted a message that may link to the previous mystery messages. It also is in coded groups, but one of the groups again is our ship's number, '33' in plain language. But this time, the strength of the signal is weaker, and the operator appears to be different, or at least I didn't recognize the 'fist'—it definitely wasn't the same sender as the past few from the trawlers. So it's possible it was not only a different operator, but sent from a different station," Jake stated.

"You're probably right, Jake. I doubt that each trawler has more than one radioman aboard, so it's origin is likely from somewhere other than the trawlers."

Stanfield thought for a moment, and said "Draft a secure message and have the ship's radioman send it to all Naval Security Group stations on the Pacific high frequency direction finding net; give them the frequency you heard the latest message on, and ask them to get a fix on any transmissions they hear on that frequency in the next couple of hours. Better to have a half-dozen ears listening and trying to locate it than us sitting here guessing. If they get a fix on another transmission, we might learn the identity of who the trawlers were keeping appraised of our whereabouts."

"Consider it done, Chief; I'll let you know if and when we get any feedback." Jake left to go to the cryptographic center to compose the message.

✳   ✳   ✳   ✳

It was the voice of his second in command, Grigory Alexinov on the ship telephone. "Captain Lishchenko, we now have a reply from Fleet H.Q. in Vladivostok; they advise that the oiler will be here by 1800 hours tonight and that we are to commence refueling immediately. They did not say why the ship was so late, Captain."

Lishchenko said "Very well" and hung up the intercom telephone. Then he had a second thought, and called Alexinov back to ask if they had received an update on the *Groveland's* location from the trawlers. When he was advised that neither the *Riga* nor the *Tallin* had yet responded to the sub's first message, the captain instructed that a second request be transmitted.

What the hell is happening to the Motherland's Fleet, Lishchenko wondered? Nobody answers messages any more. How the hell am I supposed to carry out a mission with no information?

✳   ✳   ✳   ✳

"Chief, we've got 'em!" Jake practically yelled on the *Groveland's* ship telephone.

"I'll be right there, Morton."

"Whoever the trawlers were reporting our position to just transmitted again fifteen minutes ago—same frequency, same 'fist', and they got an immediate reply from one of the trawlers. You were probably right—I recognized the sending cadence, so they probably only have one radioman. Two NSGA stations in our HFDF net were able to zero in on the transmission, and here's where we think they are," Jake said as he walked over to a wall chart of the area.

"We still don't know *who* the trawlers were sending to, but now we do know *where* he is. If the direction finders were accurate, our mystery receiving station has to be a ship, because it's located right here in the center of the La Perouse Strait," Jake said, pointing to a location on the chart.

"That's the strait between the southern end of Sakhalin Island and the northern tip of Hokkaido. And that's the route we're taking to get back to Yokosuka. I guess we'll find out who he is when we get there. Does sonar or radar show anything in the area?" Stanfield asked.

"I checked. The sonarman says we're still too far away for any accuracy. Radar says it has nothing in the vicinity of where we think the signals are coming from, but it does have a ship in the Tatar Strait about 100 miles north of there, heading due south toward that location" Jake replied, pointing to the wall chart.

After studying the navigational chart further, and marking their approximate route with a pencil, he also drew an intersecting line showing their own course, the approximate location of the mystery ship, and the other ship heading straight south from the Tatar Straits.

"Given our current speed and bearing, it looks like maybe we will know what this is all about in three days, Jake. Keep your ears open. I'm going to report what we know so far to Captain Chandler. I'm also going to recommend that we summarize this to Fleet Headquarters in Yokosuka and send a copy to both the *Oriskany* and the *King*. It might be a good idea to have them narrow the gap between themselves and us since we don't know exactly what's waiting for us in the La Perouse Strait."

CTC Stanfield left and went immediately to the bridge to make his report and recommendations to the *Groveland's* captain. Captain Chandler would agree with Stanfield's suggestions and gave instructions to make the recommended contacts.

*   *   *   *

According to the apologetic captain of the oiler, heavy seas had prevented the Russian fuel tanker from arriving on time and from completing the refueling as fast as Captain Lishchenko had wanted. The two men would warm their personal relations over a few glasses of strong Russian vodka.

It was the end of October, and in more moderate climes it would be considered to be the end of Fall—but here in the La Perouse Strait Between Sakhalin and Hokkaido Islands it was the beginning of Winter. And winter weather had arrived, with six-foot seas and winds at 20 knots. Refueling a submarine was always a dangerous operation in any weather, and the fact that it was 2000 hours local time, and dark, made the exercise go even slower.

Finally the oiler had refilled the sub's diesel tanks and had disconnected all of the umbilical hoses, and the two captains said their farewells. The oiler was continuing on to refuel another submarine located somewhere off Sovetskaya Gavan, a secondary Soviet military base some 550 miles north of Vladivostok.

During the process of refueling, one of the trawlers had reported the *Groveland's* location to the Russian submarine. The captain was satisfied that the American ship was on course, and *Groveland* was estimated to arrive at the grid location within two days. Lishchenko remained surfaced an additional three hours to complete recharging of the batteries, and to take in more air to flush the sub's stale ventilation system, and then ordered the sub to submerge to a depth of 50 feet.

"We will remain at this position until the *Groveland* is within range. I want position reports every 45 minutes until the ship arrives, and I want to be advised when she is within 20 miles," the captain ordered.

*   *   *   *

Captain Merrill Chandler was confused. It was the 24th of October, a day after they'd informed Yokosuka of the situation with the trawlers, and had requested the support ships narrow the gap between themselves and the *Groveland* in the La Perouse Strait. A priority message from Fleet H.Q./Yokohama had just arrived, advising Chandler that the trawlers had ceased trailing the *Groveland* and appeared headed back to Vladivostok. Because the shadowing trawlers were gone, Fleet H.Q. also had ordered the *Oriskany* and the *King* to maintain the 50-mile distance between them and the Groveland until the Groveland had cleared the Strait and was on a southern course back to Yokosuka.

"God damn it, I don't understand," Chandler exclaimed to his executive officer. He didn't display anger very often, and was especially careful not to openly question orders from above, so his exec was surprised. "The Russian trawlers were following us for a reason—they weren't out fishing and just happened to be going the same direction we were. We've intercepted several radio transmissions from them that indicate our arrival in the Strait is of special interest to the Soviets, for some unknown reason, and now we're being left to hang out to dry, so to speak. Get that CT Chief, Stanfield, up to the bridge on the double."

"Aye Sir," the exec said as he picked up the ship telephone to summon the chief.

Chief Stanfield entered the bridge, came to attention and reported to the captain.

"At ease, Chief. I wanted to get your input on our situation. Tomorrow morning we will arrive at the entrance to the La Perouse Strait, probably sometime around 0930. We know the Russians have been keenly interested in our exact course and location, so something or someone is waiting for us when we get there. Yokosuka has advised us that the *King* and *Oriskany* won't be closing the gap between us, and that has me somewhat concerned. If we need help in a hurry, that could pose a problem."

Stanfield acknowledged the captain with a nod, but didn't speak. He could tell by the tone of his voice that interrupting without being invited to do so could be a bad career move.

"I wanted to ask you if your operation has any new or additional information that could shed light on what the hell is going on, and—if not, to make sure you have your group on full alert and being extra diligent," the Captain stated.

Chief Stanfield tried not to show his alarm that closer support had been denied by H.Q. "I don't have any additional info, I'm sorry, Sir. We're going back over the past few days' worth of tapes of interceptions, looking for anything that we might have missed. Actually the Russian frequencies have been relatively quiet lately. The trawlers are quiet and whomever they were communicating with in the Strait hasn't been active either. You have my full assurance that we are making every effort to try and find out what's up," Stanfield said.

"Very good, Chief. I appreciate your help. I likewise will keep you informed. Please report anything you deem significant to me at any hour. And no need to repeat what I told you about the support ships hanging back to anyone; don't want any unnecessary alarm. Thanks again."

"Aye, Sir," and with that, Stanfield left the bridge and returned to the operations area to reemphasize the importance of staying alert to his men.

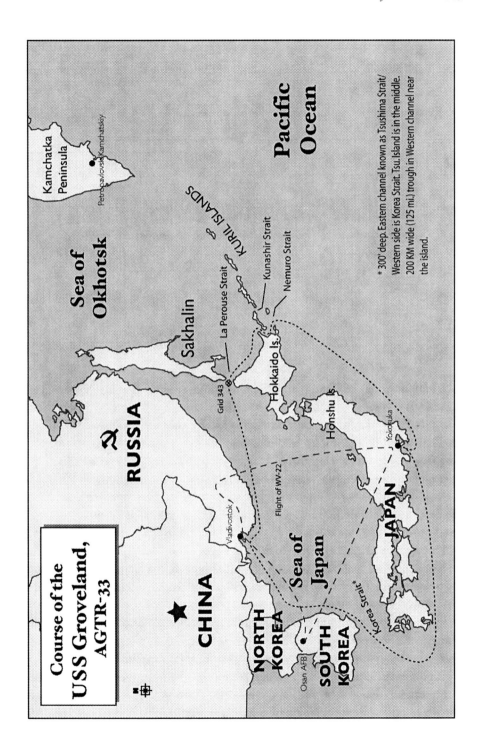

Course of the
USS Groveland,
AGTR-33

CHAPTER 12

▼

White-knuckled young sailors who never had fired anything larger than a .45 caliber pistol in boot camp again manned the guns...

At 1000 hours local time, the *USS Groveland* entered the La Perouse Strait between the Soviet Sakhalin Island to the north, and the Japanese island of Hokkaido to the south. As a precaution, Captain Chandler had ordered the Officer of the Deck to bring the ship to readiness condition II, a prelude to general quarters. The *Groveland* was cutting through relatively light seas with swells of five to 10 feet, under clear skies, with no significant weather reported in its path.

Jake and Mike were on watch in the security group operating spaces, not required to man specific ship duty stations until a general quarters, or readiness condition one was called.

During peacetime, general quarters was an order that brought a ship to a well-practiced state of peak readiness for any event. It had the advantage of assuring the captain that every possible contingency could be covered, that it was known where every single individual was at a given time, and that specific divisions or departments could be called into action depending upon the circumstances, at a moment's notice. This included fire fighting, a man overboard, or numerous other situations that demanded order and disciplined processes.

It also meant tension. The fear of the unknown was the worst kind of enemy. Fires, aircraft downed at sea, and rescues of personnel in the water—all were known entities for which drills and procedures were almost genetically implanted in every sailor on the ship. But entering unfriendly waters, alerted to danger with no clue what that might entail, was the kind of stuff that caused ulcers.

By 1200 hours, the ship had traveled some 25 miles into the Strait, maintaining an easterly course at about 10 knots. Having been on heightened readiness for two hours, some of the tension had dissipated and the crew, though still on alert, was somewhat relaxed.

Sonar informed the captain that it had detected an underwater object bearing 200 degrees off the port quarter, back about five miles, parallel with the Groveland. "I'm pretty sure it's a sub, Sir, and from the sounds of its screws, I would guess it's Russian," the sonarman would report.

"Well it sure as hell isn't one of ours, or we'd know about it!" the captain replied as calmly as he could. He was a war veteran and his experience helped him sense fear in his men, and knew when not to yell like he really wanted to. "Whoever he is, he's coming up behind us," the captain said and immediately ordered the OOD to sound general quarters. Covers were removed from the four 50-caliber machine guns located two-each fore and aft of the bridge. Ammunition was ready, and white-knuckled young sailors who had never fired anything larger than a .45 caliber pistol in boot camp again manned the guns. Specific doors were secured, and the ship was readied for what would be considered battle conditions during wartime.

All hands were at their assigned duty stations, and lookouts were posted. Sonar reports were provided every few minutes. Within 20 minutes, the submarine had come up even with the *Groveland* when the a watch yelled, "Snorkel breaking water bearing two-seven-zero degrees port!"

Jake was at his duty station on the port side of the ship and saw a yellow smoke flare or something come up out of the water where the submarine's snorkel was seen. "What the hell is *that*?" he asked aloud. His stomach was churning with nerves, and he was sure it was a precursor to ten imaginary torpedoes flying toward the ship.

Chief Stanfield was nearby. "It's a standard signal that means a submarine is about to surface, probably sent up so we wouldn't be surprised." As he said it he thought about the stupidity of his statement—*Surprised? Like a simple flare would make us feel comfortable about a submarine breeching right beside us? If we hadn't known he was there, we'd be in deep shit.*

He was right. Russian submarine K-229 commanded by Captain First Rank Yuri Lishchenko was about to surface less than 100 yards off the port side of the *Groveland*.

Captain Chandler ordered "All stop" which would bring the ship to a dead stop. As he did, K-229's conning tower broke the surface, and then the upper deck, which was flat with the surface of the ocean. It did not surface any further—possibly a precaution; the less some overzealous gunner on the Groveland could see of the sub, the harder it would be to hit, Jake reasoned.

Captain Chandler's first action was to order an urgent message sent to the *Oriskany* and the *King*, still some 50 nautical miles distant from the *Groveland*. His message would tell of the surfaced sub and request the ships to 'stand by'— about all he could tell them at this point, knowing that they'd have to get permission from Yokosuka before they could do anything anyway.

Both ships immediately would reply that they were standing by for further information from the *Groveland*.

Within minutes after the black conning tower of K-229 breaking the surface, a Russian signalman with a light appeared topside and began sending a message in broken English to *Groveland*.

"FROM CAPTAIN K-229 TO COMMANDING OFFICER AGTR-33: VERY IMPORTANT. KIND ASK YOU ALLOW CAPTAIN K-229 TO COME FOR TALK WITH COMMANDER AGTR-33. CAPTAIN COME ONLY WITH ONE ENGLISH INTERPRETER AND NO ARMS. REASON FOR IMPORTANT TALK TO CAPTAIN AGTR-33 PEACEFUL AND VERY URGENT. PLEASE REPLY. END."

"Jesus, this is extraordinary, Captain. I can't believe it. What could be so important that they would have to come aboard, and the sub's captain at that?" the executive officer asked.

"Obviously I don't know the answer to that, but I also can't think of a good reason to say no, either. If they intended anything hostile, they could have put us on the bottom a long time ago. With our ships 50 miles away, I don't believe we have much of a choice. Besides, with their captain aboard the *Groveland*, they aren't likely to do anything anyway. Return their signal and inform them that they are welcome, and that we will send a launch for them. I'm sure they don't have anything but rubber rafts on that boat, and given these seas, I wouldn't want to be in one myself," the captain ordered.

"Aye aye, Sir. We'll confirm their request and send a launch immediately if they agree."

The *Groveland* signalman replied: "FROM CAPTAIN AGTR-33 TO CAPTAIN K-229: PERMISSION GRANTED FOR YOU TO COME

ABOARD THE USS GROVELAND. WE WILL SEND A MOTOR BOAT
FOR YOU. CONFIRM AGREEMENT. END."

After a short time the sub's signalman confirmed that a boat to pick them up
would be appreciated and that they were standing by.

"Get Chief Stanfield up here. He speaks Russian, and we'll probably need
him. Launch a motorboat when ready," the captain told the Exec.

All hands watched as the motorboat was lowered and immediately departed
for the submarine. As it pulled alongside, two Russian enlisted men dressed in
black work uniforms and holding machine guns stood watch on top of the conning tower as Captain Lishchenko and a second class chief warrant officer entered
the boat. It departed the sub and quickly made the 100-yard trip back to the
Groveland, which now was dead in the water, directly off the starboard side of the
submarine. The sub still had not completely surfaced, its deck virtually even with
the ocean surface. Waves broke over the deck and smashed into the conning
tower, which rose about 30 feet above the deck of the sub.

As the motorboat approached the *Groveland*, the chief boatswain gave the
order to 'man the rail,' a courtesy involving several men standing at attention
along the side of the ship at the point where the gangplank (if there was one)
would enter the ship. The tradition was intended to honor those coming aboard,
and usually reserved for visitors of rank—which of course Captain Yuri Lishchenko was.

The motorboat tied up alongside the *Groveland* and the junior Russian
officer—the interpreter—requested permission to come aboard. Permission was
granted and the captain began to climb the short rope ladder to the deck, followed by the interpreter.

The *Groveland's* chief boatswain gave the command "Attention to port," and
the four sailor-honor guard came to attention.

First on deck was Captain Lishchenko, who smartly saluted the OOD as he
came aboard. He immediately was followed by the junior officer who returned
the OOD's salute and then reached for his hand.

"Welcome aboard, Captain. I'm Lt. Thornton. Please allow me to escort you
to the captain's wardroom," the OOD said in a slow, deliberate voice as he led
the two officers through a door and down a passageway to the captain's wardroom.

"Thank you Lieutenant. It will be our pleasure," Lishchenko replied in perfect
English.

Captain Chandler, his executive officer and Chief Stanfield were waiting in the room, seated at the wardroom's small conference table. The two Russian officers entered the door, hats in hand, and the three Americans stood. Captain Chandler extended his hand to the Russian captain, saying, "Welcome to the *USS Groveland*, Captain. I'm Merrill Chandler, commanding officer of the *Groveland*. This is my exec, Lt. Commander Neeson, and this is Chief Petty Officer Stanfield, who will serve as interpreter as necessary."

The Russian officer accompanying Lishchenko began to interpret what Captain Chandler had said when Lishchenko interrupted him saying "Thank you Starshiy, that won't be necessary; I understood the captain. Thank you for your welcome, Captain. I am Yuri Lishchenko, captain of submarine K-229 and this…"

Lishchenko didn't get to finish his sentence when Captain Chandler, looking like he had seen a ghost, interrupted the Russian saying "Did you say *Lishchenko, Yuri* Lishchenko?"

"That is correct, Captain. I am Captain First Rank Yuri Lishchenko, Navy of the Union of Soviet…"

"My God, I don't believe it!" Chandler said, interrupting again and reaching for Lishchenko's hand and gripping it and shaking it vigorously with both hands as all the other men in the room looked on somewhat quizzically. Lishchenko had a similar look of surprise on his face.

Chandler released the Russian's hand. "Captain Lishchenko, it is indeed an honor to have you aboard. I wouldn't expect you to remember, but I was the young executive officer on the American minesweeper whose crew you rescued off the coast of England 20 years ago!"

After a moment of thought, a grin slowly came over Lishchenko's face, and with it the easing of tension in the wardroom that was evident to all. "Ah, yes, I remember. We were both united against a common enemy then, weren't we? Well, Captain, I am happy to see that the unfortunate experience 20 years ago did not spoil your love of the sea."

Captain Chandler turned to the other officers and men in the room and said "Gentlemen, please be seated. This gentleman saved my bacon—and a whole lot of other guys'—when the Germans sank our minesweeper off of the coast of the U.K. in 1943. After fishing us out of the drink, this man turned his boat around and chased the son of a bitch that sank us, and sent that sorry German bastard to sleep with the fishes. I owe this man my life."

The interpreter was simultaneously reciting this back to Captain Lishchenko in Russian as fast as the American captain was telling his men.

"If I may suggest, Captain Chandler, that episode perhaps will help both of us understand why I was chosen to meet you here today. I did not know you were the commander of this ship, but evidently my superiors did, and obviously they knew of our history, but for some reason failed to tell me. I am pleased to make your acquaintance again, Captain," Lishchenko said, taking a seat at the ward-room table across from Captain Chandler.

Captain Chandler wondered to himself as to why his own senior command had not been more up front with him about this meeting. "I guess those two trawlers that have been shadowing us for a week or so were doing so at your command?" Chandler asked.

"Well, Captain, not at my command, but to make sure that if you strayed from the course that we anticipated you would take, that I would have an opportunity to alter my own course so that we could eventually meet. That is why we have been here for a few days waiting for you. We knew this is the one place in the Strait where you could not pass without our knowing it."

Chandler decided that his superiors must have known about the meeting and for that reason kept the *Oriskany* and the *King* at a distance so as to not scare off the Russians.

"I can only conclude that our two governments have discussed this behind closed doors, Captain Chandler. It was too important that we meet, as I shall soon explain, and the reason for the meeting too sensitive to have a large audience. As you know, the more people with knowledge of something, the greater the chance that something could go wrong. I am sure that our superiors on both sides have kept knowledge of this liaison limited to a very privileged few," Lishchenko said, adding "which I guess brings us to the subject of why we asked for this confidential meeting."

"Please explain, Captain Lishchenko, but first allow me to ask my exec to issue the order to my crew to stand down from general quarters." Chandler turned to his exec and said "And go to readiness condition two, Mr. Neeson."

"Aye Sir, condition two," his exec repeated as he picked up the ship telephone to call the bridge.

"Now, Captain Lishchenko, please explain why we are here together."

"It is my pleasure, Captain Chandler. I will attempt to make it brief as my English is quite rusty. As you probably know, one of your submarines—the SS *Crestfin*, was gathering electronic intelligence well within the territorial waters of the Soviet Union last July. As it was navigating a narrow, shallow channel departing Vladivostok harbor, it was unintentionally rammed broadside at a very shallow depth by one of our Coastal Defense cruisers, the *Novosibirsk*."

Captain Chandler was aware that an American sub had gone missing, but did not know the details of the incident being described. He kept quiet and allowed Lishchenko to go on. All eyes—and ears—were on Captain Lishchenko as he continued.

"We want to express our condolences. My superiors are certain that the incident was accidental. The *Novosibirsk* was moving fast and came upon the submarine before it had time to steer clear, and as a result cut through the American boat just behind the conning tower. The sub's hull was breeched at that point and your submarine SS *Crestfin* immediately sank at that spot, just two miles outside the port."

"This was an accident of monumental proportions. The relations between our two countries—once great allies—have been strained for a long time. There are many reasons why this accident was not made public by our government. On one hand our Minister of Defense was embarrassed to admit that American submarines could penetrate our coastal defense system with our superior technology, especially at the location of the headquarters of our Pacific Fleet. On the other hand, while we believe the collision was accidental, it also is not a bright spot on our military history that a modern warship such as the *Novosibirsk* did not know the submarine was there. The commander of our cruiser has been dealt with appropriately."

Chandler could imagine what that entailed.

Lishchenko continued. "As for your government, to admit that they were there, spying on our country and having lost a very expensive warship in foreign waters with many lives lost—well, you can see why your government kept it quiet."

Captain Chandler did know. He interjected: "Captain, much of what you say is true. I cannot speak to the reasons for my government's silence on this issue, and I must accept your explanation as to why your superiors have done the same. Perhaps there have been high level talks and conciliatory apologies offered on both sides. The fact remains it was an unfortunate incident that neither of us wants to ever see repeated. So why are you here, now, Captain?"

"I am here to deliver some cargo, Captain Chandler, and I mean no disrespect in using that term. We recovered the bodies of 17 crewmembers from the *Crestfin* after it sank, and we have those bodies to turn over to you. I hope that you will accept my word that these men were dead by the time we reached them, all as a result of the collision, and that we have treated their remains with the highest degree of respect. A formal state memorial service was held in their honor at the site of the incident, attended by the entire crew of the *Novosibirsk* and the vice-admiral and contra-admiral of the Soviet Ministry of Defense and the Pacific Fleet from Vladivostok."

There was complete silence in the room. The Americans looked at each other with blank expressions that belied their utter shock. It appeared that nobody knew exactly what to say.

Captain Lishchenko was about to continue when Captain Chandler broke the silence first. "Captain, as you can see, we are without words; I know you understand that this comes as a complete shock to all of us. Whatever we may have known about this incident, we did not expect to be presented with this situation. You must understand our emotions. We are extremely grateful for your sincerity and the honor you have given to our shipmates from the *Crestfin*. It would be an honor to accept the transfer of these men's' remains and know you can understand what this will mean to their families."

"Thank you Captain Chandler. We were not sure how you would react to this information, but we came here in the hopes that this action on our part would be accepted. The Soviet Navy is sorry it cannot return more of the dead to you, but most were lost or impossible to remove from the wreck. Hopefully it will help improve relations between our two great countries. These men died following orders, serving the interests—right or wrong—of their country, and they deserve a proper, honorary burial in their homeland."

Captain Chandler nodded his agreement, and glanced at the faces of his fellow officers. It was obvious that all the men in the room were shocked but pleasantly moved by the actions of their Russian visitors.

Lishchenko continued. "But there is more. You will be pleased to learn that there were three survivors of the accident. We have them aboard U-229 and wish to deliver them to you as well."

With no exception, there was incredulity among the men present in the room. Captain Chandler jumped to his feet and exclaimed "*SURVIVORS!* This is absolutely amazing, Captain! Three survivors? But how is that possible? You said your cruiser cut the submarine in half and it sank."

"This is correct my captain. But the *Novosibirsk,* though crippled, was able to maintain watertight integrity and stay in position after striking the submarine *Crestfin*. Your submarine was in relatively shallow water and some of her personnel were in compartments that were opened to the sea as a result of the accident, with close access to the surface. The commander of the *Novosibirsk* summoned assistance from a smaller commercial vessel nearby and was able to reach these three individuals before their submarine was completely unreachable on the bottom."

Captain Chandler, still somewhat shaken and numbed by the acknowledgement of the survivors, asked, "Where have these men been since the accident, and what condition are they in?"

"The three enlisted men are, for the most part, in excellent condition. One man has lost part of his leg, unfortunately, and it could not be saved despite the heroic efforts of our skilled medical technicians. They all have been well cared for, according to the Geneva Convention of course; I assure you they have received the best medical attention available in Vladivostok."

"I'm sure they have. I know you are a man of honor and your word is all I need. Let's get these sailors aboard immediately," Captain Chandler replied.

"It will be an honor, Captain Chandler."

The meeting between the two captains continued briefly, with both sides expressing gratitude for the cordial meeting, laced with the expected platitudes about peace, cooperation and mutual interest. It was agreed that the bodies of the dead seamen and the three survivors would be transferred from the submarine to the *Groveland* immediately.

"Captain Lishchenko, on behalf of the United States and the men of the *Groveland*, my sincere thanks for your effort in this endeavor. It is this spirit of cooperation and humanity that I am sure eventually will bring our two countries to a closer degree of cooperation such as that which existed during World War II. My best wishes for luck and health to you, and I hope that our paths cross sometime somewhere in the future when we're not wearing uniforms."

"Thank you Captain. I am pleased that after 20 years we are still able to communicate and reach an understanding that will benefit your country and mine. Returning these men to their countrymen was a pleasant last duty for me before I leave the service of my country and take my meager pension in retirement. My personal, and my country's condolences to the families of the deceased, and my best wishes for smooth sailing for the entire crew of the *Groveland* now and wherever they may find themselves."

The Russian and American officers shook hands and walked as a group down the passageway to the door leading to the ladder and the waiting motorboat.

As Captain Lishchenko began his descent down the short ladder to the waiting motorboat, he looked back at Captain Chandler and his exec and saluted. "Do svidaniya—good bye my friend. I hope conditions will permit you to visit me in Kiev someday," he said and entered the motorboat for the return trip to the sub.

Captain Chandler made a brief announcement on the P.A. system to inform the crew of the purpose of the Russians' visit. He then called for the entire crew to line the side of the ship and on his command, to salute the Russians out of thanks and respect for their action.

The following hour was one of amazing reverence and solemnity for the crew of the *Groveland*. Other than those assisting with the transfer, the crew had remained lining the rail, watching in silence and the black rubber body bags containing the remains of the *Crestfin* sailors were transferred from the sub to the motorboat and back to the *Groveland*.

Jake and Mike were among those watching the transfer take place. Chief Stanfield joined them. "That was one of the most amazing experiences of my life," he said. "I can't believe it happened. Wish I could tell my wife."

As the crew watched, the launch began its final trip back to K-229 for the three survivors. As it approached the sub, the crew of the Groveland could make out three individuals exiting the conning tower door to wait on the deck of the sub for the launch's arrival.

"There they are," Mike exclaimed. "I can't make them out very well but it looks like one is on crutches."

The three men boarded the motorboat and immediately sped back toward the *Groveland*. Seas were still high, the sky was overcast, and the wind was picking up. It was a cold day to be watching the historical events unfold, but somehow nobody was conscious of the weather. It was nearing dusk—the sea was awash in the gold of the setting sun as the final motorboat trip from the sub was also nearing its conclusion.

Once more the chief boatswain had given the 'man the rail' order and the sailors immediately came to the point on the rail where the ladder would bring the men on deck. "Attention to port" he again ordered as the men snapped to attention to greet the three survivors from the *Crestfin* as the three men were helped aboard.

The three survivors were all dressed in enlisted Russian work uniforms—dungarees, black wool sweaters and knit caps. The first two climbed the ladder with no problem, and then Jake noticed that the third man who had been using crutches was being placed in a sling with assistance from the motorboat coxswain and a few other sailors. As he hoisted aboard, Jake realized why—the man was missing a leg from the knee down.

The first two men cleared the top rail and stepped on deck, saluting the flag and the OOD as they did so. They paused, waiting for the third member of their party to make it to the top. As he did, all three stood in a line, saluting the flag and the OOD while standing at attention.

Captain Chandler was there to greet them and returned their salute. "Welcome aboard, men. And welcome back to the United States of America," he said, shaking the hand of each man. He then ordered the men be taken to sickbay to be checked by the ship's chief medical corpsman and then debriefed.

As the men turned to leave, they turned in Jake's direction, and he did a double take. "Holy Christ, it's *SONNY!*" exclaimed Jake, standing about 25 feet down from the men manning the rail. "I can't believe it!" he exclaimed, as he broke ranks and began running toward his former bunkmate from Kami Seya.

"Sonny! You son of a bitch! It's you!" Jake exclaimed, running up to Sonny and giving him a bear hug.

"Hi, Jake. Careful—I'm still getting used to my new balancing act. Good to see you. It's been awhile. How've you been?"

"How have *I* been? Jesus, you're a classic in understatement. I've been great. I can't believe it's you!"

"Yep, it's me. Minus a small body part, but very, very happy to be here in any condition."

As the two men stood shaking hands and greeting each other, the OOD came over to them and the other two survivors and said "Gentlemen, let's continue this below. I think a checkup and debriefing is the first order of the day."

The three men from the *Crestfin*—including Sonny Powell of Fosston, Minnesota helped by his ex-cube mate, Jake Morton, walked across the deck and through the door that would lead them to sickbay—and eventually to the wardroom in 'officer country' where the two ship captains had met in an historic moment that unfortunately would go unreported throughout the world.

*   *   *   *

In a short time after he was sure the three U.S. survivors were safely aboard their ship, Captain Lishchenko had readied K-229 for its voyage—Yuri's last—back to Petropovlosk. With one last look over at the *Groveland* through the periscope, on Lishchenko's command the sub slipped silently beneath the water almost simultaneously with the setting of the sun.

Captain Chandler and his executive officer watched from the bridge. "That was one incredible experience. With all the problems in the world, don't you think they could all be eliminated if they were worked out between equals with common goals?" Captain Chandler said—mostly to himself, and not expecting a response from his executive officer.

It would be two days later as the Groveland headed full-steam back to Yoko-suka before Jake would see Sonny again. The three survivors of the *Crestfin* acci-dent had been secluded from the first day aboard. The corpsmen had checked them over, and then security personnel, including Chief Stanfield, subjected the men to fairly intense interrogation.

Of main concern to the Naval Security Group personnel would be to learn what sensitive material from the sub had fallen into Soviet hands. Jake speculated that there couldn't have been much—the CTs aboard were monitoring transmis-sions, not making them. So, he reasoned, there would have been no classified documentation or code equipment in the NSG spaces on the sub. All of the intercepted radio traffic was contained on tape, and this would have been ren-dered useless by the salt water. Paper logs of intercept activity showing call signs, frequencies and times are about all that would have been left behind. At least as far as the SecGru personnel were concerned.

The sub's regular radio room, on the other hand, was a different matter. The sub would have been equipped with cryptographic gear to encode outgoing mes-sages and to decode incoming messages. Jake had no clue what types of docu-mentation would have been aboard. If the accident happened without warning, there would have been no time to destroy any classified material.

If the equipment and codes had fallen into Russian hands when the sub first went down, in the interim they would have had almost four months of access to a lot of U.S. radio communications. If the Russian sub commander did have advance info on the captain of the Groveland and the ship's course, there's a good chance they obtained that information from broken coded messages Jake specu-lated. On the other hand, the Navy would have been aware of that one of their ships was missing, and lacking knowledge of exactly where or how, immediately would have changed crypto codes fleet-wide as a precaution.

Security personnel also would want to know what the Americans observed while in Russian hands, what questions their interrogators had asked and what they were told—in other words, what intelligence could the Russians have learned from the Americans, and what intelligence could the Navy learn from the captives' experiences.

Jake was on watch in the operations section when Sonny entered about 1400 hours. The ship was more than a week away from arrival in Yokosuka and ship-board activities had returned to normal.

"Sonny! Jesus, it's good to see you. Sit down—Sorry about your leg; how did it happen? What was it like? How long were you in the water? Did they treat you well? I have a million questions."

"Hi Jake. Good to see you too, believe me. I don't think I will be able to tell you much. They intimated that they'd cut off another appendage—one more important to me—if I talk too much."

"I guess my first question is—what happened? You know, we were told nothing. And we never heard anything. We didn't know the sub had sunk—at least at my level; all we knew is that you were missing. When they came and cleaned out your locker, to most of us that meant you were gone—for good ."

"Like I told Chief Stanfield, I don't have much memory of the accident itself. I was on watch, heard a lot of banging, the lights went out and so did I. I remember a lot of cold—and I couldn't move away from my workstation. I remember a strange peace came over me as the water was rising—and that's about it until I woke up in the sick bay on a Russian ship."

"When I did come to, I was told that I was found literally floating on the water. My leg was severed but still hanging there, and I guess the cold water stopped the bleeding pretty much and contributed to my survival. The doc here on board said he thought the Russian medics did a pretty good job fixing up my leg—It's healing properly and there are no signs of infection at least."

"So where have you been all this time?"

"Oh, 'out and about,' as they say. I was segregated from the other two guys, who aren't CTs by the way. One's a member of the galley crew and the other guy worked in the engine room—both departments located away from where we were sliced open. I didn't know them. In fact I'd never met them until they brought us together about a week ago and loaded us on the Russian sub. They didn't tell us where we were going, or anything about the bodies of the crew they'd salvaged. Not many of the sub crew spoke any English at all, so it was a fairly intense week with a million questions of our own. Captain Lishchenko made a couple of appearances, and assured us that we were out of danger and on our way home, but that's about all he said. Somehow we seemed to sense that we could trust him, so about all we did was eat and sleep."

"Anyway, I spent the first month in a hospital bed on the base in Vlad. Not a place you'd want to spend more time than necessary. No pretty nurses, for one thing. After they sewed me up, they sent me to a recovery facility off the base somewhere. I was under guard, of course, so I didn't get to hit any of the local bars."

"If I had known where you were, I could have sent some Kirin beer."

"And I'd have welcomed it. There was vodka everywhere, but I didn't see any beer. I think they use it as anesthetic. Didn't seem to be any prohibition against it in the hospital wards either; everyone seemed to have a flask. And some rotten black cigarettes. God, I think I inhaled a carton a day just being there."

Chief Stanfield came in and interrupted them. "Well Powell, it looks like you're getting a first class ride back to Yokosuka. We were just informed that a helicopter is being sent to pick up you and the other two men. You'll be taken to the *Oriskany* and from there you'll be flown back to Yokosuka."

"I guess that's good news. I'm ready to get back to work," Sonny said.

"Well, I kinda doubt that's gonna happen. I believe the Navy will be shipping you back to the States—first for some well deserved time with your family, and then probably to the Naval Hospital to get fitted with a prosthesis. Somehow I have a hunch your career as a spook is almost over."

Sonny Powell was silent for quite awhile, reflecting on what the chief had said. "Well, I guess that makes sense. My enlistment is about up anyway. I don't think losing a couple of inches of leg is going to be a big problem. Lots of folks at home are missing limbs of some kind—mostly from frostbite or getting them stuck in a combine or something, so I'll fit in. But I probably won't be coaching the Fosston High basketball team though."

Chief Stanfield didn't say anything—what could he? He shook hands with Sonny and wished him good luck if he didn't see him before the helicopter arrived.

"Thanks Chief. Good meeting you," Sonny said as the chief disappeared down the passageway.

"I guess I'm ready to get home and get on with life. I have to get Dad another dog, you know…When I left home for the navy, he and Radar got real close. Now that Radar is gone…"

"WAIT a minute," Jake interrupted—"How did you know about Radar? I was just about to tell you that I'd had a letter from your folks telling me that Radar had died. How could you know?"

"Yeah, I know. He died on my birthday—July 17th. The same day as the sub accident. Remember I told you way back that once in awhile I'd hypnotize myself and go home? Well, I got feeling homesick when I was in the hospital in Vladivostok, so I 'went home' so to speak. That's when I learned Radar had died."

Jake just stared at him, speechless. There's no way in hell anyone else knew Radar was dead. Nobody could have told him. And he'd been incommunicado for the entire time.

Sonny grabbed his crutch and reached for Jake's hand to shake. "Now I've got to go get ready if they're sending a 'chopper for us. It was good talking to you,

Jake—I'll probably see you back in Kami Seya in a week or so before they ship me off to the States."

"Uh, yeah, Sonny, sure," Jake stammered, still flabbergasted at Sonny's knowledge of Radar's death. "I'll see you back on base. Have a good flight," he said, as Sonny left the operations area. *Why do we need radios when we have people who can communicate like that?* Jake thought, putting his headset on and getting back to work.

CHAPTER 13

▼

"I'm just trying to figure out what to do when this joyful experience ends in a few months."

Sonny already had departed Kami Seya by the time Jake returned in mid-November. According to Art, as soon as Sonny had arrived back in Japan, he'd been sent to the Navy hospital in Yokosuka, and from there was transferred to the Navy hospital in Hawaii for further examination and preliminary fitting for his prosthesis. Jake could just imagine Sonny's parents' elation when they were told that Sonny was alive and relatively well.

Time was running out for Jake in Kami Seya, and in the Navy. He had only a few months left on his first enlistment, and it was beginning to hit home. What next? He'd contemplated college, but still wasn't sure what he wanted to do with his life in general, and consequently had no idea what he'd major in at college if he went, to prepare for that unknown. Reenlistment was a possibility, but not one that he was really ready to face up to. He liked what he did in the Navy, and having advanced to E-5 in less than two years, he had enjoyed an unusually privileged Navy experience compared to the average sailor who was lucky to make E-3 on a four-year enlistment.

Jake had been off of the *Groveland* less than a month, back on duty where all seemed to be as it was before he left. But things weren't the same. The experience with the Russian submarine, Sonny's miraculous reappearance, and the total experience of the *Groveland* had affected him. He sensed his life was changed, but he couldn't figure our exactly how, or why, or what to do about it.

A stack of letters from Janice awaited Jake upon his return. Yes, he had told her he couldn't write for a few months. But that didn't mean she couldn't. And she had. God, Jake thought, how can I ever catch up with all of this mail; how can I answer all of her questions and concerns? But he'd try.

"Dear Janice,

I've been away for a few months, as I told you I would be, on a temporary assignment where it was impossible for me to write to you. Actually I could write to you, but there was no way to have the letters mailed. I was not in any danger at any time—I simply was not anywhere with mail pick-up or delivery, as I tried to explain before I left.

When I got back to base, I found a pile of letters from you. It would take a 50-page letter from me to try to answer them all. Instead, I would like to try to convey, through these few heartfelt words, that I love you, I always have, I always will, and I will see you soon. I only ask that you will understand that because of the nature of my job, I can't share day to day experiences with you, and I can't always explain what I'm doing, or where I'm doing it. Please don't misconstrue that lack of openness for anything other than what it is—an inability, by Navy regulations, to say more.

I only have a few months left on my enlistment, and right now am struggling with what to do. As you know, I have never wanted much more than to be with you. But I want us to have a good life together. On one hand, I believe that the best chance of that happening is if I get a college education. But an education in what? I still don't know what I want to do. Another option, of course, is for me to stay in the Navy. It isn't a bad life— in fact it has a lot going for it. And not just for me, but for you. The benefits for married personnel are getting better every day, and despite what my experiences may have led you to believe, there can be a normal married life for a couple in the USN. There are significant educational opportunities for me in the Navy, as there are as a civilian. I could obtain a college degree while in the service, and at the Navy's expense. I've already taken some tests to determine my eligibility, and if I pass, I could get a four-year degree in an engineering-related field at the Navy's expense. Of course I'd have to ship over to qualify.

So right now my focus is on what to do, and how to prepare for it now. I'm preparing for your future as well as mine, and it's the most important thing on my mind right now. So please forgive me for not answering your letters point-by-point after all of this time. But let me know where your heart is in all of this. I will only make a decision with your guidance and approval. My enlistment is up in February, so if I am getting out, they'll send me back to the States sometime in January—probably to Treasure Island Naval Station in San Francisco—that's where most people on duty in the Pacific are discharged from. So, I'd like to make a decision with you on this by Christmas—and that's only a month away!

With all my love,

Jake"

Jake mailed the letter with great apprehension. He had been sincere—he really didn't have a strong feeling for future direction. But he knew that Janice was very security conscious, and given her home life so far, could understand why she felt that way. He had hoped to be able to give her a more positive feeling that he had his next 50 years all planned out, but that wasn't so.

He was glad to be back on solid land. He'd heard that even though seagoing sailors got used to being at sea, without sickness, they'd suffer a similar malady as soon as they were on shore. It appeared to be true. Jake had gotten over his seasickness early on, and never had a problem with it after that first week. But now, here on land, he would awake with a slight feeling of wooziness. At first he'd written it off to a hangover from the night before, but it would occur even when he'd been a good boy, so to speak.

"Jake, snap out of it. Your tape just ran out." Walt brought him out of his daydream, whatever it was.

"Sorry, Walt. I was off at the Naval Academy or at Penn State, or selling shoes in dad's store. I'm not sure where I was. Thanks for bringing me back—it feels a lot more comfortable right here."

"No sweat, Jake. Anything going on that I can help you with?"

"Nope. I'm just trying to figure out what to do when this joyful experience of mine ends in a few months."

"Well, if you want a totally biased opinion of the decision I made when I faced the same situation—and why I chose to ship over, let me know. Of course I haven't found a honey yet like you have, so I realize you have other considerations. See you later."

"Thanks, Walt. I do want to hear your reasoning when you have a chance."

Jake fixed the free-spinning empty tape reel, scooped up the many, many folds of printer paper that had accumulated on the floor, and tried to bring himself back to the present. I can worry about all this future stuff when I'm off duty, he told himself.

*   *   *   *

"What do *you* want to do?" Janice's mother's emphasis on the word 'you' hinted at some disapproval. Mrs. Thompson was an intelligent, educated woman, but at times Janice thought her mom was too opinionated. She'd never been wild about Janice's choice of Jake Morton in the first place. Janice figured that maybe it was because her mom didn't like Jake's mother very much, and she never was quite sure why.

"If I had a good answer for you I'd tell you. I just got his letter today, for God's sake, so I need some time to think about it." *I never should have told her about it*, Janice thought.

"Well, you know you have your dad's and my support whatever you decide to tell him. But remember, you're half of the equation, and what you want for yourself is equally important. Whether Jake stays in the service or not, you have to pursue your own dreams."

"I know, Mom, but just as his decisions have to include my feelings, I have to consider his needs before I go off on some independent track myself."

Mrs. Thompson didn't reply, but continued arranging her sheet music for the next piano student who was due in a few minutes. She didn't look up at Janice, and her steady gaze at the pile of paper—with no acknowledgement that Jake's opinion mattered, spoke volumes to Janice.

With that, Janice left the room and walked to the garage. She'd only read Jake's letter once, and as usual, the first pass was a cursory one. She wanted to jog to the park and re-read it. There has to be an answer that'll make both of us happy, she reasoned.

Since returning from California some two months earlier, Janice found that little had changed at home. She was still a little girl in her mother's mind, and not capable of independent thought. Janice's dad, on the other hand, pretty much left her alone. He had been fond of Jake from the beginning, and felt that Jake had a pretty solid foundation. In a word, he didn't worry much about his daughter's future; she was level-headed and had a capable husband now, and she was on her own as far as he was concerned.

But living with the folks was not going to be an acceptable solution much longer, and Janice knew as soon as Jake made a decision, she had to be with him wherever it would be. The 'no housing on base' excuse wouldn't work again, if he decided to stay in the Navy, she thought. And if he wants to go to school, whatever career ideas I might have will have to be put on hold so I can work and pay the bills. Or we can both go to school and both work part-time. Or neither of us can work and we can live under a bridge. She laughed at that thought, realizing the possibilities were many and would take a lot of thought.

A lot of thought was being given to this subject on both sides of the world. Janice put her thoughts to paper, a brief letter that boiled down to a willingness to go with whatever decision Jake would make.

*   *   *   *

The direction Jake wanted to take was now clear, thanks to a totally unexpected letter from Sonny. He hoped Janice would agree.

"Dear Janice,

I know the recent months of indecision about our future plans have been nerve-wracking for you. I've been searching for direction, and I think I received it today in the form of a letter from Sonny.

As I told you in previous correspondence, Sonny had an accident while on duty which resulted in the loss of part of one leg below his knee. He wrote a letter to me from Balboa Naval Hospital in San Diego where he is undergoing training on the use of a prosthesis. The letter was very inspiring—I don't know if I would have the positive outlook that he seems to possess. Anyway, he discussed the decision he made about his future, and it has helped me come to a decision about my own life—and hopefully ours together.

Sonny wanted to stay in the Navy, largely because his father—a second-generation navy vet himself—told Sonny how proud he was of him, and that he thought Sonny had 'made a difference.' The activity in which Sonny was involved and the actions of those responsible for his accident indicated to Sonny's father that there was good in most everyone, and that even many of our enemies want peace as much as we do.

But his enlistment was just about up, and Sonny has been offered a civilian job with NSA at Fort George Meade, Maryland, and has accepted. He will do very well at it.

I believe that I, too, have been doing something that is important and meaningful to our country. I've told you often that I enjoy what I do, and others tell me I'm good at it. I have taken tests and have been offered the opportunity to participate in the Navy's NESEP program—an engineering and scientific program that will pay to put me through college. I want to accept the offer, with your agreement. By re-enlisting for six years, the Navy will pay for me to receive a B.S. degree in electrical engineering, and I graduate as an officer.

If you agree and I accept the Navy's offer, I will be report to Syracuse University for winter quarter after a week's leave at home. (Yes, I know—a nasty time of the year in upstate New York, but it's close to home!) We'll be provided with a living and housing allowance in addition to my full pay, and I immediately will be advanced to the rank of E6, or First Class Petty Officer. I will be a full-time student! Incidentally, Syracuse has an excellent nursing program, and I think—if you're still interested in that as a career, with the benefits that I'll receive and some part-time work, we shouldn't have any problem making it a reality.

I believe that it's a terrific opportunity for both of us, and I really think that it's a career that will enable me, like Sonny, to make a difference.

With much love, I look forward to your answer.

Jake

After no longer than it took the letter to reach Janice in Pennsylvania, Jake received an immediate response in the form of a telegram:

Jake,

Let me know when to meet your plane in Philadelphia. I already will have my snowshoes packed, ready for at least a four-year stay in Syracuse. Merry Christmas, darling!

All my love,

Janice.

- END -

EPILOGUE

▼

Arlington, Virginia—10 Years Later...

"Paging Nurse Morton. Call 366." *Damn,* Janice thought—*I almost made it...*" She was only five feet from the exit when she turned and walked back toward the emergency room. Normally she'd move faster in anticipation of an emergency, but tonight she was beat. She'd worked two consecutive shifts, and they were hectic shifts. In addition to the normal Saturday patient load of accident victims, drug overdoses and stab wounds, etc. a small plane had plowed into the river and the ER had been bedlam for 12 straight hours. It was almost 10 a.m. Sunday and she was about to collapse.

"This is Morton," she said to the duty desk nurse at the other end of the house phone. "What's up? I was almost out the door!"

"Sorry Janice, I just took a call from your husband; he called to remind you to pick up the ice cream on your way..."

"Good Lord, I would have forgotten too. It's my son's birthday and we're having a small party tonight. Thanks, Laura—see you Tuesday." With that, she hung up the phone and retraced her steps to the exit and ultimately the staff parking garage. *One stop at Baskin-Robbins and in 30 minutes I'll be home* she told herself. She collapsed into the drivers' seat of the 1975 Impala and just sat there for a few minutes. The car was only a few years old, but the starter motor was going bad and sometimes it would just 'click' when she turned the key. *Not this time, please...I'm in no mood to mess with you,* she thought to herself, with no real expectation that the car could hear her. But maybe it did, because it started on the first twist of the key, and in minutes she was picking up four gallons of rocky-road for Brian's sixth birthday party later that afternoon.

About the only good thing about getting off her shift around noon was the traffic—typically light on the expressway at that time of the day during the week, and especially so today, Sunday. Most of the government workers were home washing their cars to be ready for the next week's tedious commute. Brian was playing in the yard as Janice pulled into the driveway of their modest suburban home, and immediately ran to greet his mom.

"Hi honey, where's your dad?"

"Hi Mommy. Daddy's out back cutting the grass," Brian told her as she closed the car door with a large bag of ice cream in her arms.

"Go tell him I'm home while I go put these groceries away. Have you had lunch yet?" Brian already was halfway around the house by the time she got the words out of her mouth and didn't hear her. At six, Brian was the spitting image of his dad—thin and wiry, but with blue eyes and hair that was as thin as silk. Only it was blond like Janice's, not dark and wavy like Jake's hair.

As Janice put the ice cream in the freezer, Brian and his dad came in the back door. "Hi honey, I see you got my message." Jake said as he grabbed her from behind and gave her a peck on the back of her neck.

"Yes and you scared me at work. When they paged me I thought I was being called back. I was—and still am—so tired I probably would have quit if they'd have asked me to spend another hour in the ER," Janice said. "If you have things pretty well in hand, I'm going to go lie down for an hour or so and catch up. Make sure I'm up by four o'clock to get things ready. I have most of the stuff already prepared but some last minute things. O.K.?"

Jake understood. "Of course. But use the living room couch—not the back bedroom. I'm still cutting grass back there." Janice nodded and headed for the living room and the lumpy couch that would feel like a cloud this particular afternoon. Fortunately it was a cool day for July, and she wouldn't have to use the air conditioner.

"C'mon, Brian—you can help daddy rake up the grass for awhile," Jake said as he put his hand on his son's shoulder and went back to resume cutting the lawn. Jake wanted to give Janice as much time to sleep as possible. He didn't comprehend how she could hack two straight eight-hour shifts with no rest, eating a slice of pizza or something and copious amounts of coffee when she had a chance…But then he recalled his enlisted days and standing watch and sleeping at strange hours, and understood how the human body could adapt.

*   *   *   *

Janice would have slept for eight hours more but fortunately the doorbell would cancel that possibility. She looked at her watch and when she noticed it was 4:45, she was on her feet in seconds and running to the door.

"Oh, Sonny, it's you. Thank God. I overslept—Jake didn't wake me. The kids will be here in a half-hour or so and I'm not ready. Jake's in the backyard. Go grab a beer from the 'fridge and join him. Just make sure you both stay out of my way.., My God, I'm rambling…"

"It's O.K. Janice, ramble-on. Just keep me in beer and you can talk all day," Sonny told her as he gave her a friendly kiss on the cheek and headed for the kitchen.

"Help yourself," Janice called after him…I have to change and I'll be down in a minute.

With that, Sonny walked to the kitchen refrigerator and helped himself to a Carling Black Label beer. He went out the back door, called "Hello" to Jake and Brian, and walked down the steps off of the back porch to the shed where Jake was just putting away the lawn mower.

"Hi Sonny. Where's the family?" Jake asked, closing the rickety wooden door of the garden shed. *Have to fix that hinge,* he thought, as he turned to Sonny and shook his hand. "Good to see you, bud…"

"Same here. Sharon and Macy will be along in a few minutes. They had to stop somewhere and pick up something for you-know-who," glancing down at Brian as he spoke and winking at Jake.

"Have a seat at the picnic table. I'm gonna grab a brew myself, and I'll be right back," Jake said and turned toward the back door.

"C'mon, Jake, you don't have to keep telling me to sit down. I'm not going to fall down anymore. I actually think after all this time I've pretty well mastered this plastic leg of mine."

He's so right, Jake thought. *It's just a habit and I've got to stop it.* For the first year or so, Sonny had a tough time getting accustomed to the prosthesis. After a succession of embarrassing falls, Jake got in the habit of telling him to 'have a seat' but realized that after all these years, Sonny probably could run the Boston Marathon if he set his mind to it. He had always been athletic and initially had a difficult time realizing he couldn't do it all anymore. But he'd come a long way and was actually playing a little basketball at the YMCA again.

Returning, Jake joined Sonny and clicked bottles before taking a long gulp. "Boy, I needed that," he said, and sat on one of the picnic table benches. "So how're things at the cube?" he asked, referring to the windowless NSA building where Sonny worked.

"I'd tell you but then I'd have to kill you," Sonny replied, with a big grin. "Actually, things are going well. I just got a promotion to Section Chief and a higher GSA rating. So now we can afford that boat I've wanted since I was a kid."

"You didn't have one growing up in Minnesota? That's hard to believe."

"I know. We had a great little bass pond on our own property. As a little kid I wasn't allowed near it—I couldn't swim for a long time. Dad told me he'd buy me a fishing boat if I learned how to swim. Well, I learned, but never got the boat. I got so wrapped up in basketball that I never pressed him for it. After school, with working and practice, I never had time. Sharon hasn't been keen on the idea of any kind of boat, at least until Macy is a little older. I guess Sharon is afraid that I'll fall in and my leg will sink me, or rust, or capsize the boat or something. And how about you? I haven't talked to you for about two months; last time we talked you mentioned you were working on a new escape capsule for subs or something?"

"Well, yes, I have been. We've completed the initial design and my department has submitted it for review. I have pretty high expectations that it's gonna fly, so to speak. It's not so much a capsule as it is a combination flotation device with an oxygen supply. It's supposed to be light weight and compact enough that every compartment on a sub can have a number of them immediately available to crew members—easy to store, easily and quickly put on, and effective from considerable depths. We haven't tested the depth limits yet, but the goal is that it'll control the ascent based on pressure, and contain an oxygen supply that's good for 15 minutes."

"Wow! If we'd have had something like that on the *Crestfin*, I'm sure a lot more guys would have made it," Sonny said. "I sure hope the Navy approves it. You might even make full commander if they do!"

"Well, I guess that's possible. What I haven't told Janice yet is that if the project is funded, they may want me to transfer to New London, Connecticut to oversee product development and testing. I probably won't have any choice either."

As Jake spoke, Sonny's wife Sharon and five-year-old daughter Macy came through the gate at the end of the yard. "Hi, guys. Where's the birthday boy?" Sharon asked.

"Hi Sharon," Jake replied. "I think he's in the house—probably trying to get a head start on the ice cream."

"Go get him, and Janice," Sonny said to Sharon. "I'll go to the car and get the box." Turning to Jake, Sonny said "We wanted to bring him his present early…it's kinda special, and we wanted him to have some time alone with it before the rest of the gang arrives." With that, Sonny started walking toward the gate and the front driveway. In less than two minutes, he returned, just as the wives, Brian and Macy came out of the house to the back porch.

"Hi, Brian. Happy Birthday!" Sonny exclaimed, and sat the box down on the lawn in front of the porch. It wasn't wrapped, and Jake noticed several holes in the side of the box.

Oh no, Jake thought to himself—*I hope that's not what I think it is…*

"What is it, Uncle Sonny?" Brian yelled, as he ran down the steps and excitedly tore open the lid.

The box answered, with a "Yip."

Yep, that's what I was afraid of…a puppy, Jake told himself, already resigned to the fact.

"Daddy! It's a PUPPY!" Brian exclaimed, lifting the small black dog out of the box and cuddling it as it immediately began licking his face.

"Yes, it is, Brian. Meet 'SONAR',—Son of Radar! Just kidding—of course you can name him anything you want, Buddy," Sonny said. "Radar was the name of my dog when I was a boy."

"I like Radar," Brian said, the puppy squirming to get free. "Will you help me train him?"

"I'd be delighted," Sonny said, watching Brian and his new friend, through understanding and moist eyes…

The End

978-0-595-40902-0
0-595-40902-4

Printed in the United States
104840LV00004B/310/A